A Spanish Pact

Mark Harrison

MARK HARRISON

Copyright Mark Harrison 2016
Mark Harrison has asserted his right under the
Copyright, Designs and Patents Act 1988 to be
identified as the author of this work.
This book is sold subject to the condition that it shall not,
by way of trade or otherwise, be lent, resold, hired out, or
otherwise circulated without the author's prior consent.

For Vivien and for Pat and Les for their help and encouragement.

PART ONE

CHAPTER ONE

November 1939

A strengthening north wind funnelled through the narrow streets of Benimarta accentuating the chill that penetrated Vicenta's thick woollen coat and bit into her flesh. Doggedly she pressed on, turning a corner with her head bowed as she clasped the old felt hat she normally reserved for Sunday Mass. Pausing at a pair of massive wrought iron gates, she lifted her head and gazed along the broad stone pathway flanked by uniform rows of palm trees that reached high into the bleak night sky. Her eyes settled on the huge carved wooden door set beneath a pillared portico that gave the house a grandeur unlike any other in the village. For a fleeting moment she recalled the effort required to twist the circular clasp and swing the door open on its massive iron hinges. Other memories would have lifted her spirits; memories of smiles and laughter, warmth and joy. But the sight of a heavy chain and padlock brought her back to the realisation that those days were now past, replaced by fear and uncertainty. Her sadness deepened as she stared at the carved stone plaque at the side of the gate. Once it had read *Casa*

Pepita, now it had been obliterated by hammer blows and replaced with a painted sign that read: *Requisada por El Estado Español. Casa Cuartel de la Guardia Civil.* The sign was headed by a coat-of-arms – a bundle of sticks tied to an axe crossed by a sword and topped with a royal crown. The inscription read: *El honor es mi divisa.* Vicenta sneered at the slogan's mocking irony – honour is my motto – and cringed at the thought that her home was now the quarters of Franco's enforcers.

Casa Pepita had been the home of Vicenta's father-in-law, Julio Ripoll, a successful novelist. He lived most of his life in Valencia where he enjoyed a degree of notoriety for his work and his left wing views. His novels frequently depicted the social injustice of rural Spain and decried the repressive roles of the Clergy and the Monarchy in sustaining archaic systems of agriculture which in turn perpetuated poverty and malnutrition. His books sold well, both in Spain and abroad, but as reactionary forces strengthened their hold on power in Valencia in the early twenties, he came under increasing scrutiny and was threatened with arrest and imprisonment. Fearful, not for himself but for his family, he had left the city in 1925 and moved to Benimarta from where he hoped to pursue his literary career removed from the hotbed of politics that was spawning disorder and unrest in Valencia. Sadly his aspirations were left unfulfilled when he died of pleurisy in 1930, but not before he had overseen the construction of Casa Pepita - named after his wife who died giving birth to their only child, Eduardo, in 1910.

Vicenta turned and trudged up the hill, entering the Plaza to be confronted by a shallow flowing pool carrying the remnants of the storm across the cobbled surface of the square and down a side street to the base of the village. In the deepening gloom she picked her way on tiptoe across the pool, her path illuminated by a single candle flickering in the window of one of the adjacent houses. The electricity supply, intermittent at best before the war, was now virtually non-existent. The pool's icy water seeped through her boots and exacerbated the numbness that already permeated her feet.

The old church loomed on the far side of the square, its solid tower adorned by a simple cross hewn from a single piece of rock. Not for the first time Vicenta questioned the faith she had earnestly followed from infancy under the implacable instruction of Father Ignacio. Recent events had only served to fuel her cynicism as the Catholic Church revelled in its new-found collaboration with the Falange and cooperated fervently in enforcing the new order.

Vicenta recalled the events of the previous week when the whole of the village had been forced to gather in the square to watch the ritual humiliation of Maria Angelica Benitez whose crime had been to harbour her wounded brother, Ismael, one of the many republican soldiers forced to flee the city of Valencia when it finally succumbed to the nationalists in March that year. Ismael had been arrested and taken away two weeks earlier, herded into a truck with a dozen others denounced as republican supporters or sympathisers. No one had heard from them since. Officially they had been interned with thousands of others in a makeshift camp on the outskirts of Alicante. Though their families clung to the idea that they might one day return, quietly they conceded it was a forlorn hope. Everyone knew that in the aftermath of the war there was not enough food for the surviving population, let alone the burgeoning number of dissidents deemed enemies of the new republic. Rumours of torture and assassination by firing squad were rife; rumours which the authorities did nothing to dispel.

Having rooted out the obvious dissidents, the authorities of Benimarta next turned their attention to stifling all possible opposition and it was under this guise that vengeance was sought and old scores were settled. An anonymous denunciation from a loyal Falange supporter was all it took to justify arrest and arbitrary punishment. And that was how Maria Angelica Benitez found herself in the village square, her hair crudely shorn, stripped of clothing and bound with rope around her wrists. A group of elderly women, taking no steps to conceal their identity, appeared to take a kind of perverse pleasure as they held the struggling Maria Angelica and forced her to swallow gulp after gulp of castor oil, never relenting even as she gagged and vomited. Satisfied with their work, the women stood by and laughed heartily as Maria Angelica, fighting the pain in her stomach, defecated involuntarily, spattering her bare legs and feet and leaving a pool of liquid excrement on the cobbles. Father Ignacio had stood by and watched the degrading spectacle without so much as a flicker of disgust or distaste. Only when Maria Angelica had completed the task of mopping the cobbles with a rag and a bucket of water, did the two armed Guardia Civil officers melt away allowing the crowd to disperse in shocked silence.

The episode achieved its aim; to instil fear and suppress all thoughts of resistance against the new regime. The fact that it also instilled loathing and disgust, mattered not to the clandestine group of Falange supporters who effectively controlled the village.

Recalling the disgusting spectacle, Vicenta pressed on across the square, silently questioning. *If there is a God, a just and righteous God, how could He allow such an atrocity to transpire? How could He allow such malevolence to prevail? Why does He permit the forces of hatred to extract their revenge so ruthlessly and arbitrarily?*

She left the square by the alleyway at the side

of Bar Rull, its shuttered windows streaked with grime accumulated over the previous six months since its enforced closure – another victim of the retribution unleashed on those whose only crime was to support the wrong side in defeat.

She approached the town hall passing the studded wooden door set in a carved stone arch and looked up at the new flag flapping rhythmically in the constant breeze. The red, yellow, purple of Spain's Second Republic had been replaced with the newly decreed colours of Spain's Third Republic: red, yellow, red emblazoned with the coat-of-arms of the old Catholic monarchs Ferdinand and Isobel shrouded by a black spread-eagle whose sinister presence seemed to epitomise life under *El Caudillo*.

Until recently Benimarta had no need of a jail, but the old store next to the town hall had been hastily converted soon after the contingent of Guardia Civil arrived to take control of the village. Now it housed a rudimentary prison with a series of cells fabricated in wrought iron by the village blacksmith, Federico Blazquez, who accepted the work out of necessity, though he had laboured with a heavy heart.

Vicenta stretched to reach the heavy brass knocker at the centre of the door. She lifted it once and allowed it to fall back with a foreboding thud that shuddered through her body and set her heart racing as she waited for a response. She brushed a hand through her long auburn curls and pinched her cheeks to give them some colour. It would be the first time she had seen her husband, Eduardo, for three days; ever since he had been taken in the middle of the night by a band of men led by Juan-Martin Garcia, the local chief of the Spanish Falange.

Before the war, Garcia had been a friend of Eduardo's. They often played chess together in a corner of Bar Rull, exchanging thoughts and comments about the fractured state of Spanish politics. Garcia was a committed Monarchist and rued the day in April 1931 when King Alfonso XIII had been forced to flee Spain on the declaration of the Second Republic. Eduardo found it difficult to comprehend such dedication to the idea of rule by an absolute monarch whose only claim to power came by virtue of his dubious birthright. When most of the rest of Europe had spent the last few hundred years culling, or at least curtailing, the ancient royal dynasties, Eduardo could not see the point in perpetuating the rule of a Spanish royal family, especially one descended from the French Bourbons. He would often tease Juan-Martin about his out-dated views, decrying the rank and privilege granted to the old King and his cronies who had profiteered from Spain's crumbling Empire whilst the majority of Spain's citizens laboured in abject poverty.

Though their opinions often differed, the two men rarely argued and both enjoyed the good-natured banter that filled many an hour in the cosy comfort of Bar Rull. But as the power and influence of the Republican government fell into a chaotic decline, Juan-Martin became more enthusiastic about the prospect of revolt – a scenario that filled Eduardo with dread. When the military uprising finally began in July 1936, Juan-Martin quickly sided with the Nationalists and joined the pro-Franco forces. He ended the war on the victorious side at the siege of Valencia which finally fell one day after Madrid came under Nationalist control in March 1939.

Perhaps it was the depravities of the war or the privations suffered by both sides, but Garcia returned to Benimarta a changed man. The thoughtful intellectual had become a staunch proponent of the new dictatorship and a zealous enforcer of the repression through which Franco sought to cement his tenuous grip on power. Now he was the leader of an unelected syndicate of Falangists who controlled Benimarta, working hand-in-glove with the Guardia Civil contingent of four officers who took their instructions directly from the appointed provincial government in Alicante.

Eduardo, a journalist, made the mistake of remaining neutral. He penned several articles during the war reporting on events, but was always careful (so he thought) to avoid opinionated commentary and maintain his impartiality. But he never imagined for one moment the ruthless and systematic way in which revenge would be exacted on anyone deemed unsympathetic to the new regime. And he never foresaw the possibility that his carefully crafted words could be so outrageously distorted and misinterpreted.

Garcia's fervent support for the new repression was more opportunistic than idealistic. Unlike Eduardo's family, who had established wealth and status through his father's literary achievements, Garcia's family were poor and fashioned a meagre living from the countryside and the small parcel of land they owned on the outskirts of the village. Before the war these differences had been of little consequence; now they assumed greater importance and Garcia had realised that the new order provided an opportunity to redress the balance – even if it meant betraying his old friend in order to curry favour with the new regime.

Republican supporters, communists and trade unionists – *rojos y izquierdistas* – were routinely rounded up and arrested. But Eduardo was none of these things; he belonged to an even more dangerous class – *la inteligencia* – and the new regime feared these people more than any other. A rabble band of subversives was easily suppressed, but Franco never underestimated the power of intellectual argument or criticism. And it took little more than a malicious denunciation by his old friend to persuade the Guardia Civil that Eduardo was a threat to order and security.

A small panel in the centre of the door slid

open and a gnarled face appeared, lit from one side by the amber glow of a lantern.

'Who is it?' the gruff voice enquired.

'I am Vicenta Ripoll.'

'What do you want?'

'I have come to see my husband, Eduardo Ripoll. I have a visiting order from the Guardia.'

There was a loud clunk as a heavy bolt drew back, followed by another and the door opened.

'Let me see it.'

Vicenta handed over the paper and the man raised the lantern to read it. She studied his face, trying to distinguish the features beneath a red beret, obscured by a stubbly black beard. 'It's Pedro, isn't it? Pedro Ferrer?'

'Comrade Ferrer,' he barked.

She examined his crumpled blue shirt and her eyes settled on the embroidered emblem featuring a twin yoke and five vertical arrows. Before the war Ferrer had been a minion of the functionaries who ran the town hall. His official title was clerk, though in practice he was little more than an errand boy. Now he had swapped his stiff collar and tie for the uniform of the *Falange Española* - the only political party legally permitted in the new Spain. Vicenta doubted his right wing credentials, assuming that like so many others, he had realised that backing the new regime was the best way to keep out of trouble and put food on his family's table.

'My husband, may I see him?' Vicenta realised

that deference rather than insistence was the order of the day.

'Follow me,' Ferrer said, turning on his heels.

She followed him to the end of a dimly lit corridor where he unhooked a bunch of keys from his belt to unlock a solid wooden door.

'Third on the right. Ten minutes.'

Vicenta peered into the gloom of a narrow room illuminated by two wall-mounted candle lamps. The flames flickered in the draught. She glanced in the first two cells as she passed but could see only the contours of bodies huddled under blankets on makeshift wooden beds. She approached the third cell and could just make out the silhouette of a man sat upright on the bed, head bowed, staring at the dusty stone floor.

'Eduardo? Is that you Eduardo?'

The figure stirred, raising his head and looking sideways toward the iron-barred door.

'Vicenta, is that you?' The figure rose and stepped toward the door.

Vicenta placed her arms through the bars and grasped her husband's head as he reached to hold her waist and pull her closer. She kissed his lips feeling hard bristles scrape her face. The odour of stale sweat and foul breath filled her nostrils and she almost recoiled, but held on to stroke his lank greasy hair. He seemed to sense her revulsion and pulled away.

'You shouldn't have come, Vicenta,' he said. 'I didn't want you to see me like this.'

Beneath the unfamiliar dark stubble, Vicenta hardly recognised her husband, so gaunt was his face with sunken watery eyes. His bottom lip was swollen and split and his left cheek bore a dark scab above a black bruise. She wanted to weep, but held her feelings in check, trying to be strong.

'I had to see you Eduardo. What's happening to you? Why are they keeping you here?'

Eduardo blinked slowly and released his hold on her waist. 'There's a chair in the corner over there.' He nodded to the far end of the room. 'Bring it over here.'

Vicenta fetched the rickety chair and Eduardo pulled the end of his bed closer to the door. She sat and clasped his hands through the bars.

'It's brave of you to come, Vicenta.' His voice was strained and hoarse. 'But you must be careful. There's a new order in Spain determined to subjugate the people and the tentacles of this tyranny have reached even this small village. You must not resist it or speak out against it or even complain or you will put yourself in danger. For now at least you must just keep quiet and do as you are told. Your survival will depend on it.'

Vicenta squeezed Eduardo's hands. 'But I can't just stand by and do nothing whilst you rot in here. There must be something I can do. You have friends in this village. I will speak to them. They can protest to the Mayor, Maximo Ballester, he's your cousin after all. He must be able to do something.'

Eduardo pulled his hands away from her and lowered his head. 'Maximo isn't Mayor any more. The *ayuntamiento* has been taken over by Garcia and his cabal. They do as they are told by the provincial government in Alicante and *they* have been appointed directly from Madrid. Maximo Ballester is lucky not to be in here with me. Now listen to me, Vicenta. These are dangerous times. I don't know how long the new regime will last or how far they will go to hold on to power, but I do know that they will stop at nothing to suppress opposition of any kind.'

'Then I'll speak to Juan-Martin Garcia, he's a friend of yours. Surely he can get you out of here.'

Eduardo blinked and pursed his lips. 'You don't understand, Vicenta. The war has changed everything. People took sides in the war, friends became enemies and there's no room for reconciliation now that the war is over. Juan-Martin is the one who denounced me and he was there when I was arrested.'

'You are right Eduardo, I don't understand. What crime have you committed? You didn't fight in the war, so why are you being treated this way?'

'That's true, Vicenta, I tried to stay neutral. I knew there were dangers in showing support for one side or the other, so I was always careful in what I wrote. I took care to criticise both sides where I saw abuse or unfair treatment. But one of my articles was syndicated to *El Mundo* in Madrid. It was heavily edited so it appeared to show support for the Republicans. It was noted at the time and now they are using it against me. I've protested of course and asked them to read my work as a whole, but they are not interested. If you are not an active supporter then you are deemed to be an enemy of the new government and they want you out of the way.'

'What do you mean, "out of the way"? How long will they keep you here?'

Eduardo took Vicenta's hand once more and looked into her tearful eyes. 'All over Spain the jails are overflowing with political prisoners. There are no trials, no appeals, people are just picked up and incarcerated. I hear rumours that thousands of people have just disappeared; picked up and taken away, never to return.'

Vicenta's eyes widened. 'You mean they have been killed don't you? Oh, Eduardo, tell me this isn't going to happen to you. I won't let it happen. There must be something I can do.'

'There's nothing you can do except pray, but I fear that may not be enough. The war has brutalised people and now that it's over, there are some people who see it as an opportunity to seek revenge, right old wrongs or seize the moment to grab power and wealth.'

'Juan-Martin Garcia you mean? But surely he wouldn't do such a thing. You've known each other from when you were at school together.'

'Believe me, Vicenta, Juan-Martin Garcia is no friend of our family. He is an evil man, a fully-fledged supporter of the new order and he aims to take every advantage of his situation.'

'What do you mean?'

'He's pressing me to sign over Casa Pepita to him and all our land on the south side of the village.'

'But surely that can't be legal?'

'Legal, illegal what's the difference? There's no law any more and no justice, except that imposed by those in positions of power. Their word is law and their arbitrary decisions are justice.'

'Has he promised to release you if you sign over our property?'

'Yes.'

'Then you must do it Eduardo. Your life is worth more than all the houses and land in this village. Please, you must do as he asks.'

Eduardo swallowed hard. 'Vicenta you don't understand. I could sign the papers, yes, and Garcia could make it look like a legal transaction. For the time being that might be enough, but he knows that eventually things will settle down, even if it takes five years, ten years or more. The law will be re-established and the courts too, even though they will be ruled by the government. So he can't take the risk that I would challenge his ownership in the future.'

Vicenta understood the import of her husband's statement. 'Eduardo,' she pleaded, 'you're not saying...'

Eduardo stroked Vicenta's hands. He wanted to offer reassurance, even hope, but he knew Vicenta well enough to realise that she would see through his platitudes. He loosened his grip and began to fumble with the thin gold band on his ring finger. Tugging, he finally removed the ring and placed it in Vicenta's palm pressing her hand around it. His eyes shifted from side to side. 'Keep this safe for me, Vicenta, and remember I will always love you.'

Vicenta knew then what her husband feared. She didn't need to seek an explanation. She looked deep into his hollow eyes and saw not fear, only sadness and anxiety – not for himself, but for her and the uncertainties that lay ahead.

Eduardo reached deep into the breast pocket of his wear-worn jacket and extracted a small brass key, placing it in her hand.

'Keep this safe Vicenta,' he said in a whisper. 'In the library at Casa Pepita there are two bookcases on either side of the fire place. Behind the third shelf of the left-hand bookcase there is a false panel. It slides away quite easily. Behind it there is a small compartment with a lock. This is the key. In the compartment are all the family documents including those relating to Casa Pepita and all our land. They are important, Vicenta. Without them we may never be able to prove our ownership in the future. Even if our property is seized, there will come a time when the wrongs of the present times will be righted.'

Vicenta's brow crinkled to a frown. 'But you know that Casa Pepita has been requisitioned by the Guardia Civil. The place is always occupied, the officers even sleep there. There's no way I can get inside.'

'I know that Vicenta, but it's not important. The documents are safe for now and even if the Guardia Civil ransack the place, I doubt they will find the hidden panel. This is for the future, Vicenta. Trust me, a time will come when Spain will return to its senses. A war is raging in Europe and though Franco has aligned himself with Hitler and Mussolini, the Civil War has left the country on its knees. Spain cannot afford to become involved. The outcome of the war will determine the future of Europe and possibly the future of mankind. We must hope that Herr Hitler's vision of the future is never fulfilled for if it is, then the ownership of Casa Pepita and our land will be meaningless.'

Vicenta withdrew her hands and reached up to the back of her neck to release the clasp on a thin gold chain that held a small crucifix. It had been given to her on the day of her Confirmation when she was thirteen years old. 'Take this Eduardo and keep it safe. Remember I will always love you.'

Eduardo protested, 'No Vicenta, if they find it, they will confiscate it.'

'I don't care. Keep it, hide it. I'll make a pact

with you. So long as you have it with you, we will always be bound together, no matter what happens.'

'Time's up,' Pedro Ferrer barked from the far end of the room, jangling the bunch of keys as he spoke.

Eduardo rose and lifted Vicenta's hands. She stood on tiptoes and stretched to kiss his lips and fondle his face. She longed to pull him close and press his body against hers, but the iron bars kept them apart.

'You must leave now,' Ferrer yelled.

Their lips parted and Eduardo gently pushed Vicenta away. They looked intently into each other's eyes, fighting to restrain the tears that would betray the consternation they both shared.

As Vicenta left the room and waited for the outer door to be unlocked, she noticed Ferrer glance in her direction. She glowered at his face, her cheeks now streaked with tears. Ferrer tried hard to feign indifference, but Vicenta noticed a slight flicker of his eye lashes as he lowered his eyes for a fleeting second to avoid her unyielding stare. The moment seemed to epitomise the mood of the Spanish people.

Vicenta left the jail and trudged slowly back across the main square. The wind had eased and the sky was clearing to reveal a pale half moon and patches of bright stars between dark clouds. She lifted the collar of her coat and tried to pull down the sleeves that were riding up past her wrists. Most of Vicenta's clothes had been left behind in Casa Pepita when the Guardia Civil arrived two weeks before and gave her and Eduardo just ten minutes to leave the house. Foolishly, she had grabbed a few personal possessions, bits of jewellery and old photographs, which she bundled into a cardboard box together with her diary and a bible given to her by her parents. Before she could think about more practical things, a newly arrived Guardia officer thrust her toward the door, but not before he had rifled through the box and confiscated the jewellery. They did the same to Eduardo, searching his clothing and taking the purse that contained around two hundred pesetas – all the cash he possessed. His protests had been rewarded with a blow to the pit of his stomach from a rifle butt.

The coat she now wore belonged to her sister, Isobel Perez. It was at least a size too small. Isobel had allowed Vicenta and Eduardo to stay in her house when they were ejected from Casa Pepita, but the place was small and cramped with Isobel's husband, Francisco, his mother and two children occupying all the available bed spaces. When Eduardo was arrested, Isobel and her family had themselves come under scrutiny from the Falangists who questioned why she was giving shelter to a republican sympathiser. Vicenta had offered to leave even though she had no place to go. Isobel had refused to hear of it, though her husband had protested that Vicenta's continued presence would not be without consequences.

As Vicenta turned a corner to leave the square she was startled to be confronted by a pair of Guardia Civil officers out on their regular patrol. Before the war it was rare to see a policeman of any kind in Benimarta. Joachin Fernandez, the *policia local* officer, might occasionally visit the village, but since his patrol covered four other villages as well as Benimarta, he was pretty much a stranger. Now it seemed the Guardia Civil contingent was ever present, day and night, on the streets of Benimarta, a consequence of its designation as part of a republican zone, even though the fighting never reached its streets.

There were at least four Guardia Civil officers now quartered in Casa Pepita. They were strangers to the village – a deliberate policy of the new order to ensure they had no connections with the area over which they now exercised control. Few people even knew their names, as they deliberately maintained their anonymity.

Vicenta's heart quickened as her eyes settled on the shiny new machine guns strapped across the chests of the two officers. Their dark green uniforms were hard to pick out in the darkness, but there was no mistaking the profile of the shiny black tri-corn hats they wore with straps buckled beneath their chins. The backs of the tri-corn hats were turned up vertically and though it was never uttered in public, people joked that this was to enable the Guardia to sleep with their backs to the wall.

'What are you doing out at this time of night?' one of the officers asked.

Vicenta knew better than to tell them she had been visiting her husband in jail. 'I've been to see my uncle Antonio. He lives in Calle Mayor. He's in his eighties and he's been ill for some time, so I took him some soup.'

'Your name?'

'Vicenta Reig,' she replied, using her maiden name for fear of being associated with Eduardo's family, Ripoll.

'And where are you going?'

'Home,' Vicenta said tersely, her heart pounding.

All the while the second officer was scrutinising Vicenta with an undisguised leer and a menacing half-smile.

'Don't be smart with me, young lady. Where's home?'

'I live with my sister Isobel Perez in Calle San Juan number twenty-one.'

'Then you'd better hurry along. It's dangerous to be out after dark. It might lead us to think you are a rebel or a subversive and then we'd have to take you in for questioning. My colleague here might enjoy that, so you'd better go while you can.'

Vicenta wanted to spit in his face, gouge his eyes and kick him in the groin. Until recently Benimarta had been such a peaceful place where everybody knew everybody else and where neighbours helped each other out. Children played on the streets, safe in the knowledge that that they were under a kind of paternal supervision wherever they went. Strangers were a rare sight. No one bothered much about politics and conversations were generally dominated by benign gossip about new romances and family arguments.

Now all that had changed. Everyone, it seemed, had the designation of pro- or anti- the new regime and there was no place for neutrality. The stability of the past had been replaced by a clamour for change led by those who had wheedled their way into power and who were determined to usurp the old order. Resistance was dangerous as a word out of place could be construed as active opposition.

Relieved to be away from the Guardia patrol, Vicenta turned into Calle San Juan and headed toward Isobel's house at the end of the street. She picked her way along the dark cobbles still glistening in the aftermath of the storm. A shaft of light illuminated a section of the street filtering from the open door of Bar Rincon. As she approached, Vicenta could hear the hubbub of laughter and loud voices inside the bar, now the exclusive preserve of Falange supporters happy to revel in their new found positions of influence. As she passed by, she paused and foolishly glanced inside finding it hard to see through the dense cloud of tobacco smoke that filled the air. For a brief moment her eyes alighted on a familiar face whose attention had been attracted by her silhouette in the doorway. Immediately she looked away, lowered her head and moved along.

Within seconds she could hear footsteps behind her, keeping pace as she increased her stride. She was fifty yards from Isobel's house and safety. A hand on her shoulder pulled her up sharp and caused her heart to flutter.

'What's the rush?' a gruff voice bellowed.

Vicenta turned and looked up at the menacing face towering above her. 'There's no rush,' she said unconvincingly, 'I'm on my way home.'

'Home you say. To your sister's house you mean. Must be quite a come down from what you are used to.'

'Needs must,' Vicenta replied, wanting, but not daring, to challenge the injustice of having her home requisitioned without notice or due process.

'Still, you and Eduardo must have rattled around in Casa Pepita, I think. All that space, all those bedrooms, the grand library and dining room,' the man sneered. 'I'm glad to see the place put to good use at last. That's why I suggested it to the Guardia Civil when they were looking for suitable quarters.' His mouth twisted to a malevolent smile.

'What do you want, Juan-Martin?'

'It's Comrade Garcia to you,' he snapped. 'You've been to see your husband, I hear. How is Eduardo?'

Anger supplanted Vicenta's fear. She clenched her fists and glared at Garcia's face. 'How do you think he is, *Comrade* Garcia, beaten, starved and incarcerated in that dungeon. And for what? Not for any crime he has committed, but just to satisfy a lust for revenge and your envy of everything Eduardo's family has worked for.'

'This isn't the old republic any more. Perhaps you haven't heard, but General Franco, *El Caudillo*, won the war and your husband supported the wrong side. That makes him an enemy of the new government and that means he has no rights. In fact he's lucky to be alive, many have been executed for less.'

Vicenta gritted her teeth. 'You hypocrite. Eduardo is no enemy of Spain. It was you who denounced him and not because he has done anything wrong, just because you want to get your filthy hands on his land and property. You never had the gumption to better yourself, so now you simply want to take what others have worked for. I suppose you think that wearing that blue shirt gives you the right, but sooner or later justice will prevail and Spain will come to its senses to rid itself of fascism and trumped up tyrants like you.'

Garcia thrust himself forward so that his face was inches from Vicenta's. She could smell the foul odour of nicotine and aniseed on his breath and it almost made her gag.

'That's dangerous talk, Vicenta. I could have you arrested for sedition. Perhaps you and Eduardo could share the same cell. Now listen to me. I've offered Eduardo a way out. All he has to do is sign a few bits of paper and he could be free, but the stubborn fool refuses to accept the reality of his situation. Perhaps you should try to persuade him to see the error of his ways.'

Vicenta felt her face reddening with anger. 'And give you Casa Pepita and all his family's land. He'll never do that for the simple reason that he doesn't trust you. And why should he trust someone whom he once regarded as a friend but who has turned out to be a treacherous opportunist.'

Garcia's face turned crimson and his eyes narrowed, filled with rage. Without warning, he grabbed Vicenta by the throat and lifted her off her feet. 'Well, if he won't buy his freedom, then perhaps you can earn it for him.' He twisted her body so that her back was toward him and placed his hand over her nose and mouth, dragging her backwards into a narrow alleyway halfway down the street. She tried to scream, but all she could do was emit a muffled squeal.

It was pitch black in the alley where Garcia twisted her round once more, ramming her back against the wall and pinning her there with the full weight of his body. He grabbed her throat again, compressing her wind pipe so that she gasped for air. She started to struggle, kicking with her feet and lashing out with her hands in a fruitless attempt to prise him away. He retaliated by slamming her head against the wall. Vicenta felt an excruciating pain flow from the back of her head to the back of her eyes as she drifted into semi-consciousness and her vision became blurred.

'To the victor belong the spoils,' he snarled as he lifted her skirt and began tugging at her panties.

Instinctively she closed her legs, mustering all her energy to press her knees together. His rough hand grabbed her right thigh and lifted it high so that she stood on tiptoe with her left leg. Now he loosened his grip on her throat and thrust his face forward so that his mouth was pressing against her left ear.

'Scream and you're dead,' he snarled in a murderous tone as he dropped his free hand to rip at the buttons of his trousers and thrust his thighs forward slamming her buttocks against the wall.

Vicenta tried to twist her body sideways, but it was useless. He was inside her now and ramming his hips forwards and upwards. With his right hand he undid the three buttons of her coat, ripped open her blouse and pulled down her bra to grab at her breasts. His hand was cold and hard and she twisted her body futilely trying to turn away. He grabbed her nipple between his forefinger and thumb and pinched it hard, tugging and twisting. Vicenta let out a shrill squeal as the pain shot through her body.

'I told you, shut up.' Garcia snarled, releasing his grip of her breast and moving both his hands to her buttocks, all the while maintaining his frantic thrusts. 'Come on Vicenta, you know you love it.' With one final lunge he pinned her hard against the wall and emitted a sinister whimpering groan. He raised his head and moved forward trying to place his lips on Vicenta's mouth. She turned her head sideways to avoid the odious smell of his breath and he shoved his face against her neck, licking the soft flesh beneath her ear. 'I bet sex was never that good with Eduardo,' he whispered insidiously.

'You bastard,' Vicenta hissed. She wrenched her head to the other side and sank her teeth into Garcia's ear lobe. The warm salty taste of his blood oozed into her mouth and she almost retched in disgust. Only when a chunk of Garcia's ear detached in her mouth did she release her bite, turning her head once more to spit a gobbet of flesh, blood and spittle full into Garcia's face.

Garcia bellowed in pain. 'Bitch', he howled as he raised his right hand and slammed his fist full into Vicenta's face crushing her nose and splitting her upper lip. Vicenta felt her eyes flutter as she drifted into unconsciousness, her legs weakened and she slithered down the wall collapsing sideways onto the floor of the alley. The final image of Garcia's wild eyes and blood spattered face was etched forever on her memory.

Indistinct voices filtered through the half-open door and though she was only fuzzily aware of what was being said, she was alert enough to discern their argumentative tone. She tried to listen more acutely, but the effort was too much for her and she quickly drifted back into oblivion. Hours later she awoke again and blinked rapidly to bring her sight into focus, her eyes alighting on the blank plaster ceiling criss-crossed by cracks that seemed reassuringly familiar.

She felt a hand stroke her cheek. 'Vicenta? Can you hear me Vicenta?'

She turned her head and blinked again. 'Is that you Isobel?' she mumbled through swollen lips that stung with pain as the dry scab on her upper lip separated from the puffy flesh, causing a trickle of blood to seep into her mouth. Instinctively she spat it out leaving a trail of pink spittle to dribble from the corner of her mouth. Isobel patted it gently with a soft cloth.

'Don't talk now,' Isobel said. 'You are very weak. For a while we thought we had lost you. Just rest now and I'll bring you some soup in a little while. You've been unconscious for two days and we need to rebuild your strength.'

Vicenta's mind was racing through a jumble of disjointed images, each flashing and fading away. The lingering after-taste of her own blood suddenly registered and brought into focus those last few minutes before she had blacked out. She closed her eyes and tried to blank her mind, but the images refused to go away. She opened her eyes again and lifted her torso to sit upright in her bed. She was dripping with sweat and her heart was pounding in her chest. She tried again to gather her thoughts, but the effort made her feel faint. She allowed her body to fall back again and her head to rest on the pillow as an uneasy sleep brought temporary relief from the terror of consciousness.

Over the next three days Isobel barely left her sister's side. She bathed the cuts on Vicenta's face with salt water and fed her small pieces of bread dipped in lukewarm soup. She washed her sister's body and ran a brush through her wavy brown hair. They spoke of very little beyond sisterly platitudes and words of reassurance. Gradually, Vicenta regained her strength. Her face healed and the swelling and bruising subsided. One day she asked for a mirror and reluctantly Isobel acceded. Vicenta looked calmly at the mirror showing little emotion as she stared through and beyond her reflection with eyes that were devoid of emotion.

'We need to talk,' Isobel said one morning as she parted the curtains to allow a beam of bright sunlight to enter the room that had, until then, been kept in sullen gloom. She puffed the pillows behind Vicenta's back and straightened the blankets.

Vicenta took her sister's arm to stop her fussing. 'I don't want to talk about what happened, if that is what you mean.'

Isobel sat on the side of the bed and gripped Vicenta's hands. 'We know what happened,' she said hesitantly. 'It's not that I want to talk about.'

Vicenta stiffened and pulled her hands away. 'What do you mean, you know what happened? How can you?'

Isobel looked sheepish. 'I'm so sorry, Vicenta, but the whole village knows what Juan-Martin Garcia did to you. No one dares to talk about it, but believe me, everyone knows.'

'But how could they?'

'You left your mark on Garcia. He's missing a chunk of his ear. After… after it happened he had to explain that and… how can I say this? He says you offered yourself to him. He says you begged him to have sex with you so that he would release Eduardo from jail. He says you bit his ear when he had finished because he told you he would not release Eduardo.'

'And everyone believes his story?'

'No, of course not, but they are all too afraid to challenge him.'

Vicenta thrust the bed clothes to one side. 'Well I'm not scared of that vicious bastard. I'll challenge him. I'll accuse him in public if need be. He'll pay for what he did to me.'

Isobel placed her hands on Vicenta's shoulders

and pushed her back against the pillows.

'It's no use, Vicenta. You don't understand. Garcia runs Benimarta now. He answers to no one, not even the Guardia Civil. They know what happened, or at least they have an idea, but they just turn a blind eye. You are the wife of someone who's been imprisoned for issuing anti-government propaganda. If you make a fuss, Garcia will probably have you arrested as well, just to keep you out of the way.'

'But Eduardo's done nothing wrong,' Vicenta protested.

'I know that. Most people know that as well, but he's been denounced and people are powerless to do anything about that.'

'Afraid, you mean.'

'Yes, afraid if you like. But it's not cowardice that makes them conform, it's pragmatism. Spain is in the grip of a tyrant who holds all power to himself and who uses the force of his army and the unswerving loyalty of the Falange to suppress any act, any thought of defiance.'

'So what are you saying, Isobel? I must just stay quiet and let Garcia get away with what he has done?'

Isobel straightened and moved away. 'That's exactly what I am saying, Vicenta. Perhaps in the future things will be different. I hear rumours of resistance from Republicans who escaped to France, and there are reports of skirmishes in the mountains, but they are just that, rumours. And no one really holds out any great hope that the new regime will be overthrown. The rest of Europe is embroiled with war. Franco has bought the tacit acceptance of his regime in return for neutrality and while America and Britain focus their attention on Hitler and Mussolini, *El Caudillo* has a virtual free hand to run Spain as he pleases.'

Vicenta slumped back in her bed letting the reality of her situation sink in. She heard the heavy clump of footsteps on the stairs outside her room. Isobel moved swiftly toward the door. 'I'll be back in a moment,' she said as she left the bedroom closing the door behind her.

The voices were muffled and Vicenta strained to hear the conversation.

'Is she still here? I've told you I want her out of this house. Today.'

'Not now, Francisco, please. She's still recovering. You know what she's been through. A few more days, I beg you.'

'I don't care what she's been through. That's her own stupid fault. You know what's happening to us while she's here, and it will get worse if she stays. If she's not gone by the time I get back, I'll throw her out on the street myself.'

Vicenta heard footsteps retreating down the stairs before Isobel re-entered the bedroom. She was clearly flustered, her neck reddening and her cheeks flushed. Before Isobel could say anything, Vicenta spoke out.

'What did he mean, "You know what's happening to us"?'

Isobel strode forward and began to fuss over the bedding. 'It's nothing,' she said. 'Now settle down, you're still weak and you need to rest.'

'Stop fussing and tell me the truth, Isobel. Why does Francisco want me to leave?'

Isobel lowered her head but Vicenta could see she was close to tears. 'I don't know what's happened to the people of this village. For weeks now, there's been hardly any food. It was a struggle all through the war as you know, but we managed on what we could grow in the fields, and bits of meat the hunters brought back from the mountains. People helped each other out as best they could. Eduardo, for example, let others use his land and take water from the well to grow a few crops. As bad as things got, we still had a meagre supply of flour for bread. It wasn't easy, but no one starved. All that has changed. The syndicate has taken charge of all food supplies and distribution. No one is allowed to gather crops for themselves, everything must be handed over. Last week old Jose Rodriguez returned from the forest with a small wild boar he had trapped, but he was stopped at the edge of the village by the Guardia Civil and the animal was confiscated. It's terrible, some people are close to starvation.'

Vicenta looked puzzled. 'I read that the government had announced rationing, so why are people starving?'

Isobel looked over her shoulder, checking that the door was closed. 'Because half the food obtained by the syndicate disappears to the black market. People have seen it for themselves. All the food is taken to the municipal store which is supposed to be kept secure by the Guardia. But people have seen it disappear. A lorry turns up in the middle of the night and leaves loaded with sacks. Then when people go to ask for food they say there is not enough to meet even the meagre rations the government has promised. And all the while a few people are getting rich.'

'Garcia you mean?'

'And others.'

'And is that why Francisco wants me to leave, because there isn't enough food for your family?'

'You mustn't worry, Vicenta, we'll manage. Somehow we'll manage.'

'There's something else, isn't there, Isobel. Tell me.'

Isobel looked shamefaced and her eyes filled with tears. 'Even if there is little else, the syndicate knows that people need bread. The ration is one *barra* per person every two days. It's hardly enough, but it's better than nothing. Two days ago I went to the *panadería* and Paquita refused to serve me. She was flustered and embarrassed and when I asked her why she just said "orders." I told Francisco and he went up to the town hall to talk to Federico Blasco – he's the blue shirt supposed to be in charge of food distribution. Blasco told Francisco there was no bread for those who give shelter to enemies of the state or their relatives.'

Vicenta placed a hand on her sister's shoulder. 'Then how have you been feeding me these last few days?'

'We have a small store of dried food stashed away in the cellar. It was Francisco's idea when he saw the war coming to an end.'

'And the bread?' Vicenta asked.

Paquita came round after she refused to serve me in the shop. She gave me a couple of loaves. They were stale, but she said it was the best she could do. If she had been caught there would have been trouble for her and her family as well.'

In that moment Vicenta realised what she must do. She threw her bed linen to one side and rose unsteadily to her feet. 'Where are my clothes Isobel?'

'No Vicenta, you can't leave, you are not well enough.' Isobel took hold of Vicenta's arms to support her.

Vicenta embraced her sister, pulling her close and holding her tightly. 'You have done too much already,' she said resignedly. 'Now, where are my clothes?'

'But where will you go?' Isobel asked as she closed the top of a battered canvas suitcase.

'Eduardo's family own a small house on the edge of the village, near the washhouse. It's basic, but it has running water, I think. Eduardo always planned to repair the place, but that was before the war.'

Isobel looked concerned. 'I know the place. Half the roof is missing and the windows are rotten. You can't live there Vicenta, you'll freeze to death.'

'Don't worry, Isobel, part of the house is dry and there's an old fire place if I remember correctly. I'll be all right.'

'I wish you'd stay.'

'You know that's impossible. Now, what have you put in that suitcase?'

The clasps on the suitcase were broken and Isobel began to tie a knot in a frayed piece of rope to hold the lid in place. 'It's just a few old clothes.' She handed the case to Vicenta.

Feeling the weight of the case Vicenta said, 'There's more than a few old clothes in here. What else is there?'

'There's a little food, half a bag of rice, some dried beans and lentils and a jar of last year's tomatoes. I wish I could give you more.'

Vicenta put the case on the small table in the centre of the room and began to untie the knot. 'It's too much, Isobel. You need this for your family. Besides, what will Francisco say?'

Isobel stepped forward and placed her hands on top of the case. 'I don't care what Francisco says. He can rot for all I care after what he's done to you. For two pins I'd leave him and come with you.'

Vicenta clasped her sister's arms. 'You know you can't do that, Isobel. You have to think of yourself and your two boys. And you mustn't blame Francisco. He's a good man, and like many good men in the new Spain, he knows that compliance is the only way to survive, at least for the time being. Now, I must be going.'

'When will I see you again? I need to know that you are all right,' Isobel pleaded.

'Don't worry about me, I'll be fine, but you'd better stay away from me for a little while at least. I'll find a way to keep in touch, but we'd better not aggravate the authorities for now.'

Isobel thrust herself forward to embrace her sister, hugging her tightly. Her chest heaved as she sobbed and sniffled. She raised a hand to wipe away the tears that tracked her face. Vicenta gently eased Isobel away, fighting to hold back her own tears. She kissed her sister softly on the lips and smudged the tears on her cheeks, looking straight into her eyes.

'They may subjugate the people by fear and tyranny, but they will never repress our spirit and they will never destroy our integrity or enslave our hearts. I love you sister, always remember that.' Vicenta lifted the small suitcase and tucked it under her arm. She turned and left the house.

The door to the old house had no lock. There

was no point, it was little more than an empty ruin. Vicenta leant against the door and forced it open, scraping back a layer of rubble and broken tiles that had accumulated on the floor. Twilight penetrated the rafters above the hallway where a part of the roof had fallen in. The atmosphere smelled damp and musty. She moved to the kitchen on the right of the hall and opened a copper tap, mottled with verdigris. The pipes rattled and clanked before a trickle of brackish brown water finally emerged, falling into a stone sink covered with a layer of dust and grit.

In the living room she was relieved to find a few bits of furniture, an old sofa and a small pile of logs in the alcove at the side of an open fireplace. The ceiling to the room was intact though chunks of plaster had fallen to the floor and there were damp patches on the walls. She returned to the hall to gather a few small pieces of wood that had fallen from the roof and set a fire. The logs were moist and took a while to catch, but eventually she was able to warm her hands causing them to ache as the warmth penetrated her bones.

Cautiously she climbed the wooden stairs feeling them shift and creak under her weight. One glance along the landing convinced her that it would be dangerous to go further. Sections of the floor were missing, leaving gaping holes between the beams. The bedrooms were inaccessible and probably uninhabitable as well. She returned to the living room and placed a couple more logs on the fire, grateful that the chimney seemed to be drawing the smoke from the room. She opened the wooden shutters to a window that overlooked an inner courtyard and used her sleeve to clear a layer of grime from a cracked pane of glass. The courtyard was strewn with rocks and fallen masonry which were gradually being colonised by weeds and creepers. An ancient lemon tree in one corner bore a crop of shrivelled fruit. The light was beginning to fail as night approached. She found an old broom in a closet in the kitchen and swept an area of the floor in front of the hearth, brushing aside a layer of rubble and fallen plaster and raising a cloud of dust. She dragged the old sofa closer to the fire and, overcome with tiredness, she lay down and pulled her sister's coat over her knees. Within minutes she succumbed to a fitful sleep punctuated by reminiscences of the past and fears for the future.

Vicenta had lived in Benimarta all her life. She attended the village school to the age of fourteen and gained a solid education, excelling in reading and writing in Valenciano, the principal language in this part of Spain. She could understand Castellano when it was spoken on the radio and could read the language in books and newspapers though her vocabulary was more limited than in her native tongue. She had loved her history classes with Señor Calvo, especially his enthusiastic accounts of the centuries when much of Spain was under the rule of the Moors until the Reconquest and their eventual expulsion in the seventeenth century. She could name most of the Kings and Queens of Spain from Ferdinand and Isobela in the eighteenth century to the then ruling King, Alfonso XIII.

Vicenta was in her final year at school when she first met Eduardo. At sixteen he was two years her senior and he beguiled her with his accounts of life in Valencia, a city she had never visited. After meeting Eduardo, the local boys in Benimarta seemed plain and unsophisticated, especially since most, like her, had never ventured far from the village. She was captivated as Eduardo talked of the books he had read and the fine art he had viewed in the city. By the time she was seventeen and Eduardo nineteen they were engaged. They married a year later and moved into Casa Pepita to live with Eduardo's father, Julio. Compared to her family's modest village house, Casa Pepita seemed grand, almost too grand, especially with just three people living there.

Vicenta's own parents had died two years earlier, her mother from pneumonia and her father from diabetes that was left undiagnosed until it was too late. Eduardo's father treated her as a daughter and she soon began to relish the role of housewife – shopping, cooking and cleaning for the two men in her life. Julio had offered to engage a helper, but Vicenta wouldn't hear of it, even though the size of the house meant she was always busy. She had secretly earmarked one of the bedrooms as a nursery for the child she anticipated as a matter of course. She and Eduardo made love freely and, despite her stern Catholic upbringing, she quickly overcame the feelings of reticence and guilt she initially felt at the pleasure she derived from uninhibited sexual fulfilment.

But tragedy, it seemed, was never far from Vicenta and when Julio fell ill with pleurisy just months after her wedding, she began to wonder if her life was fated to be punctuated by sickness and death. She nursed her father-in-law for nearly six months, as his breathing became shallower and the pains in his chest grew more severe. She soothed his brow through the fevers and patted his back as he retched to clear the thick yellow phlegm that choked his lungs. His eventual death was a release from the agonies he suffered in the final few weeks. Eduardo was just twenty-one years old when he inherited the whole of his father's estate. He was devastated, for he lost not only a father, but a best friend and mentor from whom there was still so much to learn.

Though she dreaded telling Eduardo what had happened, Vicenta knew she had to see him to explain and reassure him that she was coping.

God only knew what he would do if ever he got his hands on Garcia, especially if he ever heard Garcia's version of events. For now that seemed a remote possibility, but she still needed to see him, hold him and know that he understood.

The next morning she rose early an bathed herself standing in front of the kitchen sink, shivering with each splash of icy cold water. She washed her hair using a hard tablet of soap that barely formed a lather and then rinsed it under the tap. She added a couple of logs to the embers of the fire to warm herself and dry her hair.

A rummage through the old suitcase uncovered a collection of dowdy clothes, mostly her sister's and mostly ill-fitting and showing signs of wear. How she would have loved to pick something bright and cheerful to lift her mood, but the entire collection acted as a reminder of how her life had changed, seemingly for ever. She opted for a long grey woollen skirt with a frayed hem. The waist was too tight so she left the top two buttons undone and rolled the waistband so that the hem just reached her calves. Over a cotton camisole she donned an olive green, hand-knitted sweater with a round neck. The pile of the sweater was matted from frequent washing and the fabric felt harsh against her skin. Though the body was a baggy fit, the sleeves were too short, but it was warm. She laced her only pair of ankle boots grateful that these, at least, were her own and relatively new.

Standing in front of a dusty mirror above the hearth, she crimped her shoulder-length brown hair with her fingers to enhance its natural waviness. The swelling in her top lip had subsided, and the cut had almost healed over. A dab of lipstick would have easily concealed the faint scar, but she had none. Her black eye had faded to a yellow bruising that might easily be mistaken for the kind of dark shadows induced by sleeplessness. She pinched her cheeks to bring a little colour to her otherwise pallid face. Staring at her reflection, a sudden fear gripped her. How would Eduardo react when she told him she had been raped by Garcia? Had he heard Garcia's distorted version of events already? Would her now-healed wounds suggest to Eduardo that she had not resisted Garcia's attack? Perhaps she should not tell him. Perhaps she should not go to see him at all. Quickly she cast these thoughts to one side. She loved Eduardo and she knew he loved her. She must show resolve. It was Eduardo, incarcerated in a dungeon, who needed support and she must do everything to show him she could cope and convince him there was hope for their future together, even in the crushing oppression of the new Spain under Franco and the Falange.

She tugged on her sister's old coat and pulled down the brim of a felt hat, hoping no one would see her as she strode out of the old house and climbed the hill toward the centre of the village. A chattering group of women knelt at the side of the stream that passed through the washhouse. They fell silent as she passed, keeping her head down and avoiding eye contact. The chattering resumed with added intensity before she turned the corner and moved out of earshot.

The bright winter sunshine failed to lift her gloom as she crossed the main square feeling a little too warm for comfort. A jangle of keys caught her attention and she glanced sideways to the door of the presbytery where Father Ignacio was leaving for the church next door. He looked over toward Vicenta and for a moment seemed to raise a hand. Vicenta bowed her head once more and increased her stride.

The small panel in the centre of the heavy door slid open in response to Vicenta's determined knock. She recognised Pedro Ferrer immediately and this time she was not going to grovel.

'I'm here to see my husband, let me in,' she demanded.

Ferrer blinked and stuttered. 'Do you have a visiting order?'

'No I do not. And I don't know why I would need one. This is not a prison, my husband has not been convicted of any offence, he's not even been charged. I want to see him... now.' Despite her bravado, her heart was pounding and she could feel beads of sweat forming on her brow.

'I can't let you in without a visiting order,' Ferrer persisted.

Vicenta decided to change tack. 'Pedro, this is

Eduardo we're talking about. He's an old friend of yours for God's sake. I really need to see him. Please let me in.'

The panel slammed shut and for a brief moment Vicenta thought she had failed. Then she heard bolts sliding and the door opened. Ferrer stuck his head out to glance furtively up and down the street.

'Quickly, come inside,' he whispered, closing and bolting the door behind Vicenta as she entered the dingy passageway.

'Oh thank you Pedro, you have no idea what this means to me. I just have to talk to Eduardo.'

Ferrer shuffled and lowered his eyes. 'He's not here.'

Vicenta gasped. 'What do you mean, he's not here? Where is he?'

'I don't know,' he mumbled, still looking at the floor.

Vicenta grabbed his face with both hands and forced him to look into her eyes. 'Pedro, please tell me what's happened to him. Where is he?' Her voice was gruff, faltering with anxiety.

Ferrer swallowed hard. 'If I tell you, you must promise not say you heard it from me.'

'I promise. Now tell me what's happened.'

'He was taken away last night.'

'Taken away? By whom? Where to?' she demanded, the desperation now clear in her voice.

'I'll tell you all I know, but you must promise...'

'Yes, yes, I promise. Now tell me.'

'Just before midnight two blue shirts arrived. They said they were acting under orders from the Provincial Governor. They said something about under the new Law of Political Responsibility all dissident prisoners were being transferred to Alicante to be tried.'

Vicenta froze, open-mouthed for a second, waiting for more, but Ferrer said nothing.

'Is that it? You just let them take him?'

'What else could I do? They waved some papers in front of me and one of them had a gun. They just brushed me to one side and took the keys. They went through to the cells and returned with Eduardo. They bundled him out through the door and into a truck that was waiting outside.'

'And what was Eduardo doing as they dragged him out?'

'Nothing. He looked dazed and half asleep. The two men had hold of his arms and they just shoved him forward then climbed in the back of the truck with Eduardo. He wasn't resisting if that's what you mean.'

'These men, did you know them?'

Ferrer blinked and looked to one side. 'No. They were just blue shirts with red berets. It was dark and I couldn't see their faces. They were in and out so quickly, I hardly had time to think.'

'And this paper they showed you. Did they leave it with you?'

'No.'

'Did you even read it?'

'I told you, it was dark and they came and went so quickly.'

Vicenta was exasperated. 'Pedro how could you possibly let these people take Eduardo. You have no idea who they were or what they were up to. You don't even know that they had any proper authority to take him.'

Ferrer pushed Vicenta away. 'They were blue shirts and that's all I needed to know. The Falange are running this country now and it doesn't do to get on the wrong side of them. For all I know, if I'd refused to let them in then I'd be sitting in a cell right now accused of helping a republican supporter.'

Despite her anger, Vicenta understood what Ferrer was saying. Fear makes cowards of even the strongest men. Tyranny and repression can cause a nation to accept subjugation when the alternative is arbitrary arrest and persecution… and worse.

Where was Eduardo now she wondered? She pictured him bouncing in the back of a truck, guarded by two strangers intent on delivering him to an internment camp somewhere in Alicante, if that was indeed his destination. A sudden thought grabbed Vicenta. She took Ferrer by the shoulders and gave him a cold hard stare. 'You said the two men went in the back of the truck with Eduardo?'

Ferrer frowned. 'Yes.'

'Then who was driving?'

'I... I'm not sure. I... I told you it was dark.'

Ferrer's hesitation was revealing.

'Was Juan-Martin Garcia driving the truck?'

Ferrer looked away. 'I've told you all I know. Now, you must leave before someone sees you here.' He turned away and pushed Vicenta toward the door.

Vicenta knew then the instigator of Eduardo's forced removal and she feared the worst. Eduardo's imprisonment had been hard enough to bear, not knowing his fate was even worse. With panic and dread overwhelming her emotions she knew there and then what she must do. She would not rest until she had found Eduardo and secured his freedom.

CHAPTER TWO

An old man and his son found Vicenta lying exhausted by the side of the road between Senija and Benissa. Even the rattling motor of the mula mecánica failed to rouse her as she lay motionless with her head resting on the battered suitcase, her clothes damp in the aftermath of an overnight shower. Their first impression was that she must be dead.

Lifting her to a seated position, the son swept the hair from her face and held her shoulders firm while the father rubbed her hands in an attempt to generate some warmth. Vicenta's eyes fluttered as she struggled to focus on the rough bearded face that confronted her. She flinched in fear.

'Don't worry,' the old man said, 'we're not going to rob you. What are you doing here, out in the open?'

Vicenta pulled her hands away and scrutinised the two men, noticing their muddy boots and shabby, wear-worn clothes. They must be farmers, she thought, though she new better than to trust any stranger, especially in these uncertain times.

'I'm heading for Benissa,' she said in a faltering voice.

'Then you've a long way to go,' the old man said. 'And by the looks of you, you'll never make it. Where have you come from?'

'I'm from Benimarta,' she said hesitantly, not wanting to divulge too much.

'Benimarta, that's a distance from here. How long have you been on the road?'

'I left on Wednesday.'

'That's two days – and two nights,' the son declared. 'No wonder you are exhausted.'

'We need to get you somewhere warm,' said the old man. 'We have a casita just along the road. Come with us and we'll light a fire. When did you last eat?'

In a different age, an age that seemed all too distant now, Vicenta would have thought nothing of accepting the hospitality of fellow country folk. Such benevolence to travellers was the norm in a part of Spain where public transport was virtually non-existent and a mule was the only alternative to journeying on foot. Picking an orange or a caqui (the fruit of the persimmon tree) or a handful of almonds as sustenance for a journey was an accepted convention. But now, all food supplies had been effectively commandeered by the State and picking just a single fruit could be construed as theft. Accepting the charity of strangers would never have bothered Vicenta in the past, but now such altruism gave rise to suspicion.

'I must press on,' Vicenta said as she struggled to her feet and clutched the suitcase defensively. Stiff from the damp, her legs buckled and she stumbled forward. The son grabbed her waist and held her tight to prevent her from falling. At the same time the old man took hold of the suitcase and wrenched it from beneath her arm. Bolstered by fear, Vicenta wriggled free from the son's grip and straightened her legs, striding forward to snatch back the suitcase from the old man.

'Give me that,' she demanded, 'and leave me alone. I don't need your help. Get away from me.'

The old man raised his hands and took a step back. 'I can see you're afraid,' he said. 'I can also see that you are in no fit state to continue your journey. We'll leave you alone if that's what you want, but my guess is that your journey is important or you wouldn't be out here in the open at this time of year. Without food and warmth, I doubt you'll survive another night.'

The breeze stiffened and a shiver reverberated through Vicenta's spine. She examined the two men, carefully scrutinising their features. The old man's leathery, pock-marked face was scoured with deep-set wrinkles. His greying hair, though thinning, fell untidily over his brow overlapping bushy brown eyebrows conjoined at the centre. The backs of his hands were speckled with age spots and a thick layer of reddish dirt was ingrained beneath jagged finger nails. Raising her eyes she noted his conspicuous crooked nose that twisted incongruously to the left side of his face. It must, she assumed, have been distorted by a blow or collision, until she noticed the son's equally misaligned nose. Indeed, on closer study, the son's face was a facsimile of the father's though its narrowness and angularity contrasted with the father's more rotund profile. His wiry hair was darker and thicker and flopped wildly about his head in an unruly mop. Still suspicious, Vicenta looked into the young man's hollow eyes, framed by stubby lashes and glistening with moisture. She thought they reflected a kind of sorrowful benignity that engendered trust. She could have been mistaken, but as weariness overwhelmed her, she felt compelled to accept the help that had been offered.

Wedged between the two men, Vicenta clutched her suitcase and bounced uncomfortably on the hard metal seat of the trailer hitched to the mula mechánica as it chugged and rattled its way along the rough gravel track approaching the casita. The final fifty metres took them through an olive grove where small shrivelled olives bore testament to the unusually long hot summer only recently brought to an end by late autumn rain.

'I'm Mario,' the old man said as he dismounted and offered a hand to Vicenta. 'Mario Revilla. My son is Rafael.'

Vicenta took Mario's hand as she shuffled along the bench seat and slid to the ground, still clasping the suitcase. Rafael rounded the now silent contraption and offered to take the suitcase.

'Here let me help you with that,' he said. Vicenta strengthened her grip on the case prompting the young man to step back apologetically.

'You haven't told us your name,' he said.

For a moment she thought of lying, inventing a name, but it seemed an unnecessary falsehood. 'Vicenta,' she stated, not willing to offer more.

'Come Vicenta, let's get you inside and set a fire,' Mario said.

The casita was tiny, just a few metres square, constructed of roughly hewn rocks held together with uneven layers of mud-coloured mortar flecked with small stones. The mono-pitch roof comprised irregular rows of overlapping half-round tiles stained with blotches of black lichen. At one side of the structure Mario approached a low door fashioned from rough-cut planks of wood, cracked and bleached by the sun. He pushed a key in a rusty padlock and pulled the door outwards, lifting it slightly on loose-fitting hinges to clear the weed infested ground.

Vicenta peered into the pitch-dark interior and waited for Mario to enter. Once inside he lifted a piece of sackcloth covering a small pane of opaque glass allowing a shaft of watery sunlight to penetrate the space and highlight a cloud of floating dust particles.

'After you,' Vicenta said, declining Rafael's invitation to enter the confined space. Rafael, much taller than his father, ducked beneath the frame of the door and Vicenta followed.

'Sit,' Mario implored, dragging a rickety wooden crate from a corner and standing it on its side. 'I'll light a fire and see if we can find you something to eat.' He raked the ashes from a small hearth set beneath a makeshift stone chimney and gathered a few twigs from the side of a small log pile setting them alight with a flip-top petrol lighter.

It was half an hour before Vicenta began to feel the benefit of the fire's warmth. She removed her sister's old woollen coat and Rafael placed it over the handle of a broom leaning against the wall to one side of the fire. A heavy black metal pot hanging from a hook above the fire began to simmer and steam.

'It's just dried beans, a carrot and few pieces of cardo (the celery-like stalks of the artichoke plant) I'm afraid, but that's all we have here. There's a scrap of bread, too, but it's stale. It will take a while for the beans to cook, and then you can eat.'

'I shouldn't be taking your food,' Vicenta said, 'if this is all you've got.'

Don't worry about us,' Rafael replied. 'We ate some bread and olives before we left home this morning.'

While the pot simmered, Vicenta reflected on the wisdom of her journey. Alicante was still many days away and yet she had faltered on the first leg and been forced to accept the help of strangers. Perhaps she should turn back and return to Benimarta. But her home town held nothing for her now; as the wife of someone deemed an enemy of the state she was a virtual outcast. And the thought of facing Juan-Martin Garcia was impossible to bear. Her thoughts turned to Eduardo and her spirits were lifted momentarily as she recalled the love they had found and the sublime ecstasy of sharing his bed and nestling up against his naked body in the afterglow of their ultimate intimacy. Her temporary reverie was quickly replaced by fear and anxiety. Not knowing where he was or what was happening to him was the cruellest cut of all. She needed him and she knew he needed her. Whatever hardship she faced along the way, Vicenta knew she must continue her journey and her quest to find Eduardo and fight for his freedom.

The aroma of the cooking pot struck her nostrils and she felt suddenly queasy. Her stomach churned and she began to gag. Outside the casita she bent forward, one hand against the stone wall and retched as her stomach went into spasm and she disgorged a mouthful of yellow bile. She heaved unproductively several more times until she felt empty and spent. She realised then that what she had suspected for the last few days was true. It meant her journey to find Eduardo had assumed a greater importance. It had also acquired an added burden.

The broth was insipid, but she managed to force it down, knowing she needed sustenance for what lay ahead.

'You say you are heading for Benissa,' Mario said as he took away the empty bowl.

Vicenta was reluctant to reveal too much about her mission, but she had begun to trust the father and son, believing that their generosity was devoid of any ulterior motive. They might even be able to help her. 'Benissa and then Alicante.'

Mario's eyes widened. 'Alicante! What on earth takes you to Alicante? Your journey has barely begun and we find you virtually exhausted. You've covered just twenty kilometres and there must be more than eighty to go. Are you sure you are fit to continue?'

'I have no choice. Whatever it takes, I must get there.'

'Then you must indeed be desperate,' Mario said. 'But how do you propose to get there.'

'There's a train line from Benissa, I believe.'

Mario scoffed. 'The trains were intermittent before the war and from what I hear the whole network is in ruins now. The rail lines were bombed and sabotaged by both sides and the engines have broken down through lack of maintenance. You'll be lucky to find a train to take you anywhere near Alicante.'

'Then I'll have to take the coast road.'

'I doubt you'll find a bus either. Fuel is in short supply, what little there is has been commandeered by the authorities and not for running bus services.'

Vicenta was growing impatient. 'I don't care what you say, I have to get to Alicante.' She rose from the wooden crate.

Rafael stood and blocked her way to the door. 'Don't be rash,' he said. 'If you're determined to press on, we won't stand in your way, but rest a while.' He looked toward his father. 'We can take you to the outskirts of Benissa if you want, but not until tomorrow. We have a load of almonds to deliver to the central stores near the coast road, but we have to finish baling them today.'

Mario frowned, his bushy brows knitting even closer together. 'My son has a very kind heart, but he doesn't fully understand the dangers that exist in these difficult times. The Guardia Civil are everywhere and the motive for every journey is questioned because they suspect rebels or subversives of trying to link up and mount an insurrection. Every cargo is liable to be searched. I'm not saying we won't help you, but we need to be sure you are not on the run from the authorities or involved in any kind of subversion. Good luck to you if you are, but I'm afraid we can't help you. Perhaps we should, but everyone knows the consequences and I have a family to support – my parents, my wife's mother and three sisters of Rafael.'

Vicenta understood only too well the fear and subjugation imposed on ordinary Spanish people by a regime whose tentacles spread through every fibre of society. 'I'll be honest with you,' she said at last. 'My husband was denounced to the authorities in Benimarta. Not because he's a rebel, but because he is a journalist, and not because he supported the Republicans. The man who denounced him used to be his friend, but now he is a leading light in the Falange. Eduardo's family own a fine house and land in the village but this man is trying to steal it from him. Already the house has been commandeered by the Guardia Civil. My husband was arrested and jailed in Benimarta and his accuser tried to coerce him into handing over his property in exchange for his release. Eduardo refused because he didn't trust the man. The next thing I knew, Eduardo had been taken away in the middle of the night and sent to Alicante. Now you understand why I must get there. I cannot just abandon him, I must be with him, I must try to secure his release. He's committed no crime and surely someone will see reason and release him, but only if I can get there to plead on his behalf.'

Mario and Rafael exchanged glances and an awkward silence ensued before Mario spoke again. 'I have no doubt you are in earnest in your quest, but I fear it's a foolhardy mission.'

Vicenta straightened. 'I won't be deterred, if that's what you're trying to do.'

Mario looked again toward Rafael. 'You'd better tell her, Rafael,' he said at last.

Reluctantly Rafael began to speak. 'We have a

cousin who lived in Alicante until the final days of the war. She witnessed what happened and fled the city to come here shortly afterwards. If what she said is true, then I fear not just for you, if you make it that far, but also for your husband.'

'What do you mean?' Vicenta pleaded.

Rafael recounted what he had heard.

Madrid fell to the fascists in March 1939 and everyone knew that Valencia was only days from surrender. Rumours spread through the city that relief ships from France or even a republican fleet were on their way to Alicante to take people to safety, so thousands of refugees fled there. A few managed to escape on small boats, but the hoped-for fleet never arrived. Instead a fascist battleship blockaded the seaway. By that stage the pier was packed with more than 15,000 refugees; there was barely room to stand. The city itself was under the control of Italian troops so there was no means of escape. The battleship began to broadcast by loudspeaker telling people to lay down their arms or be shot. Many of the republican soldiers did so, throwing their weapons into the sea, but others knew what awaited them. Stories of the ruthless execution of republican soldiers in Barcelona had been rife for months. They knew that they, too, would be executed if they surrendered and rather than face that end, many committed suicide. Some comrades shot each other; others jumped into the sea and drowned. Eventually the battleship fired warning shots over the pier. Surrender was inevitable, but there was another wave of suicides before the remaining refugees finally succumbed to their fate. Two hundred soldiers were shot where they stood. The remaining refugees were separated into groups. The women and children were taken to various locations in the city. The men were taken to a prison camp not far away at Albatera.

Vicenta listened intently as Rafael recounted his story. 'It's a dreadful account,' she said, 'but it has nothing to do with my husband. He wasn't a soldier and he wasn't there on the pier.'

Rafael pressed on. 'It wasn't just soldiers who were arrested, there were many civilians as well; leftists, writers, officials and intellectuals.'

Vicenta was losing patience. 'I still don't see what any of this has to do with my husband.'

'I'm explaining this because if your husband has been taken to Alicante, then he's probably been sent to Albatera. It's the only prison camp in the area. And I'm sorry to be the one to tell you this, but by all accounts it's a dreadful place.'

'What do you mean?'

'Well, you won't read anything official of course, but there are rumours. A few people managed to escape and what they say confirms what we'd already heard. The place is terribly overcrowded; it was built for around eight hundred, but there are said to be many thousands in there now. Hygiene and shelter are primitive and there's hardly any food or water. People are said to have died from disease or starvation and there is talk of executions by firing squad. I even heard rumours that some of the guards had refused to work there after an outbreak of typhoid. I'm sorry, Vicenta, but if your husband is in Albatera then I fear for his safety.'

'All the more reason why I must go there,' Vicenta replied.

CHAPTER THREE

Vicenta slept fitfully in the damp casita with only a couple of musty hessian sacks acting as a blanket to ward off the chill. Eduardo was constantly in her thoughts and she imagined him confined within the dreadful concentration camp at Albatera. Did he have a bed to sleep on? Was he healthy or had he, like so many others, succumbed to disease? Had he eaten or was he starving? Was he still alive? She refused, resolutely, to allow her doubts and fears to overwhelm her. Eduardo was young, strong and determined. He was alive; she could feel it and she knew that wherever he was, he would be thinking of her. With freezing hands she pulled out the short length of cord that hung around her neck and fingered Eduardo's thin gold ring and the small brass key. They were warm from the heat of her skin and their warmth percolated through her body, momentarily halting her shivers. A twinge in her abdomen reminded her of the importance of her mission and dispelled any doubts she had about the wisdom of her quest.

True to their promise, Mario and Rafael returned at first light, their mula mechánica chugging and rattling along the narrow camino and belching out a cloud of blue diesel fumes. The trailer hitched to the engine was piled high with sacks of almonds lashed together with a sturdy length of rope. Vicenta sat squashed between the two men on the hard metal bench at the front of the trailer as Mario steered the contraption with a set of long handlebars using the various levers and cables to control the motor. As the road twisted and inclined steeply, Vicenta feared the ancient motor would grind to a halt, but it progressed, creaking and clanking, at little more than walking pace. As they reached the summit of the hill, the early morning mist began to clear and the sun emerged bringing with it a feeble warmth. In the distance a car approached and Mario became suspicious – only the police or figures of authority had the luxury of travelling by car these days.

'If we are stopped,' Mario said, 'you'd better say you are my niece. And don't mention you are headed for Alicante, it will only raise suspicion.'

The dusty Citroën slowed to a stop as it neared them and the driver's door opened. A bulky figure emerged to stand in the centre of the road and raised a hand holding a slender walking cane. A double breasted raincoat was tightly belted at the waist, the collar drawn high around the neck. A prominent bulge at his hip distorted the otherwise symmetrical line of his outfit. His round bespectacled face was framed in close-cropped black hair and topped with a black felt beret placed centrally on his head, the leather band pulled horizontally across his forehead.

The man's flabby jowls disguised an almost non-existent jaw that disappeared into the folds of a flaccid double chin.

Mario halted the mula mechánica just a few metres from the authoritative figure, noticing the blue shirt beneath the raincoat and the small lapel badge featuring a twin yoke and crossed arrows. Falange.

'Cut the motor,' the man demanded.

Mario did as he was told.

'And you are?'

'Mario Revilla of Senija and this is my son Rafael and my niece Vicenta.'

The stranger scrutinised the three of them squashed side by side on the bench seat of the trailer. His hard stare moved slowly from one to the other settling on Vicenta with a sinister leer. Vicenta felt her heart skip a beat and fought to maintain a blithe expression disguising her inner consternation.

The man rounded the trailer and prodded one of the hessian sacks with the ebony cane.

'What's your cargo?'

'Almonds,' Mario answered, loath to say more.

'And where are you headed?'

'To the central food depot in Benissa.'

The man raised an eyebrow.

'A bit late for almonds isn't it. They would have been harvested when? In September I think. You haven't been hoarding them I hope. You know it's an offence to stockpile food that is the property of the provincial food syndicate.'

'Our dehulling machine broke down and we haven't been able to get the parts to repair it so we've had to remove the hulls by hand. It's a laborious process as I'm sure you will understand.'

'And this is your entire crop?'

'Yes.'

'Are you sure about that? If I were to search your house might I find a sack or two stashed away for your personal consumption?'

Rafael murmured as if to speak, but Mario restrained him by grasping his thigh.

'This is all we have harvested this year,' Mario said.

'Is that so? You mean to tell me that you haven't kept even a handful for your family?'

Mario shifted uneasily on the bench seat.

'Well maybe a jar or two to keep until Christmas, but no more than that.'

A wry smile distorted the man's face.

'So you lied to me?'

'It's a small reward for a whole year's work, just a couple of kilos that's all.'

'And now you protest against the government's food laws. You'll have me thinking you're a rebel or a subversive. You're not a Red are you?'

Mario knew better than to demur or issue a denial that might simply prompt further questioning.

The man tapped the top of the load with his cane.

'It seems to me this trailer is overloaded. If you're not careful this ancient contraption isn't going to make it to Benissa.' He cast a glance in Mario's direction as if to gauge his reaction. Mario remained silent.

'How many sacks do you have here?'

'Eighteen,' Mario replied.

'Seems to me that's too many. But you're in luck, I can help you. I have room in the boot of my car for a couple of sacks. If you'd just oblige me, you can be on your way and we need say no more about the fact that you've withheld some of your crop.'

Rafael rose from his seat and started to speak. 'You can't...'

Mario grabbed his arm. 'Keep quiet Rafael.'

'Is there a problem?' the man enquired, glowering at Rafael.

'No problem. My son will help me unload the sacks and put them in your car.'

'I think that would be best all round. I'm just glad I'm able to help you out. I'll open the boot for you.'

The man returned to the Citroën and lit a cigarette as he waited by the open boot.

Rafael muttered something under his breath as he and Mario unlashed the trailer and removed the two top sacks, carrying them over to the car.

'For Christ's sake, just keep your mouth shut,' Mario whispered to his son, 'or we'll be in more trouble and he'll confiscate the whole load.'

The man slammed the boot shut and dropped his cigarette to the road, stamping it out with a polished boot.

'On your way now,' he said. 'And don't delay on your way to the central depot. All food supplies are vital in these hard times and it's important they are distributed equitably. I'm sure your efforts will be appreciated by the authorities in Benissa.'

He slid into the driver's seat and started the motor. As he passed the trailer, he wound down the car window. 'Drive carefully,' he said as he sped off into the distance.

'You corrupt bastard,' Rafael yelled as the car disappeared over the brow of the hill. He turned to his father. 'And you? Why did you let him get away with it? You didn't even protest. You just did as you were told like a meek little peasant.'

'You've a lot to learn about the new Spain, son. And you'd better learn fast if you value your freedom.'

'Freedom? What freedom? The only freedom we have is to live in fear and accept the tyranny of shits like him. What gives him the power to order us about like that?'

'Victory is what gives him the power, son – that and being on the winning side. But remember this; repression only fosters dissent. Now is not the right time, but the people of Spain know what it's like to be truly free, and they have long memories.'

CHAPTER FOUR

Ten pesetas a sack was all Mario and Rafael received for their cargo in line with prices fixed by the Ministry of the Interior. Before the war their value would have been ten times that amount and Mario knew that on the black market they would command an even higher price. Such was the devastation wreaked on Spain's agricultural economy that production had fallen to less than fifty percent of pre-war levels and the cost of living had tripled. Hunger and malnutrition, always the scourge of rural Spain, had now spread to the masses and even the petite bourgeoisie were finding it hard to source basic commodities such as oil, flour and meat. Yet speculators made their fortunes, oblivious to the needs of the population at large. The new government sought to make an example of some of these speculators by imposing fines and even jail sentences on a few black market merchants. But in truth, the official infrastructure for the collection and distribution of food was so decrepit that it was only the speculators who had the means to move things around. So the system was allowed to prevail with the tacit approval of the authorities so that unrestrained greed and corruption became virtually endemic.

Despite the paucity of their reward, Mario and

Rafael gave Vicenta ten pesetas, overruling her protests.

'We may be poor,' Mario said, 'but at least we have food. Even our evil friend from the Falange cannot account for every almond or olive or orange we produce. We are lucky to have land and we can feed ourselves one way or another. Where you are going things will be much worse from what I have heard.'

The sun had faded and its meagre warmth dwindled to a dank chill by the time Vicenta reached the old railway station at Benissa. To her consternation the small station hut had been gutted, its windows smashed and the door twisted on its hinges. The short gravel platform was overrun with weeds and several of the concrete edging stones had crumbled and fallen to lie by the side of the track. The single, narrow-gauge track was itself engulfed in weeds and fallen leaves. For a moment Vicenta's heart sank as she supposed the line must have fallen into disuse. Then she noticed the rails themselves were not dull or rusty, but showed signs of recent use. She prayed there would be a train before too long and settled on an old cast iron bench at the side of the hut. Hungry and exhausted, she fell asleep clutching the old suitcase on her lap. By the time she woke, dusk had turned to darkness and her coat was covered in a layer of fine drizzle. Stiff from her sleep, she moved inside the station hut and made an attempt to close the rickety door to keep out the draught.

She wished now that she had cleared a space in the room before darkness had fallen. In pitch blackness she shuffled around the room, feeling her way along the walls to find the rearmost corner. She scuffed her feet across the floor to clear away the debris and then sat in the corner, her back propped against her suitcase. A combination of cold and hunger made sleep virtually impossible. Finally tiredness overcame her and she began to doze. She was aroused suddenly by a scraping sound that in her drowsiness she imagined to be rats scratching around for food. She tensed and pushed herself hard against the wall as her eyes gradually adjusted to the weak twilight that vaguely illuminated her surroundings. The scraping sound recurred and she flinched again. The narrow shaft of light that penetrated the space between the door and its frame suddenly began to broaden. A vague shadow moved across the beam of light as the door opened further and in the silhouette Vicenta realised it was the figure of a man. Instinctively she screamed and yelled, 'Get out, go away.'

The shadow disappeared in a single swift movement and in the dim light Vicenta looked round for a weapon or something to protect herself. In the far corner she spotted a wooden shaft propped against the wall. She rose to her feet and crossed the room realising that the shaft was little more than a flimsy piece of broken window frame. She grasped it in both hands trembling as she shuffled along the wall to stand at the side of the door. The shadow reappeared in the weak shaft of light and the door moved again, creaking on its twisted hinges. Vicenta's heart pulsated in her chest as she raised the shaft to shoulder height, pressing herself against the wall and preparing to strike. The shadow lengthened and a booted foot appeared, just crossing the threshold. Vicenta tightened her grip and raised the shaft above her head.

'Don't be afraid, I won't hurt you.'

It was the voice of a child.

'What do you want?' Vicenta shrieked, alarm etched in her voice.

'I don't want anything,' the child said. 'I just noticed the door had been closed and wondered why. I didn't know you were inside.'

'Then move back,' Vicenta ordered. 'I'm going to come out.'

The shadow slipped backward and stopped. Vicenta lowered her stick to her side but maintained a firm grip with her right hand. With her left hand she pulled the door back, dragging the bottom edge across the floor until it was wide enough for her to get out. She stepped into the doorway.

Noticing the shaft, the child cowered and took a step backward looking rapidly from side to side as if preparing to scarper.

'Don't run away,' Vicenta said, her voice now

calmer.

The child, a boy Vicenta now realised, froze and pulled his scuffed brown boots together as if standing to attention. One boot lacked a lace and was pulled together with a short piece of string drawn tightly around the ankle. Crumpled grey socks clung at different heights to spindly legs protruding from a baggy pair of shorts with badly frayed hems. The grubby cuffs of an oversized jumper projected from the sleeves of a tight-fitting jacket, too small even for the boy's scrawny frame. His face was blotched with dirt and his lank greasy hair fell haphazardly about his head.

'I didn't mean to scare you,' the boy said.

'That's all right. I was startled that's all. What's your name?'

'Felipe. What's yours?' the boy relaxed and recovered his poise placing his feet apart and thrusting hands on hips in an assured posture.

'My name is Vicenta. How old are you?'

'None of your business.'

'Okay, I didn't mean to pry. Do you live near here?'

'You said you didn't mean to pry.'

A steady drizzle began to fall.

'Do you want to come inside? We'll both get soaked if we stay out here.'

'Just for a minute then, until the rain stops.' The boy strode past Vicenta and shoved the door until it was fully open. The brightening dawn now illuminated the inside of the hut and the boy, seemingly knowing his way around, picked up a wooden crate and set it on one side.

'You can sit here,' he said.

'Where will you sit?' Vicenta asked.

The boy settled cross legged on the floor on the opposite side of the room away from Vicenta. He noticed the suitcase propped against the wall.

'Is that yours?'

Vicenta eyed him suspiciously, wondering if the boy was a thief. 'Yes it's mine, so keep your hands off it.'

'Hey lady, I just asked the question, that's all.'

'Okay, I'm sorry. We seem to have got off on the wrong foot. It's just that I'm in a strange place here and a little nervous. You said your name was Felipe?'

'Yes.' The boy folded his arms across his chest. 'Vicenta, you said?'

'Yes.'

'So what are you doing here, Vicenta?'

'I'm on my way to Alicante,'

The boy scoffed. 'What, and you thought you'd just catch a train?'

'That's the general idea.'

'There hasn't been a passenger train on this line for almost two years.'

Vicenta's heart sank. 'Then it seems I'm wasting my time.' She began to stand.

'Hold on lady, I said there had been no passenger trains, but that doesn't mean there are no trains at all.'

'I told you, my name is Vicenta. So what trains use this line?'

'There's a freight train three days a week. Goes all the way to Alicante and back.'

'And when is the next one due?'

'Well, there ain't no timetable or anything like that. What day is it today?'

'Wednesday.'

'There's one due today then, usually about half past ten.'

'And can I get on this train?'

'Depends.'

'On what?'

'Well for a start, it depends on whether it stops.'

'Does it usually stop?'

'Most times, yes.'

'Then if it stops today, I'll be able to get on it?'

Felipe chuckled to himself. 'Vicenta you can't just put your hand out and get on the train. It's a freight train remember.'

'Why don't you explain?'

Felipe shuffled uncomfortably on the floor.

'Here, come and sit on this crate,' Vicenta said. 'I can sit on my suitcase.'

They swapped places and Felipe settled on the crate, his feet barely reaching the ground.

'Have you got anything to eat?' he asked.

'Sorry, no.'

He reached to the inside pocket of his jacket

and tugged to release a half bocadillo wrapped in grease stained tissue paper.

'You can share this if you like. The bread's a bit stale, but there's some ham on it.'

Vicenta looked at Felipe's grubby hands with dirt encrusted fingernails. 'No thanks, you eat it.'

Felipe grabbed the bocadillo in both hands and broke it in half, tearing the tissue paper at the same time. 'Take it,' he said, thrusting his right hand forward.

Reluctantly Vicenta took the bread and bit hard to break a piece free. He was right, the bread was stale and hard and the thin sliver of cured ham was dry and chewy. Even so it was welcome to Vicenta's empty stomach.

'You were going to explain about the trains?'

Felipe munched enthusiastically on his sandwich, picking up the crumbs that fell on his lap.

'The train comes from the port in Denia with provisions for Alicante. Most of the goods come from Italy. It's one of the few places that will supply the new government. It's mostly poor quality, oil, wheat and rice, the stuff the Italians don't want. Some things come over by boat from the Balearics, but not so much these days. I guess they are struggling like the rest of Spain. There are usually a couple of wagons loaded with better stuff, vegetables, cured ham, salami and sometimes cheese. It's meant for the top brass in Alicante, but not all of it gets there.'

'What do you mean?' Vicenta asked, marvelling at the boy's knowledge.

'It's the same all along the line. There are guards on the train supposed to protect the supplies, but at some of the stations there are people waiting and the guards take money to offload some of the cargo.'

'Who are these guards?'

'Falange soldiers usually, sometimes Guardia Civil, but they're all the same.'

'And who are the people who buy the goods?'

'Mostly they're racketeers, sometimes they're local Falange officials. They're the only ones with money these days.'

'You seem very well informed for a boy of your age. How old did you say you are?'

'I didn't.'

'So how do you know all this? About the trains I mean.'

Felipe's expression changed suddenly. Despite the dirt and greasy hair, Vicenta saw an almost cherubic face with chubby cheeks and bright eyes. Now he looked sullen and downcast.

'My father,' he said quietly. 'He used to work the railways before the war. He was a fireman and sometimes he'd let me go with him on the footplate, mostly in the holidays and on some Saturdays depending on who the driver was. Some drivers wouldn't have me on the engine so I sat on the coal tender and kicked the coal down to dad. Mum used to hate that because I came home black.'

'Where are your parents now?'

Felipe lowered his head and mumbled into his chest. 'Mum died two years ago. She was pregnant but there were complications, Dad said. The baby died as well.'

Vicenta wanted to reach out to the boy and hug him, but something told her he was not the sort of kid to appreciate molly coddling.

'And your father?'

Felipe raised his head, his face set in a stern scowl. 'Those bastards killed him.'

Vicenta stiffened in surprise. 'Who do you mean?'

'The Falange and their cronies in Benissa. He was accused of harbouring his brother, my uncle Ernesto. Ernesto fought for the republicans in Valencia and he came home wounded. He had a leg amputated and the gangrene set in. He was dying, so what else could my Dad do? Someone denounced him and Dad was arrested. They threw him in the rat infested jail and left him to rot. When I asked what had happened to him, they told me he had been sent to work in the north, but another prisoner later told me he had seen Dad taken out on a stretcher covered in a blanket. That's all I know.'

Felipe's story struck a chord with Vicenta. Instinctively she rose and moved toward him holding out her hands. 'You poor thing,' she said.

Felipe straightened and recoiled, pushing her hands to one side. 'Leave me alone, I don't need your sympathy. I don't need anyone's sympathy, I can look after myself.'

Vicenta returned to sit on her suitcase. 'But I need your help, Felipe. I need to get to Alicante.'

'What's so important in Alicante that you end up stranded at this station without a clue as to how to get there?'

Vicenta thought of explaining the events that had led her to this desolated spot. Instead she simply explained, 'My husband is there and I need to find him. Can you help me?'

'If you're sure,' he said, 'but it won't be easy.'

'I'm sure. You said there was a train due this morning.'

'If the train stops we may be able to get on, but you'll have to do exactly what I say.'

'You said "we"?'

'You'll never make it on your own. I was heading in that direction anyway. First we have to get out of this hut and across the tracks.'

Following Felipe, Vicenta dropped down from the platform and stepped over the track to the other side of the rails. It was a single line and there was no platform on the other side, just an embankment overgrown with shrubs. They slipped through the thicket and clambered down the slope until they were just below the brow, but able to view the station on the other side. Felipe gave instructions to Vicenta telling her to be ready to move quickly and follow him exactly.

An hour passed in virtual silence before a car

swung into the gravel area at the back of the station. A tall man wearing a great coat and a fedora hat emerged from the car and walked toward the platform.

'We're in luck,' Felipe whispered. 'That's Antonio Gallego, head of the local Falange syndicate. It means the train is going to stop.'

Fifteen minutes later they heard the distant rumble of an approaching train. Peeking through the shrubs Vicenta could just make out the billowing smoke and steam of the engine as it chugged laboriously up the incline of the narrow track. As it neared the platform Gallego waved his hands over his head and the driver responded with a shrill blast on the engine's whistle. Brakes squealed and couplings jangled as the locomotive and its fourteen wagons gradually drew to a halt. Between the wheels of the slow moving bogies they watched Gallego's polished shoes moving up the platform coming to a halt by one of the central wagons. The locomotive released a blast of steam from a safety valve and the engine simmered as a steady stream of smoke drifted from its chimney.

A door slid open on the carriage immediately behind the coal tender; the only carriage with windows ahead of the remaining goods wagons. Two sets of booted feet dropped to the platform and walked in Gallego's direction. A metal clasp creaked on its hinge and slammed back against the solid wooden carcass of the fourth wagon from the front. A door slid open. The guards' booted feet climbed into the wagon while Gallego remained on the platform. Two small crates were placed at Gallego's feet along with a small sack and a leg of ham wrapped in muslin. The guards jumped from the wagon, the door slid shut and the metal clasp slammed back into place. From behind the bushes Felipe and Vicenta could hear a muffled conversation unable to discern the words except the parting call from Gallego, '*Hasta la proxima*,' as the guards moved back toward their carriage.

'Now,' Felipe said, rising to his feet. 'Follow me. Quickly.'

Vicenta followed Felipe along the ridge of the embankment toward the last of the wagons, a close-boarded tender covered with a heavy tarpaulin stretched over a ridged frame. As Felipe emerged cautiously from the bushes he looked up and down the line then dashed across the track to the rear of the last wagon. Vicenta followed in close order.

The locomotive let off a burst of steam and its wheels screeched, slowly gaining traction on the track. The wagons lurched forward and heavy chain couplings clanged and stretched before the wagons slammed back on their buffers.

'Hurry,' Felipe shouted, his voice almost inaudible above the din of the train. The metal frame of the rear wagon comprised a series of horizontal bars riveted to wooden boards. Felipe climbed on one of the projecting buffers and began to climb the metal struts until he had a grip on the top edge of the wagon. The train and all the wagons lurched forward again and gradually began to pull away. Vicenta was just a few of metres from the end of the wagon as it began to move. She panicked. Clutching her suitcase she began to run, but her foot snagged on one of weed-shrouded sleepers and she tripped and fell. She flung her hands forward to break her fall, releasing her grip on the case which slid sideways coming to rest on the far side of the track. As she hit the ground, her hands grazed on the gravel ballast and her chin thudded against a sleeper. Dazed, she pushed herself up and on to her knees, but the train was now beginning to accelerate away.

'Run,' Felipe shrieked, 'Run.'

'My case?' Vicenta yelled.

'Leave it.'

Vicenta rose to her feet and began to run, gingerly stepping on each of the sleepers in turn. Still the train moved away, the distance increasing. For a moment Vicenta feared she would never reach it as her heavy skirt dragged around her legs.

'Come on Vicenta, you can make it.'

She hitched her skirt and redoubled her effort, taking the sleepers two at a time. Legs aching and gasping for breath, she finally drew close to the wagon.

'Grab the chain and swing onto the buffer,' Felipe said, his voice calm and reassuring.

Still running and without thinking, Vicenta followed Felipe's instructions and heaved herself up until she was sitting astride the cylindrical buffer, her chest pressed against the frame of the wagon.

Felipe, still clinging with one hand to the top edge of the wagon reached down toward Vicenta. She reached up, but their hands were a distance apart.

'You'll have to stand up,' Felipe said.

The train was still gathering momentum and Vicenta looked down as the sleepers flashed by with increasing rapidity.

'I don't think I can,' she replied.

'You can do it Vicenta. Just grab the first strut and pull yourself up.'

Vicenta pushed on the buffer with her hands trying to raise her body to reach the first metal strut. But the buffer was covered in a thick layer of grease and her hands came away slimy and black. She wiped them on her skirt and tried again, just managing to reach the first metal bar. With greasy fingers and only a tentative hold she heaved herself up with both hands until she stood upright, her shoes resting on the slippery buffer. If the train lurched now she would surely fall.

Felipe reached down again, but still he was inches away from Vicenta's hands where they clung to the lowest strut.

'Let go with one hand and reach up. I'll grab you.'

Vicenta could feel her heart thumping and for a moment she froze, looking down at the track beneath her feet. She realised she had no alternative but to do as Felipe instructed. She released her right hand and reached up toward Felipe's outstretched hand. Immediately she felt her feet slip on the greasy buffer. She leaned backward in an attempt to maintain her balance but this pulled her hand further away. She could feel her feet slipping further and screamed, convinced she was about to fall. Just as her feet lost contact with the buffer, Felipe's hand grabbed her right wrist and clasped firm. She was now dangling in mid air and Felipe took her full weight as he strained to maintain his hold on the top edge of the wagon. Realising the strain on Felipe's spindly arms, Vicenta re-found her footing on the buffer and pushed upwards, at the same time gripping the second metal strut with her left had. Now Felipe was able to pull her arm upward until she, too, was able to grip the top edge of the wagon.

'Now what do we do?' she asked.

'Just hold on with both hands and keep your feet on the strut.'

Vicenta had no alternative but to do as she was told. Felipe gradually moved his hands, shuffling to the corner of the wagon. Releasing one hand, he tugged at a rope and managed to peel away one corner of the tarpaulin which covered the wagon. He hauled himself up to sit astride the top of the wagon and beckoned Vicenta to do the same. With the cold air and smoke from the locomotive blasting their faces the two of them looked at each other with startled relief. Inside the wagon Vicenta could see piles of hessian sacks stacked almost to the top of the wooden panels.

'Come on,' Felipe said, 'we better get inside before someone sees us.'

They both dropped to squat on the sacks and Felipe pulled back the tarpaulin, leaving them in semi-darkness. A sweet musty smell filled their nostrils.

'It smells like chocolate' Vicenta said, a note of hope in her voice.

'We should be so lucky,' Felipe declared. 'The sacks are full of carob pods, fit only for animal fodder.'

'What do we do now?'

CHAPTER FIVE

As the train reached full speed Felipe and Vicenta shuffled the sacks to find comfortable positions and catch their breath. Felipe seemed quite excited to be embarking on his new adventure, but Vicenta was full of trepidation, wondering what dangers they might face between here and Alicante and what she might encounter when, if, they reached their destination.

Felipe explained that the journey could take up to four hours depending on how many halts they made, and that depended on how many times the guards were beckoned to stop to offload goods to corrupt officials. There were about twenty stations along the route, but Felipe was sure they would not stop at all of them, probably just two or three.

Vicenta was dismayed at the thought of spending the whole journey amongst the smelly sacks of carobs especially as the brittle carob pods made a very uncomfortable mattress. Felipe had other ideas. They should aim to reach the wagon from which the guards had unloaded the booty at Benissa. Here they would find food and that, Felipe explained, was the reason he made the journey every week or so, pilfering just what he could easily carry, enough to sustain him for a few days at least.

Vicenta visualised the two of them crawling along the roofs of the moving wagons, taking death defying leaps from one to another, just like in an American movie she had once seen when the travelling picture show came to Benimarta before the war. Felipe roared with laughter at the very idea. His plan was much simpler than that. They would wait until the train stopped then climb out of the wagon and creep alongside the carriages to the fourth one from the front, then slide back the door and get in – easy.

Surely, Vicenta suggested, they would be seen or heard by the guards or the engine driver. And if the train only stopped to offload the illicit goods, wouldn't the guards be in the wagon they wanted to enter? Again, Felipe had it all figured out.

The train chugged through two more stations at Ferrandet and Calpe without stopping by which time the musty smell or carobs was making Vicenta feel queasy. She did not know if her nausea was caused by her claustrophobic surroundings or by her condition, but it served as a reminder of the importance of her mission.

After almost an hour, the train began to slow. Felipe peeled back the tarpaulin and poked his head out to see where they were.

'This is it,' Felipe said as he ducked back. 'The water stop just outside Altea. We need to be ready, but there's no need to rush. The train will be here about ten minutes.'

When the train drew to a halt Felipe stood and peaked through the tarpaulin toward the engine. Just as he had predicted the fireman climbed down from the right hand side of the locomotive and moved toward the water tower, a large metal tank mounted on a cast iron stanchion. The fireman grabbed a chain that dangled from the tower and used it to swing a long length of metal tube over and across the engine. The driver, meanwhile, had climbed a short ladder and stood atop the tender to receive the tube and direct it over the open hatch of the water intake. All the while the two guards leaned out of the windows of their carriage watching proceedings.

'We need to move quickly, but quietly,' said Felipe as he peeled back the rearmost corner of the tarpaulin and clambered out and down the back of the wagon using the metal struts as footholds. He rested on the left hand buffer and helped Vicenta as she, too, climbed down from the wagon and jumped onto the track. Crouching, they moved carefully along the left hand side of the carriages until they reached the fourth from the front, another metal-framed wooden wagon, but this one with a solid boarded roof. There was a heavy sliding door at the centre of the wagon, held shut with a hinged metal hasp closed over a staple designed to take a padlock. The hasp was beyond Felipe's reach so he climbed on Vicenta's shoulders and silently swung it back to rest against the flat side of the door. Vicenta lowered Felipe back to the ground. The two of them grabbed the edge of the door with their finger tips and slid it back just a few centimetres to be sure it would move.

'Stop there,' Felipe said. 'If we open it now they're sure to hear us. We have to wait until the engine starts up again. For now we have to get out of sight.'

The pair of them crawled between the heavy wheels and crouched underneath the wagon. Vicenta had never been so close to a railway train before and the enormity of the wheels and axles and the springs of the bogie made her feel very small and frightened. How, she began to wonder, had she embarked on such a dangerous enterprise. Before she could deliberate further on the wisdom of her escapade, the train's whistle let off a shrill blast and the locomotive awoke from its wheezing slumber and huffed back into life.

'Now,' Felipe said, grabbing Vicenta's hand.

They crawled out from beneath the wagon and two pairs of hands wrenched back the door which slid begrudgingly, screeching on its rusty rail. When the door had moved about a foot it suddenly jammed. Frantically they pulled and pushed, but the door was fast. The wagon lurched forward, and thudded into the next carriage before bumping back on its buffers. Without a word, Felipe jumped up and squeezed through the narrow opening, standing in the wagon and pulling back on the door with every meagre ounce of strength he could muster.

'Push, Vicenta,' he yelled as the train rumbled into motion.

Not again, Vicenta thought as she pushed for all she was worth, stepping sideways to keep up with the movement of the train.

Suddenly the door jerked and slid back to its full extent. Vicenta placed both hands on the floor of the wagon and levered herself up. Felipe pulled her in and slammed the door shut leaving both of them in total darkness.

'Do me a favour,' Vicenta said. 'Next time you decide to hitch a ride on a train, don't invite me.'

Felipe laughed. 'I thought you were doing okay – for a woman.'

'I don't understand, Vicenta said when she had calmed down. 'Why don't the guards lock the carriages?'

'They're stupid, that's why,' Felipe replied. 'When my dad worked on the railway, every carriage was locked with a padlock. He knew every single key. But these guards haven't a clue, so the keys have been lost, or they just can't be bothered.'

'But won't they notice that the hasp on the door has been left open?'

'So? If they do, they'll just think it has swung open and close it.'

Vicenta's alarm was clear in her voice. 'And then we'll be locked in.'

'Relax,' Felipe said disdainfully. 'All the stations are on the right hand side of the train in this direction and the guards are too lazy to walk along the other side.'

'What now?' Vicenta asked, now shouting to be heard above the rhythmic clackety-clack of the wheels as the train reached full speed.

'First we need some light,' Felipe replied, standing to open the door just a fraction to allow a narrow shaft of light to enter the wagon.

Vicenta looked around to see the space piled high with all manner of crates and boxes stacked untidily around the perimeter.

'We need to find somewhere to hide.'

'What do you mean?' Vicenta exclaimed with some alarm.

'We'll be at Altea in a few minutes time. If the train stops, the guards are sure to come in, so we need to get out of sight.'

'But how?'

'It's easy,' Felipe said cheerfully. 'We just need to shuffle a few of these boxes to create a hidey-hole in the corner. There are plenty of boxes and so long as we don't move them about to much, the guards will never notice. Here, I'll show you how.'

Felipe moved to one corner and began sliding out the bottom layer of boxes that rested against the wall placing them neatly on top of the stack. They were loose boarded crates all identically labelled, "Queso Manchego." When he had removed six boxes there was a narrow tunnel at the back of the pile.

'That should be enough,' he declared. 'See if you can crawl into the space.'

Once again Vicenta wondered about the wisdom of her quest and how she had found herself to be part of a young boy's escapade. It was like something from Mark Twain's Adventures of Huckleberry Finn, a book she had read as a young girl. But with seemingly no choice she crossed the wagon and crawled into the space and hitched up her knees. Felipe slid back one of the crates to seal the space and Vicenta was once again thrust into total darkness.

'Felipe,' she yelled. 'Don't leave me in here.'

He slid out the crate. 'Don't panic. That was just a practice run.'

'But where will you hide?'

'I'll have to shut the door and then I'll be in there with you,' he said nonchalantly.

'Then let's just hope the train doesn't stop before Alicante.'

They passed through the stations at Altea and Alfaz del Pi without stopping and Vicenta and Felipe took the opportunity to eat. Felipe used a penknife to prise open one of the cheese crates and remove a full round of cheese, paring off chunks which they chewed away from the hard crusty rind. Felipe was careful to replace the top of the crate and position it amongst the others.

Of the remaining crates, most contained tinned goods – beans, asparagus and artichokes, which Felipe deemed too difficult to open. In another corner he found a pile of cardboard boxes containing layers of chorizo sausages. Carefully he slit open one of the seals and removed four of the long thin sausages handing one to Vicenta. They were not the freshest with a white crusty bloom on the outer skin, but inside the cured meat was a deep orangey red. They both munched away, savouring the spiced meat flavoured with smoked pimentón. Vicenta had not eaten so well since the end of the war and gorged herself, not knowing when she would dine so well again. Next Felipe attacked a case of tomatoes and removed a couple of large, green striped specimens wiping them on the front of his jacket to remove the preservative sulphur powder. The skin was tough and leathery, but inside the flesh was sweet and succulent and Felipe used his sleeve to wipe away the juices that trickled down his chin.

'Look, there's wine if you want it,' Felipe said, pointing to another stack of boxes.

'Better not,' Vicenta responded, thinking the boy was far too young to be drinking alcohol, especially as he needed to keep his wits about him.

'You're probably right,' Felipe said. 'It's crap anyway, all the good stuff goes to Madrid.'

For the next forty minutes they chatted and laughed, almost forgetting the dangers that might lie ahead or the dire repercussions that would undoubtedly befall them were they to be discovered. In answer to Vicenta's cautious questioning, Felipe revealed that he was just fourteen years old.

'Nearly fifteen,' he protested.

Since the death of his parents he had lived an itinerant existence occasionally resting his head at the houses of an uncle and two aunts, none of whom had the space, let alone the patience, to accommodate him on a permanent basis. In between times he travelled the railways and slept in whatever shelter he could find, usually in empty goods wagons shunted into sidings.

Without warning the rhythmic clank of wheels on rails began to slow. Felipe was quick to his feet, poking his head through the narrow opening of the door.

'Shit! It's Benidorm. The train doesn't normally stop here as it's just a small fishing village, but we're definitely slowing down.'

He tossed the hulls of four tomatoes through the open door together with the uneaten rinds of the Manchego cheese.

'Quick, you'd better get in the hidey-hole,' he urged.

Vicenta complied, squeezing into the cramped space beneath the crates. Felipe slid the door shut and then felt his way in darkness across the floor to crawl, feet first, into the opening and slide back a single crate to seal their bolt-hole.

Vicenta was breathing hard and trying not to

panic. Felipe snuggled up against her and she hugged him, more for her own comfort than his. In the confined space their breaths mingled and Vicenta feared they might suffocate. Despite the cold of the wagon she began to sweat. Felipe sensed Vicenta's alarm and feared she might become hysterical.

'Keep calm,' he urged. 'We'll be fine, but we need to be absolutely quiet.'

Vicenta tensed as they heard the sound of the wagon door sliding back on its rail. Heavy boots thumped on the wooden floor. Vicenta took a deep breath and held it.

'Good day, Mr Mayor,' a voice within the wagon said. 'How can we help you today?'

'What have you got?'

'What would you like? Cheese, ham, salami, wine? We even have some biscuits.'

'How much?'

'How much have you got?'

'I have two hundred pesetas.'

'Then here, take this Serrano ham and a box of salami. Do you want a case of wine?'

'No thanks I have plenty of that in the bodega. Those biscuits sound good. And some cheese.'

The boots clonked across the floor and boxes were dragged toward the door. A crate was lifted from the pile above the hidey-hole and a tiny shaft of light penetrated the space below. Vicenta tensed and felt Felipe's grasp tighten.

'What more can you give me?'

'For two hundred pesetas you have a good deal, I think. Besides, we have to deliver something to the depot at Alicante otherwise the food superintendent will get suspicious.'

The boots stepped down from the wagon onto the platform.

'Hey, this crate has been opened, Look, there's a cheese missing.'

Feet shuffled on the platform.

'You're right. That's terrible. You just can trust anyone these days. Now, two hundred pesetas we said.'

The door slammed shut.

'Remind me never to go on a train journey with you again,' Vicenta said, relieved to be emerging from darkness of their hideaway as the train picked up speed.

'It may not be over yet. There are six more stations between here and Alicante.'

Felipe began to make preparations for their eventual arrival. He explained that they could not remain on the train until the final stop at Alicante port. It was a busy terminus packed with people and trains and it would be almost impossible to disembark without being noticed. The train would stop at a coal depot, just outside Alicante to take on fuel for the return journey. It was a quiet place, normally, with just a couple of workers to operate the loading machinery. The workers would be preoccupied with the noisy process of loading coal and it would be easy to leave the wagon without being noticed.

The train passed through five of the six remaining stations without stopping. As the locomotive approached the last stop, El Campello, it began to slow and Vicenta readied to re-enter the black hole. Much to her relief, the train picked up speed again and passed through the station.

As instructed, Vicenta began to put together a small supply of food to see her through her first few days in Alicante. Without her suitcase it was difficult to carry much and Felipe explained that she must take only what she could hide away in her clothing; anything more would attract attention and in these difficult times anyone found with more than a meagre ration of food would be assumed to be a thief and liable to be arrested.

Just as Felipe predicted, the train drew to a halt at the coal depot and they left the wagon without being noticed, scurrying across the tracks to a siding that housed a small collection of empty carriages. The dim light of a dreary day was fading fast as twilight fell. Felipe tried several of the covered wagons before finding one with an open door. They clambered aboard and prepared to bed down for the night.

'You said your husband was in Alicante?' Felipe said as he propped himself up in a corner and munched on another tough-skinned tomato.'

Vicenta's first thought was to say as little as possible for fear that revealing her true purpose would label her as a dissident. But she had come so far and learned so much of Felipe's own plight that she knew he could be trusted. 'I have to find him first,' she said at last.

'Alicante is a big city. Don't you know where he is staying?'

'All I know is that he's in prison somewhere.'

Felipe looked stunned. 'You're telling me you've come all this way to see your husband in prison?'

'No. I mean to get him released. He's done nothing wrong, you see.'

Felipe scoffed. 'Like everyone else arrested since the end of the war you mean?'

'No, he's not like everyone else. He never took sides in the war. He was victimised and denounced by someone who used to be his friend but now just wanted him out of the way.'

'The Falange, you mean? If that's the case then you'll be lucky to find him.'

Vicenta marvelled at the young boy's understanding of Spain's new political reality and wondered if it wasn't more rational than her own sentimental appraisal of her situation. Doubt engulfed her and she began to whimper. 'You may be right Felipe, but I only know I have to try. You see, without Eduardo, my life has no meaning and I could never rest without knowing what has become of him.

CHAPTER SIX

Felipe shunned the embrace proffered by Vicenta as they parted the next morning and put forward his hand for a formal handshake that symbolised his self-ordained status as an independent young man. His intention was to hang around the coal yard for a few days, sniffing out what sustenance he could find amongst the wagons that were shunted in and out. In a few days time he would make the return journey to Benissa riding the wagons once again, avoiding the attentions of the guards and hoping to pilfer a few day's supplies to take back to his kinfolk.

Vicenta's heart wept for Felipe as he waved then turned away to shuffle off into the distance and disappear amongst the grimy detritus of the yard. For all his bravado and resourcefulness he was just a young boy left to fend for himself in a world fraught with danger and menace.

Arriving in Alicante courtesy of a kindly truck driver who had seemingly believed her story that she was a widow seeking work, Vicenta was overwhelmed by the cacophony of sights and sounds that confronted her. She had never been to the city, or any city, for that matter, having spent her entire life in Benimarta and the surrounding villages. Just walking along the palm lined Explanada de España was a formidable experience. People scurried along, alone or in groups, seemingly determined to get to their destinations in a hurry and more than once Vicenta took a sideways step to avoid what she perceived to be the possibility of a collision.

The streets which flanked the Esplanade were congested with all manner of vehicles; cars, buses, trams and horse-drawn carts, all competing chaotically for space on the congested street. There were even a few hand-drawn carts which mingled with the faster moving traffic prompting angry horn thumping from impatient drivers.

The promenade at the centre of the esplanade was tiled in waves of red, black and cream that resembled the sea tumbling over a shallow beach. The effect made Vicenta feel giddy as she struggled to know what to do or where to go next.

As she meandered between the pedestrians, she came to a section of the promenade populated with cafes and stalls selling handicrafts, clothes and bric-a-brac. The clear blue sky allowed the sun to emit a wintry warmth and the palm trees cast well defined shadows across the pavement. Confused and bewildered, she began to feel faint and decided to rest at one of the cafes, taking a seat at a wicker table, one of a matching group containing plastic napkin holders advertising Café Bon Aire.

Despite her dishevelled appearance, her arrival aroused little interest amongst the other patrons who ranged from smartly suited businessmen, smoking and taking brandies with their coffees, to workers in overalls sipping small glasses of beer and groups of smartly dressed young women nibbling from plates of tapas. At an adjacent table she heard a smart young couple talking in a foreign language; German she thought, though her knowledge of the language came only from speeches by Herr Hitler which had been broadcast on national radio. They must be tourists, she thought, though she could not imagine anyone wanting to visit war torn Spain at this particular time. And then it dawned on her how normal things were, on the surface at least. She had expected to see troops on the streets, even tanks, to maintain order in the face of anticipated rebellion, but it seemed there was a collective resignation to the new order and a determination to get on with life in the new Spain. A sense of disappointment overcame her. Where were the rebels fighting against fascism? Where were the campaigners for freedom and liberty? Where was the true spirit of the Spanish people? Above all, she feared for Eduardo, incarcerated unjustly, while the rest of Spain passively accepted its fate.

An elderly waiter appeared at the side of her table prompting her to look up and squint at his silhouette framed by the sun's low arc.

'Senora?'

Vicenta would have liked simply to stay and rest, but felt obliged to order something even though her meagre resources could be put to better use.

'Café con leche,'

The waiter hovered, glancing from side to side evidently troubled by something.

'Is there a problem?' Vicenta enquired.

The waiter cleared his throat. 'Your badge, madam, you have no badge.'

Vicenta was confused. 'I'm sorry, I don't know what you mean. What badge?'

'You are new to the city, I think. Everyone must buy a blue badge from the Auxilio Social. Without one, I should not serve you or the restaurant could be fined.'

It was only now that Vicenta noticed that all the other clients, including the German tourists, wore a small blue paper flag pinned to their clothing depicting the cherubic face of a young child on a blue background with the words Auxilio Social overprinted in red.

'You are right, I have just arrived in Alicante and I didn't know. What is the Auxilio Social?'

'They are part of the Sección Femenina of the Falange Español. They raise funds for victims of the war, especially women and orphans and run soup kitchens for the poor and hungry.

Quietly, Vicenta was pleased to hear of an organisation helping the needy people of Alicante, even if it was part of the Falange. After all, she realised, she may have need of their help. 'Then I must buy a flag,' she said enthusiastically. 'Where can I get one?'

'Leave it to me,' the waiter said as he returned to the café, negotiating the traffic that circulated around the esplanade.

He returned a few minutes later with the coffee and a small paper flag attached to a pin which Vicenta attached to the lapel of her coat.

The coffee was weak and watery with barely a dribble of milk, but she sipped it contentedly, taking her time and enjoying the radiant warmth of the sun's rays. Briefly she closed her eyes and imagined herself back in Benimarta taking coffee on the terrace of Bar Rull in the days before the Civil War when life was simple and carefree. She was aroused by a tap on her knee and looked down to see a small boy crouching at her feet holding a wooden box with a carrying handle. His hands were grubby and his fingernails caked with black wax.

'Señora, I clean your shoes?' he intimated, lifting the lid on one side of his box and extracting a dirty rag.

Her scuffed old boots could certainly have done with a polish, but she had better things to do with what little money she possessed.

'No, no,' she protested, flustered by his presence.

The boy stuffed the rag back into his box then looked sheepishly up and down the esplanade before lifting the lid on the other side.

'You want cigarettes, lady?' He lifted out three packets of cigarettes each a different brand. 'I give you good price, cheaper than the estanc.'

'No, now go away,' she said tersely.

The boy scurried off to the next table to pester the group of suited businessmen.

After half an hour the waiter reappeared to enquire if she wanted anything more. It was a none too subtle way of suggesting she must move on or buy another cup of coffee.

'La cuenta,' she said reluctantly.

As she waited, two men sauntered between the tables of the bar. One, a portly figure, wore a heavy black leather coat belted tightly at the waist. The other, taller and much slimmer, sported a thick brown woollen coat, unbuttoned to reveal a grey pin-striped suit over a crisp white shirt neatly fastened at the neck with a bright paisley tie. They approached the table occupied by the Germans who greeted them warmly with handshakes and hugs. As they took their seats, the waiter interrupted his return to the bar and hurried over to their table, standing almost to attention to take their orders. The two Germans now spoke to the men in Spanish and Vicenta began to realise that they were not tourists after all, but perhaps had some other, more sinister, reason to be in the city. She also noticed that neither of the new arrivals wore the blue flags of the Auxilio Social. Her curiosity aroused, she could not help staring at the group until, suddenly, she realised the man in the leather coat was returning her stare, eying her suspiciously. Quickly, she lowered her eyes and fussed with the collar of her jacket, glancing back toward the bar and relieved to see the waiter returning.

The bill arrived, clipped to a small metal plate. It comprised twenty-five céntimos for the coffee and a further thirty céntimos for the flag. Vicenta presented the waiter with a one peseta coin which she extracted from the pocket of her skirt. He seemed peeved when she did not indicate that he could keep the change and rummaged through the purse attached to his belt to extract a couple of coins which he tossed haughtily onto the plate.

'Tell me,' Vicenta enquired bashfully. 'Where might I find the Auxilio Social... should I have need to?'

The waiter now eyed her suspiciously, noticing for the first time her bedraggled appearance. 'They operate a soup kitchen from a building near the old market in Calle San Jaime.' Then, recognising the puzzled look on Vienta's face he added, 'It's not far from here. Turn right at the end of the esplanade into Avenida de la Constitución. Calle San Jaime is the third street on the left.'

'Thank you,' Vicenta said, pushing back her chair.

The waiter's demeanour changed unexpectedly. 'You say you are new to the city?'

'Yes, I've just arrived. I... I'm looking for work.'

'Do you know anyone in Alicante?'

'No.'

The waiter pursed his lips. 'Then I wish you good luck,' he said, adding, 'and be careful. Alicante is a dangerous place these days... especially for a woman on her own.'

Vicenta frowned, but refrained from seeking further explanation. 'Thank you,' she said. 'Good day.'

'Vaya con Dios,' the waiter replied, ominously.

As she trudged slowly to the end of the esplanade, Vicenta considered her options. Reluctant as she was to encounter anyone associated with the Falange, she realised that without food or clothing, with very little money and nowhere to sleep, she was unlikely to survive for long on the streets of Alicante. Perhaps the Auxilio Social might offer her assistance or at least a resting place whilst she devised a plan to find Eduardo.

Following the waiter's directions she turned into Calle San Jaime and began the climb away from the coast. There was less traffic here, just an occasional lorry noisily pumping out clouds of noxious diesel fumes. The tall buildings, grander than anything Vicenta had ever seen before, blocked out the sun and formed a wind tunnel that accentuated the effect of the chill breeze. She pulled up the collar of her jacket, lowered her head and pressed on up the hill.

Rounding a sharp bend in the street, she entered a small plaza flanked on three sides by more impressive stone buildings with grand entrances, carved stone sills, ornate balustrades and moulded cornices. The other side of the plaza was occupied by the bombed-out remains of another lofty building. Only the façade now stood upright with broken window frames and shattered panes of glass. Behind it Vicenta could see piles of crumbling masonry, twisted metal and splintered wood. As she passed by the building's former entrance, a gothic stone arch enclosing a pair of battered wooden doors, she noticed the inscription carved in a tablet to one side. Mercado Central. Now she remembered something she had read in the republican press. In May 1938, after Franco had authorised the indiscriminate bombing of republican strongholds, the Italian Aviazione Legionaria attacked Alicante. With obsolete anti-aircraft artillery and a non-existent air-alarm system, the city was virtually defenceless. More than ninety bombs had fallen, many on the central market, resulting in around three hundred deaths and more than one thousand wounded. The catastrophe was less infamous than the earlier obliteration of the Basque town of Guernica in which the Legionaria had joined the German Luftwaffe's Condor Legion, but it provoked an almost equal outcry at the time.

It wasn't hard to find the relief centre run by the Auxilio Social from the ground floor of an old department store. It was distinguished from the neighbouring buildings by a queue of around fifty bedraggled people, mostly women and children, which spewed out of the entrance and spread along the pavement in front of the building and around the corner into the next street.

Vicenta considered her options and wondered whether to join the queue. She had just a few morsels of food left in her pockets from her journey with Felipe and she knew that would not last long. Since losing her suitcase she couldn't even change her clothes which by now were grubby and noisome. She also needed a bath. Above all, she realised she was just at the beginning of her quest to find Eduardo. She could not expect to find him in the next few hours or days, so she needed to establish herself in Alicante and work from there. So, despite her reluctance to ask for help, especially from an organisation associated with the Falange, she joined the dismal procession of hungry and forlorn people forced to accept whatever charity was on offer.

As the column shuffled slowly and silently toward the entrance she began to concoct her story. She knew she dare not divulge the true purpose of her presence in the city for it would almost certainly lead to her arrest. She dare not even say that she was from Benimarta for sooner or later someone would check with the authorities there. She would say she was from Castell de Castells, a remote farming village inland from Benimarta which, as far as she knew, had been largely untouched by the hostilities of the war though it would not have escaped the privations that had since come about. She would continue to describe herself as a widow even though she feared it might be tempting fate. She would say she was the daughter of a farming family, whose parents had died in the last two years, though not as a result of anything associated with the conflicts of the Civil War. She would not, under any circumstances divulge that she was pregnant.

Approaching the entrance to the building she was gripped by a sudden panic as if taking the next step would mean beginning a voyage of no return, but she took a deep breath and calmed herself, knowing she had no other option. The broad entrance hall, showed signs of a former grandeur, its walls lined with polished wooden panels centred in richly carved frames. An imposing chandelier hung from the centre of an ornate stucco ceiling, though only a few of the countless light bulbs were illuminated to give a cheerless yellow glow. On each side of the hall a symmetrical staircase curved upward, rising from matching carved newel posts by means of polished wooden handrails that culminated in a central balcony overlooking the lobby. Festooned across the front of the balcony was a large banner bearing the symbol of the Auxilio Social above giant letters spelling out: Woman-Wife-Mother.

As she trudged through the entrance hall and into the sales floor of the former department store, she was struck by how quiet it was. More than a hundred people sat at wooden trestle tables set out in uniform rows that stretched the full length of the room, but barely a word passed between them. There were a few older people amongst the gathering, but in the main they were women and children. Heads were bowed and the predominant sound was the clanking of metal spoons against pottery bowls, interrupted by the occasional admonishment or encouragement to eat. It was as if, forced to demean themselves by accepting charity, the spirit of the people had evaporated, to be replaced by a sullen mood of despair.

Vicenta now approached a long serving table centred by a steaming metal cauldron alongside an assortment of bowls and dishes. Behind the table stood three stout ladies looking prim and proper with tightly coiffured hair pulled up and plaited into buns at the back of their heads. They looked almost identical in uniforms of grey ankle-length skirts and blue blouses covered by crisp white aprons. Taking her cue from the woman in front of her, Vicenta lifted a bowl from the pile and moved on to the cauldron where the first of the ladies lifted a precise ladle of soup and poured it into her bowl. As she moved along with the flow, the second lady passed her a shallow metal spoon. At the end of the table the third lady handed out roughly cut chunks of bread, careful to ensure that there was just one piece per person. As Vicenta waited for her bread to be handed over, the lady paused, eyeing her suspiciously.

'You're new here, I think?'

Surprised, Vicenta answered, 'Yes, I've only just arrived in Alicante.'

'And you are alone?'

'Yes.'

The lady handed over a chunk of bread and Vicenta moved on, following the line of people to take a seat on the far side of the room next to a woman whom she presumed to be the mother of the two boys who flanked her. On the opposite side of the trestle table sat an elderly couple both shabbily dressed in ill-fitting clothes. The woman's face was pale and drawn and her watery eyes seemed to focus on infinity as she spooned her soup methodically and broke away bits of bread. The man was equally pale with hollow eyes and jutting cheek bones. His hand shook almost uncontrollably as he lifted the spoon to his mouth and left a dribble of soup trickling down his stubble-encrusted chin. Noticing his difficulty, the woman pulled a grimy handkerchief from her pocket and gently dabbed the man's cheek. He swatted her away in a gesture that was born more from embarrassment than irritation. They seemed, to Vicenta, to evince an aura of dignity despite the degradation of their circumstances and Vicenta couldn't help wondering what fate had brought this couple to the ignominy of the soup kitchen. Briefly, she made eye contact with the man and felt awkward, as if she were intruding on his private anguish. Quickly, she lowered her eyes and began sipping her soup. A few pieces of potato and cabbage were submerged beneath a layer of grease floating on some lukewarm liquid that was virtually tasteless. Vicenta spooned it up slowly, dunking the dry bread to make it more edible.

As she finished her meal Vicenta began to realise that most of the gathered assembly were now sitting quietly as the hubbub of clanking spoons died away to be replaced by an eerie silence and yet no one was leaving the room. It was as if they were all waiting for something to happen.

A middle aged woman mounted a makeshift stage at the far end of the room and strutted to its centre. She did not wear the uniform of the serving ladies, but sported a heavy ankle-length skirt with a tightly buttoned tweed jacket. Her wiry brown hair was swept up from her face and twisted into a tidy French bun. She set her feet apart, facing the audience and placed her hands on her hips. Taking a deep breath, she began to sing. Instinctively the assembly of people rose to their feet. Reluctantly Vicenta joined them, not wanting to stand out.

"Cara al sol con la camisa nueva, que tú bordaste en rojo ayer..." (Facing the sun in my new shirt that you embroidered in red yesterday...).

Vicenta recognised the words of the official hymn of the Falange Español which had been broadcast ad nauseum on national radio since the end of the war. A few of the women joined in, though in less than enthusiastic tones, whilst the woman on stage pressed on in a bold patriotic voice, singing acapella.

"Volverán banderas victoriosas al paso alegre de la paz..." (Victorious flags will return to the merry steps of peace...)

Vicenta stood silently, watching the downcast faces of most of the audience as the woman reached her rousing crescendo.

¡España una!
¡España grande!
¡España libre!
¡Arriba España!

With a wave of her hand the singer signalled for the audience to sit. The sound of scraping chairs echoed around the room, gradually dwindling to an uneasy silence as the woman began to speak in a confident booming voice.

'Women of Alicante give thanks to the Sección Femenina of the Falange Español and to our leader Pilar Primo de Rivera for the food that we put in your bellies. Give thanks also to El Caudillo by whose leadership and inspiration Spain will rise once more from the threats of communists and trades unionists and take its rightful place in the world.

'Many of you are widows and mothers who have suffered through the sacrifices made by our gallant soldiers. Your sadness may be deep, but it must only be transitory. Move on from the slough of despair and despondency and take up the challenges of New Spain.

'Your single mission in the service of the Fatherland is to be a homemaker. Those of you who are widows should not wallow in mournfulness and self pity, but move on to resume your family life. Just as our men folk have done their duty, now it is your turn to serve your country by becoming obedient wives and diligent mothers.

'Our homes today are vital to the economy of our country. It is your duty to relieve your men of the routine chores of family life in order to free them to work and build our nation. It is your obligation to make family life so agreeable that they will find within the home everything they previously lacked. Raise your children as much in the knowledge and love of God as in the service of the Fatherland.

'Above all be feminine, not feminist, and cast aside the misguided philosophies of the old republic that sought, through so-called emancipation, to emasculate women with notions of equality.'

Vicenta recognised these sentiments from speeches she had heard on the radio and propaganda promulgated by the state controlled press. The new government was clearly intent on reversing the hard won reforms introduced by the second republic which had given women equality within marriage and the right to vote for the first time in 1933. Now it seemed there was a movement to return to the Penal and Civil Codes of the 19th Century when women were denied education and the right to enter into contracts and bound by law to be obedient to their husbands.

The orator's exit from the stage signalled an end to proceedings and people began to stand and shuffle toward the way out. Vicenta was anxious to join them. Grateful as she was for the paltry meal, she found the whole experience stifling and manipulative. Clearly the motives of the Auxilio Social were as much political as they were altruistic.

As Vicenta stood to join the exodus, she was approached by one of the blue-bloused ladies.

'A word please,' she said as she took hold of Vicenta's arm and led her against the flow of the departing assembly.

Surprised, Vicenta followed the lady though her anxiety grew with every step. For a brief moment she thought of bolting, but the crowd was bottlenecked at the exit and she realised she would not get far without being blocked. In a corner of the hall Madam Blue Blouse opened a wooden door which framed a panel of etched glass inscribed with the word "Cajero."

'Wait here,' the woman said abruptly as she ushered Vicenta into a small office and closed the door behind her.

All signs of the room's former use as a cashier's office had been removed with the exception of a heavy, cast iron safe located on a reinforced wooden plinth in the far corner. Three solid metal bolts protruded from the edge of the safe's door which had been left ajar to reveal its empty innards. Vicenta was faced by a substantial desk with an inlaid leather surface which was worn and curling at the edges. Two leather upholstered chairs were positioned behind the desk, both showing the same signs of wear and tear. In front of the desk there was a single hard chair with an upright back.

Before she could decide whether to sit, the door behind her flew open. The lady orator strode purposefully across the room to take up her position on one of the leather chairs. She was followed obsequiously by a frocked priest whose head was adorned by a black, three peaked biretta surmounted by a tufted pom pom.

'Please sit down,' the lady said. It was more of an instruction than an invitation.

Vicenta obliged and watched as the priest placed a notebook on the desk, turned a few pages and began scribbling.

'My name is Maria del Carmen López del Hierro. I am Secretary of the Alicante Branch of the Auxilio Social. This is Father Lorenzo, our Chaplain. You are?'

Flustered by the terseness of the woman's introduction, Vicenta wondered how to answer and decided to fall back on her previous practice of using her maiden name. 'I am Vicenta Reig.'

'We haven't seen you here before. Are you new to Alicante?'

'Yes, I arrived this morning.'

'Then it is good that you found us so quickly. I'm glad that we have been able to offer you some food, even though our rations are rather limited at this time.' The woman's tone was friendlier now, but still peremptory. 'I see you are wearing one of our flags.'

'Yes, I bought it this morning.'

'We are grateful for your support, every céntimo helps in these difficult times. Where are you from?'

'I'm from Castell de Castells.'

The woman frowned. 'I don't think I've heard of this place.'

'That's not surprising,' Vicenta said, trying to lighten the conversation. 'It's a small pueblo in the mountains of the Marina Alta about forty kilometres inland from Denia.'

'Then you've come a long way. How did you get here?'

Vicenta hadn't prepared for this question. She knew that she couldn't say she had travelled by train without prompting further questions. 'My journey has been difficult,' she said. 'I walked some of the way and some local farmers gave me a lift on their tractor as far as the coast road. From there I walked some more but picked up a couple of rides, one from a family travelling to Altea and then from a man driving a beer wagon who dropped me off near the port.' She wondered if her story sounded plausible and scrutinised the face of her inquisitor who met her gaze with a blank expression.

'That's quite a journey. What brings you to our city?'

Here Vicenta was on more certain ground having prepared for this particular enquiry. 'As you said, these are difficult times. Food is scarce in my village, there is very little money and no work. I heard there was work here in the city so I decided to come here in the hope of finding a job.' Vicenta hoped her story sounded believable, but she knew it was unconventional for a lone woman, especially one from a backward little hamlet, to leave her family and travel such a long way. Her self-doubt was well-founded and prompted a quizzical look.

'You have no family in Castell de Castells?'

'No, my parents are both dead, some years ago.'

The woman's expression darkened. 'And you have no husband?'

'I'm a widow.' Vicenta could have said more since her answer begged the question of who her husband was and what side, if any, he had supported in the war. She also realised that to volunteer further information might make her seem defensive, as if she had anticipated the suspicion her answer would arouse.

'A widow? I'm sorry to hear that. How did your husband die?'

Vicenta did her best to look downcast. 'My husband, Antonio, suffered from a congenital lung problem. When he contracted influenza in the winter of 1937 it turned to pneumonia and he never recovered.' She began to fret about the lies she was telling and just hoped that the truth of her story would never be checked. Castell de Castells was, she hoped, sufficiently remote to make that unlikely. Even so she felt uneasy as the priest continued to scribble in his little book.

'You have no children, I presume.' Maria del Carmen López del Hierro seemed relentless.

'No.'

'You have papers, I presume?'

Vicenta was flustered and it showed. 'Papers?'

Maria del Carmen's frown deepened to a scowl. 'Identity papers. Everyone must have identity papers from the Guardia Civil and a permit if you wish to travel from one place to another.'

Vicenta was on the verge of panic and wondered if she should just come clean and confess the true purpose of her mission. She just about held her nerve. 'I'm sorry, I didn't know. There are no Guardia Civil officers in our village. They visited once or twice but there is no permanent barracks.'

Finally relief came when Maria del Carmen appeared to soften her approach. 'You're a very brave young woman,' she said with sincerity. 'You are not the first person I have come across who has left a rural home to seek a new life in the city. Times are hard, I understand that. It's very courageous and you have my admiration, but I have to tell you that finding work and somewhere to stay is not that simple, especially as you have no papers.'

'Oh?' Vicenta looked despondent.

'But don't despair, the Auxilio Social was formed to help people like you and many others who have suffered through the war.'

'I'd be very grateful for whatever help is on offer,' Vicenta said, not knowing what else to say.

'Good, I hoped you would, but what we offer is not charity, especially for someone young and vigorous like you. What we offer is a chance to serve your country and rebuild the New Spain following the ideals of our great leader General Francisco Franco. Our men folk have done their duty and served their country, now, more than ever, Spain needs young women to do their duty as well. And through such service women can better themselves and prove their worth as citizens. Indeed completing one's service with the Auxilio Social is the only way for women to fulfil their potential and participate in the rebirth of our nation.'

Vicenta heard in Maria del Carmen's words the Nationalist propaganda that had been promulgated relentlessly since the end of the war.

'I see,' she said innocently. 'I could think about it, of course.'

Suddenly the priest was roused from his scribbling. 'You don't seem to understand young lady.' His voice was tinged with anger. 'You cannot simply wander the streets like a vagrant begging for alms. No one will employ you, especially as you have no papers. Service in the Auxilio Social is not a matter of choice. It is your duty; in fact it is required by law. Every healthy young woman must complete six months service.'

Maria del Carmen placed a hand on Father Lorenzo's arm as if to calm him and cease his ranting.

'Please, do not fret Vicenta.' Her tone was conciliatory. 'I know all this will come as a shock to you. I have seen many young women, especially from areas that were relatively untouched by the war, who, like you, are ignorant of new Decree. But within the Nationalist zones such service has been established for quite a few years. Women see it not so much as a duty, but as an opportunity; an opportunity that will provide you with legitimate documents, a passport even, and such things are essential if you want to participate fully in the development of the new Spain.'

Vicenta's head was spinning. She felt trapped, as if she had inadvertently fallen into the clutches of the very people who were responsible for Eduardo's arrest and detention. But then a second thought occurred to her. She had made it this far, but she was still a long way from finding Eduardo, let alone securing his release. She knew she could not simply roam the streets of Alicante without running the risk of being questioned or even arrested and that would serve no purpose whatsoever. Perhaps, she thought, if she could legitimise her presence in the city and establish a base it would be easier to find a way to Eduardo.

'I am sorry,' Vicenta said at last. 'I did not know of the new Decree, I must seem very naïve. I am anxious to do my duty if it means I will have work and a place to stay.'

'Excellent,' Maria del Carmen said, her face contorting to a perfidious smile. 'I'll leave you with Father Lorenzo to go through the formalities and get you settled in.' She stood and left the room.

CHAPTER SEVEN

'And God caused a deep sleep to fall upon Adam, and he slept. And He took one of his ribs and closed up the flesh instead thereof. And the rib, which God had taken from man, made He a woman and brought her unto man.'

Vicenta tried hard to disguise her unease as she sat behind a rickety desk in an old classroom alongside eleven other young women all identically dressed in blue blouses covered by white aprons.

Father Lorenzo continued in his stern authoritarian voice. 'And what must we understand from the text of Genesis?' His question was purely rhetorical and he did not pause for an answer. 'Woman was created from the body of man, from a single rib. As such woman is not equal to man, but merely a part thereof and subservient thereto. A woman can never aspire to be the equal of man and must accept her natural role as that for which she was originally conceived – wife, mother, homemaker.'

Vicenta chanced a glance at some of the other women in the classroom looking for signs of dissent or disagreement. She saw nothing but faces rapt in concentration, either too absorbed, or possibly too frightened, to signify any form of dissension. She looked back to Father Lorenzo who seemed to meet her eyes with a stern scowl.

'And deviating from these essential truths was the primary failure of the old Republic. The so-called emancipation of women was as evil as its attempts to organise the working classes and weaken the authority of the Church. In perpetrating this devilry, the Republic was consciously anti-Spain. Now we must rebuild the New State, adhere conscientiously to its tenets and hierarchies and return to the spiritual and patriotic values of the Golden Age and bring about a return of Hispanidad.'

Vicenta was overwrought, not just by the priest's reactionary message, but by the confidence in his voice and the fervour of his delivery. Here was a man, she thought, who clearly believed that the Church and the State were one inseparable entity. Only now did she begin to realise that the end of the war had brought about not just a victorious leader in the shape of General Francisco Franco, but it had prefaced a revolution that had placed the Spanish people in the hands of a regime that was not content with power in itself, but which wanted to dictate the very thoughts and feelings and aspirations of its citizens. And the Church was the principal pedagogue in disseminating the dictates and dogma of new Spanish Nationalism.

Vicenta had spent the previous night sleeping fitfully in a makeshift dormitory on the first floor of the old school not far from the soup kitchen. The room was divided into small cubicles separated by a series of flimsy screens that looked as if they had seen previous life in an army hospital. Although she had been briefly introduced to the other women, little in the way of conversation had passed between them. Like Vicenta, it seemed they were all strangers in their new surroundings and lacked the confidence to do anything but follow the terse instructions routinely issued by the nun who had introduced herself as Sister Asunción.

Her clothes had been taken away with a promise that they would be laundered and returned and in their place she had been issued with a heavy ankle-length skirt in grey wool that already showed signs of wear. There was also a blue, button-front blouse with long sleeves and a white cotton apron, crisp with starch. One corner of the bib of the apron had been neatly embroidered in red with a twin yoke crossed by five arrows. In the other corner, the letter Y was embroidered ornately in a yellow gothic script. Vicenta understood the symbolism of the yoke and arrows, but not the letter Y.

She had relished the chance to wash away the grime of her journey even though the water was barely lukewarm and there was no privacy in the communal shower room. Now she lay uncomfortably on a musty mattress resting on a metal framed bed that, like all the others in the dormitory, creaked with every restless move. At least the nightdress she had been given smelled clean and fresh.

Although there was no lock on the door of the dormitory, Vicenta couldn't help feeling imprisoned, as if she had inadvertently surrendered her liberty in return for a meagre bowl of soup and a rickety roof over her head. At least she now had an identity card bearing her name and issued by the Guardia, though the bold overprinted word *"Temporario"* suggested her actual status was still in question and possibly subject to further checks. Naively, she hoped she would be able to conclude her mission in Alicante long before anyone discovered the falsehoods she had used to get this far.

Sister Asunción had explained that the first week of their initiation in the Auxilio Social would comprise an intensive induction into the aims and objectives of the Sección Femenina and its role in enabling women to support the development of New Spain. After that they would be given work in one of the institutions run by the SF to aid the sick, the poor and the victims of the war. The work would be unpaid, but food and accommodation would be guaranteed for all those who continued to the end of their six months service.

After Father Lorenzo's long preaching lecture, Maria del Carmen entered the classroom striding purposefully to the central dais. The priest was dismissed with a perfunctory gesture and left the room hastily, clutching a bible and a bundle of papers under his arm. The tails of his cassock fluttered behind him as his boots clattered loudly on the boarded wooden floor.

A sinister silence reigned as Maria del Carmen removed a pair of gold-rimmed spectacles from a small leather case and placed them on the end of her nose, peering intently over the lenses and scanning the faces in front of her.

'You will have to forgive Father Lorenzo his monastic overtones. He is a devoted priest and his message is well founded and well meant if a little scholastic. But when all is said and done, he is just a man and not a very worldly wise one at that.'

Vicenta was as surprised as the rest of the class at this seemingly dissentious introduction.

'You will have seen on your bibs the symbol Y. Does anyone here understand its significance?'

There was silence.

'It is the icon of our great Queen Isabella I of Castile, wife of Ferdinand II of Aragon – the Catholic Monarchs who first unified Spain after centuries of division and discord. It was through the foresight and guile of Isabella that she was able to steer Spain toward the Golden Age. It was an age that marked the Christian Reconquest of Spain, ridding it finally of the iniquitous influences of the Moors and the Jews and ending the lack of religious and national unity that had weakened Spain throughout the ages. And it was Isabella that had the foresight to commission Columbus to seek out the Americas and build the empire that gave Spain its former wealth and status within the world.

'Isabella achieved all this, not by campaigning for emancipation or insisting on equality within her marriage to Ferdinand, indeed she was a devoted wife and mother and a committed Catholic. It was only from the strength of her dedication to her husband and family that she was able to exert her influence over the Kingdom and bring about such momentous change in her lifetime. That is why she is such an icon to the modern Spanish woman who, like Isabella, can influence the future of Spain through dedication to the home and family. Politics and economics should be left to the men of the world who are better suited to the intellectual rigours of business and government. But it is the women of Spain who will bring about the changes that matter – improvements in health and social care, a strengthening of morals and the upbringing of a new, more spiritual, generation of Spaniards, resolutely diligent, earnestly patriotic and unswervingly constant to the Catholic faith.'

Despite her cynicism, Vicenta found herself almost spellbound by the evangelical fervour of Maria del Carmen's sermon. She recognised the clear undertones of Falangist propaganda, though she detected an implicit scepticism in the prevailing message. However, this impression was quickly dispelled as Maria del Carmen continued.

'We are a religious militia and when we feel as much spirituality for the Fatherland as the Falange does, then by serving our country in procreating children and tending our duties as wives and mothers we shall be serving God.'

Vicenta thought then of the child within her womb and wondered what future it would find within Maria del Carmen's vision of Spain. She felt suddenly alone, not knowing what she should do and how she would cope with the travails of motherhood. She knew only one thing; she must find Eduardo and secure his release so they could face the future together. Only with him at her side could she imagine any future at all.

Her mind wandered from Maria del Carmen's continuing diatribe and consternation rose in her heart. She did not even know where Eduardo was. If, as she had been led to believe, he was in the camp at Albatera, how would she get there? How would she find him? What could she do to secure his release? A sense of frustration grew as she sat through another half an hour of hectoring and haranguing from Maria del Carmen. All she wanted to do was escape the clutches of the Falangist functionaries and find Eduardo.

Finally the sermonising came to an end as

Maria del Carmen appeared to reach a kind of crescendo.

'You, all comrades of the Women's Section, you are going to take on a momentous task in modelling the soul of man through docility and domesticity and obedience. You will be like a fruitful vine in the room of your house. Around your table will be your children like olive seedlings. And it will be your task to nurture those seedlings and imbue in them a devotion to the twin pillars of New Spain – National Syndicalism and National Catholicism.'

With that, Maria del Carmen lifted a bundle of papers from the dais and walked between the rows of desks placing a pamphlet in front of each woman as she passed.

'You will read this tonight and we will discuss it in the morning. Class dismissed.'

Vicenta looked at the pamphlet and studied the words printed over a drawing of a smiling housewife with impeccable hair, dressed in a smart frock and pinafore and sweeping a floor. "*Una buena esposa siempre sabe cual es su lugar.*" (A good wife always knows her place.)

The women in the class returned to the dormitory and waited for Sister Asunción to call them for supper. Vicenta picked up the pamphlet and began to read.

> Have a delicious meal prepared for when your husband gets home from work. Especially his favourite dish. Offer to take off his shoes. Speak in a

low tone, relaxed and enjoyable. Prepare for his arrival by retouching your makeup; put a colourful ribbon in your hair to make your self a little more interesting to him. After his hard day at work he may feel a little downhearted and one of your duties is to cheer him up.

During the coldest days prepare and light a fire in the fireplace so that he may relax in front of it. After all, catering for his comfort will provide you with immense personal satisfaction.

Minimize all noise. At the time of his arrival be sure the house is calm and quiet. Greet him with a warm smile and show your desire to please. Listen, let him talk first; remember his topics of conversation are more important than yours. Never complain if he is late, or goes out to dinner or other places of entertainment without you. Try, instead, to understand his world of strain and stress, and his real needs. Make him feel at ease, allow him to rest in a comfortable chair, or lie in the chamber. Prepare a hot or cold drink for him. Do not ask for explanations of his actions or question his judgment or integrity. He is the master of the house.

Encourage your husband in his hobbies and interests and serve to support him without being too pushy. If you have any hobbies, try not to bore him by talking about these, since the interests of women are trivial compared with those of men.

Clean the house in the morning so that it is tidy when he returns for lunch. Lunch is vital to your husband if he is to meet the outside world in a positive mood. Clean the house again in the late afternoon.

Once you both retire to your room, get ready for bed as soon as possible, taking into account that while feminine hygiene is of the utmost importance, your husband does not want to wait for the bathroom. You must look at your best at the time of going to bed. If you should apply face cream or hair rollers wait until he is asleep, as this may be shocking for a man late at night.

As regards the possibility of intimate relationship with your husband, it is important to remember your marriage obligations. If he feels the need to sleep, so be it, do not push or stimulate him intimately. If your husband suggests a union, then humbly accede, taking into account his satisfaction is more important than your own. You can then set the alarm to get up a little before him in the morning. This allows you to have a breakfast ready for when he wakes up.

Vicenta found it hard to believe the text she read. She felt sure it must be something from the previous century, until she saw the footnote on the back page which read, *"Publicada por la Sección Femenina 1938."*

A giggle erupted from the cubicle opposite where two young girls, teenagers Vicenta thought, sat side by side on one of the single beds.

'What's so funny?' Vicenta said, approaching the two girls.

Immediately the girls sat upright and looked

serious, one of them stuffing the pamphlet under the pillow.

'Nothing,' one of them said.

'Don't worry,' Vicenta said, 'I found it amusing as well. Which bit were you laughing at?' She joined the girls on the edge of the bed.

One of the girls, a fresh faced blond, looked embarrassed, her face gradually turning crimson. 'It was the bit about stimulating a man intimately,' she said, giggling once more. 'We were thinking about what that might involve.'

The girl was called Aurora and her friend Maria-Ángelica. As Vicenta had thought, they were seventeen and eighteen years old respectively. Both were from Alicante and had joined the Auxilio Social the week before. Aurora was an orphan, her parents having died in the bombing raid at the central market. Maria-Ángelica's father had died fighting for the Nationalists at the siege of Valencia, but her mother was still alive. She had joined the Auxilio Social to do her duty and to better herself. Her mother had told her that completing her service would give her an education and training. Both seemed content in their current surroundings, though Aurora confessed to being bored by the induction process and she was looking forward to doing some proper work in the next week or so.

Another woman poked her head round the screen. 'What are you talking about?' She was older, more like Vicenta's age with an angular face and hard features that were at exaggerated by the severity of her swept-back blond hair.

The two girls looked nervous, as if they had committed an indiscretion of some kind.

'We were just discussing the pamphlet,' Vicenta said.

The woman smiled. 'Amusing isn't it? Or at least it would be if it weren't meant to be taken seriously.'

Vicenta stood and left the cubicle, returning to her own space and ushering the woman to join her.

'My name is Vicenta Reig, what's yours?

'I am Maite Giménez.'

'Are you not a little bold to comment in such a way about the instruction pamphlet?'

'Don't tell me you go along with that crap.'

Vicenta was surprised by the woman's bravado. 'I didn't say that. It's just that I'm new here and so far I haven't heard anyone utter a murmur about our induction... or should I say indoctrination?'

Maite peered around the edge of the screen and pulled the end closer, virtually enclosing the space. 'Brainwashing is the word I would use.'

Vicenta warmed to her new companion recognising someone who shared her scepticism for the process they were both enduring. She had found, it seemed, a kindred spirit.

At thirty-two, Maite was five years older than Vicenta. She was an Alicantina by birth and had lived all her life in the city. Her husband, Juan, was originally from Castellon in the north of the Valencia region, but had moved to Alicante when they married in 1933 where he worked as a stevedore at the docks. He was, as Maite put it, always a bit of a hot head and played a leading role in organising Alicante's participation in the general strike of 1934 called to protest against the reforms of the then right wing government. He was arrested at the time and imprisoned for a short while before being released in 1935. The experience left him with an even greater hatred of the fascists led by José Antonio Primo de Rivera. When the civil war broke out in 1936, Juan was quick to join the local militia defending Alicante, a Republican stronghold at the time. He saw action in the many unsuccessful attacks mounted on the city by the Nationalists and survived them all until the very end of the war. Juan had rejoiced when Primo de Rivera, who had found himself stranded in Alicante at the outbreak of the war, was arrested and eventually executed in November 1936. But as the Republicans gradually crumbled in the early months of 1939, Juan had refused to accept the inevitability of defeat. Even as Franco's tanks rumbled through the outskirts of Alicante, Juan and a dwindling band of Republicans had mounted a fruitless offensive. He died when the building from which he was sniping was blasted by tank shells. His body had never been recovered.

After the end of the war Maite continued to live in the small apartment block in the suburb of San Vicent del Raspeig which she and Juan had rented since their marriage. Now jobless, she was struggling to pay the rent. She had joined the Auxilio Social three months ago but she hated every minute and left after just three weeks. Before the war she had been a teacher in a secondary school in the suburbs of the city. Since quitting the Auxilio Social she had tried to find work but a lack of official papers and her husband's reputation made it impossible to gain employment. Reluctantly she had reached the conclusion that completing her service with the Auxilio Social was the only way to re-establish her credentials and move forward in her life.

'But don't they know about your husband's support for the Republicans?' Vicenta asked.

'Of course they do,' Maite replied nonchalantly, 'but they don't care. Most Alicantinos supported the Republican side, men and women alike. So if they excluded us all, there would be no one left. To them the war is a thing of the past. They believe that all women have a part to play in building New Spain and training people in the Auxilio Social is their way of disseminating their message. They are not trying to convert everyone to fascism; to them being a good Catholic and a faithful wife and mother are more important.'

'But don't you find that terrible – I mean being

told what to think and how to behave?'

'I don't like it any more than you do, but for me it's a matter of practicality. It's a passport to the future. Without legitimate papers I don't stand a chance of finding work, travelling or renting a house. Besides, not everything the Auxilio Social does is tied in with political indoctrination.'

Vicenta was surprised. 'I don't understand.'

'Well, there's the religious stuff and their outdated views on feminism, but they actually do a lot of good.'

'What do you mean?'

'They run orphanages for hundreds of children and give health and child-care training to lots of young mothers. On top of that, they are feeding hundreds of people who might otherwise starve.'

'Yes, but at the price of humiliation. I witnessed that on my first day at the soup kitchen – singing the Falange anthem and listening to all that guff about women being subservient to men.'

Maite scoffed. 'Gosh you really are a little revolutionary. You'd better be careful what you say, especially around here.'

'I just don't like being told how to behave or what to think, that's all.'

'And you think I do? Look, the secret to survival here is to listen without questioning, but that doesn't mean you have to believe what you are told. You can learn a lot here and take what you want from it. Do your duty and keep your thoughts to yourself, that way you can maintain your independence.'

'But I just hate the thought of these young women being used to further the political agenda of the new government.'

Maite's face darkened to a scowl. 'Do you think you are unique – something special? Don't imagine that everyone else here is stupid or naïve enough to be taken in by everything they are told. Most of these women are like you, here out of necessity not conviction. History is full of people who think they can mould the thoughts and beliefs of entire nations and most of them fail because the human spirit is stronger than all of them. Spain is weak right now; the people are tired of war, but mark my words, Spain will emerge a better and stronger country. Sooner or later it will rid itself of tyranny, not by fighting or active rebellion, but by the strength and determination of the human spirit.'

Vicenta found herself rapt by Maite's tirade. She had clearly under-estimated the intelligence of her new found companion. Could what she said really be true? Were these bleak times merely an interlude before Spain came back to its senses. She wanted to believe Maite, but somehow she felt that Maite's aspirations were born more from hope than any realistic expectations. Even so, she took comfort from the knowledge that there were people like Maite who saw beyond the stifling repression of Franco and the Falange to a better future.

Though inspired momentarily by Maite's determined optimism, Vicenta quickly returned to the reality of her situation, remembering that she was not in service with the Auxilio Social to further her own future, but simply as a means to an end – to find Eduardo and secure his release.

Perhaps Maite could help; she knew Alicante and understood the way the authorities work. But could she trust Maite? For now she decided to wait and see.

CHAPTER EIGHT

For the next three days Vicenta, Maite and the rest of the group sat through hour after hour of instruction from Maria del Carmen López del Hierro and pious preaching from Father Lorenzo. The message was relentlessly consistent – women were different from men; weaker, subservient. A man's social purpose was different from a woman's and therefore their education should not be the same. He should be a tough fighter for his country and she must be the devoted wife and mother; respectful, loving and submissive.

Father Lorenzo urged them to follow and defend the Catholic faith with fervour. 'If someone laughs or insults the name of God, or Spain, or the Virgin Mother, do not hesitate to attack him with your fists, your feet, your teeth. If you do not defend your faith you are no longer fit to wear the yoke and arrows on your shirt.'

Maria del Carmen espoused her own version of a woman's annual duties.

'In January count and review the household clothing, repair what is serviceable or buy new if resources permit. In February sort and tidy the drawers and cabinets. In March beat the carpets, clean the ceilings and lamps. In April wash the curtains and cushions and in May clean the hearths and fireplaces. In June clean the blankets and shake the pillows and mattresses. In July and August use the holidays to catch up on sewing and participate in the fiestas, taking the opportunity to help the church celebrate the blessings of the patron saints of your town or village. In September prepare for the return of your children to school, cleaning their clothes and putting together supplies for the next term. In October stock up on supplies of wood and charcoal. In November review all boots and shoes, making sure they are fit for winter. In December remind yourself of the miracle of the birth of Our Lord and prepare the new year's budget.'

Vicenta found it hard not to scoff. She glanced surreptitiously in Maite's direction. Maite raised her eyes briefly to the ceiling before resuming her expression of studious concentration.

On the final Friday morning, Maria del Carmen made a great fuss of welcoming a guest speaker to the class. Her name was Mercedes Sanz Bachiller and she was introduced as the founder of the Auxilio Social. What Maria del Carmen did not say was that Mercedes Sanz Bachiller was also deputy and rival to Pilar Primo de Rivera, sister of José Antonio and leader of the Sección Femenina.

Mercedes strode purposefully to the rostrum, planting her feet wide apart and gripping the lectern with both hands. She was a sturdy woman with an ample bust, tightly enveloped in a sage green twin set, accessorised by a triple string of pearls. Her bubbly brown hair was flecked with grey and she peered at the class over the top of her half moon spectacles. For all her sternness, she greeted her audience with a benign smile as she began to talk of the work of the Auxilio Social in the aftermath of the fall of Madrid in March of that year.

'We found that almost every house was infected with parasites and we had to decontaminate and disinfect them. But it was not just lice and cockroaches we were forced to sanitize; we had also to eradicate the infestation of Marxism and Liberal ideas of parliamentary democracy.'

Mercedes glared at the class at this point as if to reinforce the analogy and be sure its import was not lost on the audience.

'And it is to you that we entrust the task of continuing this work by immunizing the spirit of Spaniards against unhealthy doctrines. Our motto must be "clean bodies, clean clothes, clean souls." We must rebuild the spirit of Hispanidad and recreate the virtues of chivalry, steadfastness, spirituality and faith. Foreign influences have permeated the country and caused Spain to fall into a quagmire of atheism, liberalism and feminism. Our very genotype has been put in danger of extinction because of these alien influences first sown by the Jews then by the Moriscos and more recently by radicals and rationalists. These have bred negative traits such as malice, resentment and moral degeneration.

Armed with soap, disinfectant and whitewash and strengthened by our faith and a clear understanding of our place in society, it will be the women of Spain who will extinguish the corruption of our ideals. And through moral re-armament, we will bring about a return to the values of the Golden Age when Spain was clear in its ideals, steadfast in its self-belief and unswervingly loyal to is leaders and to the Catholic church.'

When Mercedes stepped back from the rostrum, Maria del Carmen stood and applauded enthusiastically, glowering at the class until they, too, applauded as Mercedes left the dais without further ceremony. It was the end of their induction.

That evening, after supper, Vicenta sought out Maite and found her sitting on the bed reading a copy of the magazine "Revista Y"

Seeing Vicenta, Maite tossed the magazine to one side. 'More anti-feminist twaddle,' she said.

Vicenta looked around the room to be sure no one was within earshot and then joined Maite on the edge of the bed. 'I wonder if I can ask you something,' she said hesitantly.

'Ask away.'

'Well, you are from Alicante and I wonder if you know anything about the prison camp at Albatera.'

Maite looked surprised. 'Why do you ask?'

Vicenta paused, wondering again if she could trust her new found companion with her secret. Finally she overcame her reticence. 'My husband is there. I need to see him and secure his release.'

'Well, you really are a dark horse aren't you? Not just a poor country girl looking for work. You'd better tell me all about it.'

Vicenta recounted her story in every detail, omitting nothing except the fact that she was pregnant. Maite listened intently without interruption. At the conclusion Maite said, 'What bravery you have shown to get this far. You must love your husband very much.'

Vicenta lowered her eyes. 'He means everything to me and I will not rest until I have found him.' She looked up again, meeting Maite's eyes with a watery gaze. 'Will you help me?'

Maite paused for a moment and looked thoughtful. 'How can I refuse? I would do the same for Juan were he still alive. But you must realise that your mission is fraught with danger, not least because you are here under false pretences. The Auxilio Social does not demand absolute commitment to their ideals, but they certainly wouldn't take kindly to anyone using them as a means to another, more subversive, cause. We will have to be extremely careful.'

Vicenta took comfort from Maite's use of the word "we" and knew instantly that she had found a true and steadfast friend. 'Thank you,' she said taking and squeezing Maite's hands.

Saturday, like Sunday, was a free day for the women of the Auxilio Social and Vicenta woke early, feeling anxious about the day ahead. She dressed in her old clothes which, as promised, had been laundered and returned to her. Maite, too, was ready and waiting, dressed in a plain white cotton shirt and a pair of baggy green linen trousers pulled tight at the waist with a broad leather belt. Her wavy blond hair hung lose about her face, a contrast to her previously severe style, pulled up and back to form a bun at the back. It was the first time Vicenta had seen it that way and she realised now what an attractive woman Maite was. Vicenta had no make-up of her own, having lost what little she had in the suitcase abandoned on the railway track at Benissa. Maite allowed her to use a little of her powdered rouge and held a small mirror as Vicenta applied a thin layer of bright red lipstick and crimped her own curly brown hair.

'We must have you looking your best if you are to see your husband,' Maite said.

Vicenta's heart fluttered at the very thought.

The town of Albatera lay about 40 kilometres south west of Alicante. There were no direct transport links to the town in the Vega Baja region so Maite and Vicenta would have faced an arduous journey except that Maite had enlisted a little help. Her brother Ramón, a blacksmith by trade, owned a truck which he used for his work in and around the Alicante area, making and repairing all kinds of wrought ironwork. His work was in great demand in the aftermath of the war and his trade gave him a legitimate reason to travel. He had agreed to meet the women on the outskirts of Alicante, it being less likely that they would be stopped by the Guardia Civil once outside the city limits. Maite made sure Vicenta had her temporary papers and they agreed a concocted story about visiting an elderly aunt in the town of Elche.

They boarded a bus just outside the port and sat side by side at the back of the vehicle as it rattled its way through the suburbs. After ten minutes a group of four army soldiers boarded the bus all wearing the same brown uniform and side caps. The epaulettes of their pocketed jackets were edged in the red and yellow of the new Spanish flag and the right sleeves all bore an embroidered badge of green felt displaying an open-winged eagle centred by a red cross and topped with a royal crown. Their uniforms were crumpled and their lace-up boots looked worn and dirty. The only thing tidy about their appearance was their polished leather belts and pistol holsters.

Vicenta flinched as the four men took their seats at the front of the bus.

'Don't worry,' Maite whispered, 'They are regular army troops, returning home by the looks of it. They won't be interested in us.'

The troopers sat in virtual silence and by the time Vicenta and Maite left the bus two of them were fast asleep.

As promised, Ramón was waiting for them by the bus terminus in the district of San Blas. His battered old flat-bed truck was parked side-on and Vicenta could barely read the hand-painted words splashed in red on the driver's door which was pock marked with dents and patches of rust - *"Ramon Turell, Herrero. Instalaciones y reparaciones de hierro."*

Vicenta squeezed between Maite and her brother on the bench seat in the cabin of the truck as Ramón fired up the motor and crunched through the gears to get them underway. The cabin was musty and smelled of a combination of tobacco smoke and diesel fumes to which Ramón seemed oblivious as he munched on the end of a bocadillo stuffed with tomato, alternating mouthfuls of bread with deep drags on the stub of a thumb sized cigar. Everything in the cabin rattled, from the loose-fitting door handles to the knobs on the dashboard and the glass in the door windows. The long gear stick wobbled from side to side as they moved and Vicenta had to shift her knees to one side as Ramón waggled it up, down and across to find the gears.

'I have some news for you,' Ramón said as he dropped through the gears, climbing a steep incline in the road that meandered through the urban sprawl of dilapidated apartment blocks interspersed with workshops and warehouses. 'There has been some activity at the prison camp in Albatera. A friend passed there last week and told me he'd seen a fleet of army trucks lined up outside the prison gates. He didn't stop so he doesn't know any more than that.'

Vicenta was alarmed 'Were they bringing people in or taking them away?'

'Your guess is as good as mine.'

As they neared the town of Albatera, Ramón explained that he would have to drop Vicenta some distance away from the prison as he did not want to be seen too close to the place for fear of being stopped and questioned. Anyone associated with the prisoners was likely to be regarded as a Republican sympathiser and he did not want to put his business at risk by being seen in his truck. He stopped at the side of a disused warehouse about half a mile from the prison and gave Vicenta directions saying he would wait until she returned. Maite offered to walk with her at least part of the way, but Vicenta said she had done enough already. The two women hugged as they parted.

It was a clear day and even though the sun was low in the sky, its warmth caused Vicenta to perspire beneath her heavy woollen jumper. Despite her trepidation she could not help but imagine what it would be like to see Eduardo again and to feel his touch. She rounded the corner of a high stone wall enclosing a factory of some kind and caught her first glimpse of the prison camp. A three metre high chain link fence topped with coils of barbed wire stretched out into the distance. The fence was interspersed with watch towers crudely constructed of criss-crossed angle-iron supporting a small open-sided platform covered with a bent sheet of corrugated metal. Inside the fencing, Vicenta saw row after row of dilapidated wooden shacks, many with broken windows and some appearing to be on the verge of collapse. Between the rows, the parched earth, devoid of vegetation, blew up into small clouds of dust. Vicenta looked beyond the end of the fencing to a large stone building in the distance supposing it must be the entrance to the prison. As she hastened her steps she began to realise that something was seriously wrong. The watch towers were unmanned and the rows of huts were deserted. Where were the guards? Where were the prisoners?

In near panic Vicenta reached the end of the fencing and approached the stone building she had seen in the distance. Still there was no one in sight. Only when she reached the heavy ironclad gates at the centre of the building did she encounter a human presence in the form of a wiry old man in a scruffy grey uniform sitting on a foundation stone at the side of the entrance. His head was bowed forward and he seemed to be staring at his own scuffed brown boots. He did not notice Vicenta's arrival until she was standing directly in front of him. He raised his head and then his hands to shield his eyes as he squinted at the silhouette before him. Even then he did not move or stand, but simply scowled as Vicenta came into focus.

'What do you want?' he barked from behind his swarthy black beard.

'Are you a guard here?' Vicenta asked.

'What business is it of yours who I am?'

This was not the reception Vicenta had envisaged. A phalanx of guards, an office full of people checking paperwork was what she had expected to encounter, not a solitary guard slumbering on a rock. Bemused, she regained her resolve. 'My husband is a prisoner here, I believe. I was hoping to see him.'

Now the man stood and stepped forward confronting Vicenta head on as he laughed dismissively revealing a mouth with more gaps than teeth. 'Ha,' he smirked, 'then you're wasting your time.'

'What do you mean?'

'Isn't it obvious? The prison has been closed and not before time. The last of the surviving prisoners were shipped out last week.'

'I don't understand.'

'What's to understand? Can't you smell it? The stench of death is all about the place. The whole camp was ridden with disease and infestation it was like a plague. The staff were refusing to work here and even the rats moved on.'

In desperation Vicenta pleaded, 'But what happened to all the prisoners? Where have they gone?'

The man shrugged and sat down again. He rummaged through the pockets of his jacket to extract a crumpled pack of cigarettes. He placed one between his lips and shielded the end from the breeze with cupped hands as he struck a match and dragged hard before belching out a billowing cloud of smoke.

Vicenta was losing patience. She leant forward and took the man by his shoulders, shaking him into life. 'Tell me,' she demanded. 'Where have they sent the prisoners? My husband is amongst them and I need to know where he has been sent.'

The man pushed Vicenta's hands away and took another drag on his cigarette. Vicenta stood her ground and gave him a cold hard stare. Glowering, she said, 'Well, are you going to tell me?'

'I'll tell you, but it won't help you. They are all over the place. Some have been dispersed to other parts of Alicante, some have been sent to other prisons in their home regions and the rest have been sent to work camps in Murcia and Almeria – those that were fit enough to work.'

Vicenta was on the edge of despair. 'But my husband, his name is Eduardo Ripoll. Do you know what happened to him?'

'Listen lady,' the man growled, 'there were thousands of prisoners crammed into this place.

It was built for just eight hundred but there must have been three or four thousand at one time. Every day more arrived, but very few left, except in coffins – those that were lucky enough to get a decent burial. If they didn't starve to death or die of typhoid they were just as likely to be executed by the firing squads. As for your husband, I never heard of him. But then I never knew the names of any of the prisoners, they were just numbers herded about the place. As one man died, another took his bed, if he was strong enough to fight for it. You have no idea how bad things were and you don't want to know. I've told you too much already. Next week the bulldozers arrive and the whole place will be razed to the ground and wiped from the map like as not.'

Anguish suddenly overcame Vicenta and she wobbled on her feet. The man stood and steadied her, easing her onto the stone and sitting at her side. 'I'm sorry,' he said, 'but this is what life is like in Spain now. If your husband was an opponent of the regime then he got what was coming to him, like everyone else in here.'

'Eduardo was not an opponent of the regime. He didn't even fight in the war. He was denounced by someone who was jealous of his standing in our village and wanted to get his hands on our land. His only crime was to stand up for his rights.'

The man sighed. 'I wish I had a peseta for every time I've heard that story. I would be a very wealthy man.'

'But it's true,' Vicenta implored.

'I don't doubt it, but what difference does it make? If he was in this hell-hole and if he survived then God only knows where he is now.'

'But surely someone must know. There must be records of some kind listing the names of prisoners and where they have been sent.'

The man thought for a moment and scratched his chin. 'I was just a guard here, you understand. I didn't like my work, but I did as I was told and for the most part that meant circling the perimeter or doing a shift in one of the watch towers. There were others, however, who worked in the reception block. Their job was to search the prisoners on arrival and assign them to one of the blocks. There was an office there as well. I only went in it once, but I remember it was full of cupboards and filing cabinets. There were papers everywhere.'

Vicenta felt a brief glimmer of hope. 'Where are these papers now? If I can find them, perhaps there is a record of my husband.'

'Don't get your hopes up, lady. All I can say is that the office is empty now. I have no idea what happened to all the papers. They may have been taken somewhere else or just as likely destroyed.'

Vicenta despaired. She had come this far only to find a dead end. What would she do now? How would she ever find Eduardo? Despondency overcame her and she began to weep.

The man remained silent for a while and puffed on his cigarette, coughing as he took a last drag and dropped the stub on the ground, crushing it with his boot. 'There's one possibility,' he said at last. 'I know one of the guards who worked in the office. He lives in Albatera, not far from here. He wasn't of any high rank, just a clerk as I recall, but he saw all the prisoners as they arrived and booked them in. He may remember your husband or at least he may know what happened to the records.'

Vicenta's hopes rose again. 'Who is he? Where can I find him?'

'His name is Silvestre Moreno, but there's something you should know – he's a blue shirt. He may not be too willing to help the wife of a dissident prisoner, innocent or not.'

'I don't care if he's one of Franco's personal bodyguards. He's my only hope of finding Eduardo. I have to see him.'

'Fine. Just don't say I never warned you.'

As Vicenta returned to Ramón's truck, Maite could see by her demeanour that all was not well. In tears Vicenta recounted her conversation with the guard. When she mentioned the clerk from the prison office, Maite's reaction was instant. 'Then we must go there now,' she said.

Ramón was more sceptical, especially when he heard the man was a blue shirt. Even if he had no particular status or rank, the fact that he was a supporter of the Falange meant he was dangerous. It would be risky for Vicenta to approach him, particularly as she would have to reveal the purpose of her visit. The very fact that Vicenta's husband had been imprisoned would mean the man would assume he was a Republican sympathiser – and Vicenta, too, for that matter. Why would he want to help her even if he could?

'I don't care,' Vicenta screamed in frustration. 'He's my only hope. I haven't come all this way just to give up on Eduardo.'

Maite calmed her and after a little persuasion Ramón agreed to drive to the address given by the guard. It was only a short journey, less than fifteen minutes through a rabbit warren of apartment blocks. It was early afternoon and Ramón was relieved that the streets were virtually deserted – even in the New Spain, siesta was sacrosanct. He was conscious that his lorry bore his name and he was uneasy that he might be spotted in the area.

They found the block they were looking for and Ramón drove by slowly so they could take a look. It was a non-descript concrete building four storeys high with narrow balconies overlooking a small strip of rough ground that separated it from an identical block the opposite side of the road. An assortment of washing fluttered in the breeze on several of the balconies, pegged to the metal balustrades. The entrance to the block was located at the far end and comprised a pair of metal framed glass doors sheltered beneath an overhanging concrete canopy. Ramón parked the truck just around the corner from the entrance in a place where it could not be seen from the main road. Reluctantly he offered to go with Vicenta, but she was adamant he had done enough already.

Inside the entrance Vicenta found a small lobby with a terracotta tiled floor and beige painted walls. The space was surprisingly tidy, Vicenta thought, and smelled of strong disinfectant. The apartment she wanted was on the third floor and accessed by a gloomy stairwell at the far end of the lobby. With some trepidation she climbed the stairs slowly until she reached a sign that read *"Piso 3."* A narrow walkway stretched past the front doors of the different apartments and Vicenta walked slowly along its length looking for number four. With every step she grew more anxious and her heart pounded in her chest. What am I doing here in this strange place trying to talk to a man I have never met? He's a blue shirt. He could have me arrested just for being here; just for daring to ask about Eduardo. She took a deep breath and straightened, stiffening her body as well as her resolve. I'm here for Eduardo. I cannot rest until I have found him. I must go on.

A first timid knock on the door brought no response and her first feeling was one of relief. At least she had tried. From somewhere she plucked up the courage to bang again on the door, harder this time. From behind the door she heard a movement and every nerve in her body jangled with fear.

The man's bulky frame virtually filled the doorway and Vicenta, overawed by his intimidating presence, took a step back. His curly, jet black hair was dishevelled and fell like an unruly mop about his head. The equally black stubble on his face covered bulbous cheeks and flabby jowls that converged into a sagging double chin. The top buttons on a collarless shirt were open to expose his hirsute chest that appeared shallow compared with the bulging belly that overhung a pair of beige twill trousers spattered with stains.

He squinted and rubbed the sleep from his eyes. 'What do you want?' he growled.

Vicenta took a deep breath and composed herself once more. 'Are you Silvestre Moreno?'

'What's it to you,' he scowled.

'I'm looking for one of the prisoners who may have been in the prison until it was closed. I was told you worked in the office there and you may know where he is now or at least what happened to the records.'

Silvestre Moreno leered at Vicenta scrutinising her carefully from head to toe. A simpering smile crossed his face. 'Are you alone?' he asked, stepping out of the doorway and glancing along the walkway.

'Yes.'

'You'd better come in,' he said, retreating into the apartment.

Vicenta followed him along a short hallway that led to a sparsely furnished lounge. A coffee table pulled close to a sofa was strewn with the residue of a meal – a plate littered with crumbs and a half empty bottle of beer.

'Sit here,' Moreno said, gesturing to the sofa.

Reluctantly Vicenta complied, careful to position herself in the centre of the seat. Moreno sat down on a loose-covered armchair on the opposite side of the table, sitting back and crossing his legs to reveal bare feet inside a pair of worn, foam-soled slippers.

Vicenta sat rigid on the edge of the sofa cushion.

'You're looking for one of the prisoners you say?'

'Yes, his name is Eduardo Ripoll.'

'And who is this Eduardo Ripoll to you?'

'My husband.'

'I see. And what was his crime?'

'He committed no crime, but he was denounced without just cause by someone in our village.'

'I see, so he is innocent of any charges laid against him.' The scorn in his voice was meant to be detected.

'I'm telling you the truth,' Vicenta pleaded. 'He was never even charged and as far as I know he has never been to court.'

'No charges? Never been to court? Most irregular,' he said with mocking surprise.

Vicenta ignored Moreno's derision. 'He was held for a few days in the jail in our village then taken away in the middle of the night. The guard at the jail was shown some papers and told he was being sent to Alicante. That's all I know and that's why I need to find out what has happened to him. I was told that the camp here in Albatera was the main prison for political prisoners and that's why I've come here to find him.'

'Political prisoners?' Moreno jibed. 'Is that what your husband is? What is he – a Republican fighter, an atheist, a Red?'

'He's none of those things,' Vicenta insisted. 'He's a journalist, a writer. He never took sides in the war.'

'So, he's a member of the inteligencia, is he?'

'That's not how I would describe him. He's just an ordinary man doing his job. He was always careful to remain neutral.'

'Neutral,' he derided. 'There's no room for neutrality in today's Spain. Those Republican bastards executed thousands, hundreds of thousands of innocent people during the war. And those who failed to condemn them are just as guilty as the perpetrators themselves. Your husband was a journalist, you say. Tell me, did he denounce the Terror Rojo? Did he criticise the degradation and murder of Catholic clergy and the desecration of churches and monasteries?

Did he disapprove of the attacks on landowners and industrialists and the murder of right wing sympathisers?'

Vicenta knew there was some truth in the tales of atrocities perpetrated by the Red Terror, though they had undoubtedly been exaggerated since the end of the war, perhaps to divert attention from the fascists' own barbarity. Wherever the truth lay, she knew she had to tread carefully.

'My husband is no threat to the new regime. He did not fight in the war and he did not and would not campaign for one side or the other. All he ever wanted to do was to get on with his life and support his family. I've told you, the only person who has accused him acted not to protect the government, but simply to line his own pockets.'

Moreno leant forward and sneered. 'And if what you say is true, what do you expect me to do about it?'

'I just want to find him. Its so distressing not knowing where he is or what is going to happen to him. I just want to find him and talk to him, to know he is safe and well. If I could explain that he has been wrongly accused perhaps I could secure his release.'

Moreno stood and walked around the low table then sat alongside Vicenta on the sofa forcing her to move along. 'Your husband is a lucky man to have a wife like you prepared to fight for him. And such a handsome wife at that.' He shuffled along the sofa forcing Vicenta against the arm rest. 'And just how do you think I could help you?... you haven't told me your name.'

'Vicenta.' His face was so close to hers she could smell beer on his breath. 'I... I just thought that if you worked in the office, you might remember him or have some knowledge of where he was sent when the prison closed.'

'It's true, I worked in the office. I saw all the new prisoners as they arrived and booked them in, writing details on record cards. I don't know what has happened to those records, but luckily for you I have a very good memory. Tell me, your husband, Eduardo Ripoll you say, when was he sent to Albatera?' His face twisted to a sinister smile and he shuffled further along the sofa so that his thigh was pressing against Vicenta's.

'Four weeks ago.'

'Quite recently then. It shouldn't be too hard for me to remember.'

'So you can help me then?' she said, flinching.

'Well, Vicenta, I could help you, but such information is very valuable, I think, especially to such a dedicated wife so desperate to find her husband,' He placed his right hand on her thigh. 'It ought to be worth something, don't you think?' His hand grasped at her skirt and began sliding it upwards.

Vicenta placed her hand on his and held it firm. 'I have nothing to offer you except my gratitude. Now, please tell me what you know about

Eduardo.'

Moreno pulled his hand away. 'I don't need your gratitude. Perhaps there is some other way you could encourage me to tell you what I know about your dear Eduardo.' He leant sideways rolling his body over Vicenta, grabbing at her left breast and squeezing hard. His right leg lay across Vicenta's thighs virtually pinning her to the sofa.

Vicenta pushed with all her might, but he was like a dead weight. 'Get off me you brute,' she yelled, pushing hard once more.

'Oh come on Vicenta, a kiss would do no harm. I promise I won't say anything to Eduardo.' He thrust his face toward Vicenta's, forcing her to turn her head to one side.

'Please, just tell me what you know and let me go,' she pleaded struggling beneath his weight.

Moreno's face twisted with rage. 'You stupid little bitch. Why should I help you find that Red husband of yours? You stuck up cow, you'll give me what I want or you might be joining your dear Eduardo sooner than you think.' Moreno raised his body a fraction placing his left arm across Vicenta's throat, pushing her into the back of the sofa. With his right hand he tugged at the bottom of her pullover lifting it to expose her bra which he grabbed and pulled down to expose her naked breasts. 'Nice tits,' he sneered, fondling her left breast and squeezing the nipple. 'Your Eduardo is a lucky man.'

Vicenta's mind filled with recollections of Garcia's brutal assault and her whole body stiffened with fear. For a fleeting moment she thought of submitting to Moreno's onslaught if it meant he would tell her what she wanted to know. She stared into Moreno's bulging lustful eyes and her fear was overtaken by nausea and revulsion. Bile rose in her throat as she mustered all her strength to raise her right hand and jab her fingers into Moreno's eyes.

Moreno winced and pulled back, releasing his grip on her breast. 'You evil bitch,' he yelled, raising his hand and forming a fist.

Vicenta pushed his other arm from her throat and screamed – a shrill piecing shriek that boomed through the whole apartment as she closed her eyes and moved her face to one side anticipating Moreno's blow.

The intended blow never came. Instead it was Moreno who shrieked in pain as his raised arm was twisted behind his back and shoved up between his shoulder blades. The force of the attack made Moreno slide sideways until he knelt on the floor in front of the sofa, his head pressed into the back cushion.

Shocked, Vicenta opened her eyes to see Ramón leaning over Moreno with his knee in the small of Moreno's back. He lifted his free hand and placed a finger vertically across his lips. Vicenta understood and remained silent.

'Has he told you what you wanted to know?'

Ramón asked.

Vicenta shook her head.

'It seems you have been reluctant to cooperate, Mr Moreno.' Ramón shoved Moreno's arm a little higher prompting him to squeal again. 'Keep your head facing the cushion and don't try to look round. Now would be a good time to tell the lady what you know of her husband.' He gave the arm a further tweak to reinforce his demand.

'Please,' Moreno simpered, 'you're breaking my arm.'

'That would be very easy. Now talk.'

'Okay, okay, I'll tell you what I know. I've never heard of Eduardo Ripoll.'

'That isn't good enough Mr Moreno.'

'I'm telling you the truth. I remember all the prisoners' names. If he was supposed to have been sent to Albatera in the last few weeks, then he never arrived. I would remember, believe me.'

'You'd better not be lying.'

'It's the honest truth. Why would I lie? He's probably better off anyway. If he had been put in that hell hole he'd probably be dead by now, like most of the rest of the prisoners.'

Ramón looked over to Vicenta raising his eyebrows as if to ask if she believed Moreno's story. Vicenta shrugged.

'You'd better be telling the truth, Mr Moreno. If I find out you lied to us, I could always pay you a return visit. You wouldn't want that would you?'

'It's the truth, I swear.'

Ramón looked at Vicenta and gestured toward the door. She stood and walked in that direction.

'Very well. We are leaving now and you'd better not report what happened here. Even your blue shirt friends don't take kindly to men who try to rape vulnerable women. Now, I suggest you stay here and keep your head down for five minutes until we're well clear of this place.' Ramón pulled the cushion from the back of the sofa and shoved it over Moreno's head. 'Remember, stay put.'

Out of breath and panting, they finally reached Ramón's truck.

'What happened?' Maite asked. 'Are you all right?'

'Just get in the truck,' Ramón instructed. He gunned the motor and they sped away just as quickly as the ancient motor would permit, not stopping until they reached San Blas on the outskirts of Alicante.

As they left the truck Vicenta walked over to Ramón and gave him a hug that lasted a moment longer than it might have done. 'I don't know how to thank you,' she said. 'You probably saved my life.'

'That's a bit of an exaggeration,' he said.

'I don't think so.'

'You're a very brave woman, Vicenta. I hope you find Eduardo, wherever he is. He's a lucky man.'

'Right now, I'm not sure I would agree with

you, but thank you for everything. I will always remember what you did.' She stood on tiptoe and kissed him gently on the cheek. 'You're a good man Ramón. Farewell.'

CHAPTER NINE

Vicenta felt wretched as she and Maite returned to the dormitory at the Auxilio Social in Alicante. The distress of her experience with Moreno was bad enough, but she could cope with that. What caused her to feel more despondent was her failure to find Eduardo. And if what Morena had told her was true, she was now further from finding him than before. The only certainty was that he had been taken from Benimarta. But where was he now? Could he have been sent to some other prison in Alicante or in another part of Spain? She had heard stories that Republican prisoners had been sent to work camps and given an opportunity to earn their freedom by hard labour. Could Eduardo be in one of these camps? Perhaps he had been sent to the infamous Valle de los Caídos (Valley of the Fallen) on the outskirts of Madrid; Franco's idea of "a national act of atonement." Eduardo was fit and strong and he could endure hard work if that was his fate. Vicenta was convinced Eduardo was still alive, but how could she find out where he was now?

Maite brought a ray of hope explaining that even Republican prisoners were usually allowed to write to their families. Perhaps Eduardo had been able to write to Vicenta at Benimarta. The idea set Vicenta thinking she should return home, but as Maite pointed out, if she returned to find no word from Eduardo, she would be back to square one. Besides, if she quit the Auxilio Social now, she would be persona non grata once again, with no papers or travel documents. But if she did return home, perhaps she could confront Juan-Martin Garcia and demand to know what had happened to Eduardo. The idea evaporated as Vicenta realised Garcia would never lift a finger to help her, especially after she had bitten off half his ear.

It was Maite who convinced Vicenta to stay in Alicante and write to her sister to see if there had been any word from Eduardo. It seemed such a hopeless step, but Vicenta realised Isobel did not even know where she was, so she needed to write to her anyway. The letter was posted the next day, but it didn't stop Vicenta from agonising about Eduardo and brooding over the uncertainty as to his whereabouts.

On Monday morning Vicenta was told she had been assigned to work in the industrial laundry just a few blocks away from the dormitory. At seven in the morning Sister Asunción walked with her to the stone-clad building which even at this early hour had steam rising from a profusion of vents and chimneys. Inside the cavernous bowels of the laundry, forty or so women, all in their blue uniforms and white aprons, scurried about between isles delineated by metal columns stretching up to the arched roof. The space echoed to the sounds of motors whirring and steam hissing from pipes threaded along and between the columns.

The boss of the laundry, Señor Alvarez, greeted Vicenta with a grunt and a perfunctory hand shake before passing her on to Paquita, a slip of a teenager who would, as he put it, show her the ropes in the distribution department. Vicenta's assigned task was to move laundry from a loading bay at the back of the building to a long row of washing machines running the full length of the hall. Each machine consisted of a three metre long cylindrical metal barrel with a sliding hatch running along its complete length. Two women worked together to operate the machine with familiar efficiency, loading laundry through the hatch and sprinkling powder throughout. They slid down the hatch and locked it in position with a series of giant wing nuts before operating a series of buttons and levers to flood the machine with hot water and set the drum rotating by means of a series of cogs and chains connected to a separate electric motor. The noise was ear-splitting as the grinding of the motor competed with the clanking of the barrel and the sloshing of water from within.

The first consignment to arrive at the loading bay was a canvas-covered army wagon loaded high with khaki uniforms. Paquita was one of a team of two others and showed Vicenta what she should do. As the driver of the lorry stood by smoking a cigarette, the women dragged the clothing from the pile, shoving it into large wicker baskets mounted on wobbly wheels. The clothing reeked of dirt and sweat and as Vicenta pushed her basket to the washing machines she was almost overwhelmed by the foul stench. A machine operator helped her stuff the barrel and then she returned to repeat the task until, after four more journeys, the lorry was empty and the driver moved off.

A steady stream of vehicles arrived at the loading bay throughout the day bringing more uniforms, soiled sheets and filthy blankets. In between unloading wagons, it was Vicenta's job to help remove the damp laundry from the machines and take it in the trolleys to a vast yard criss-crossed with washing lines where she hung the items out to dry. Once dry, the laundry was gathered up again and moved in the trolleys to various work stations to be pressed. A dozen women stood in front of large steam presses comprising a long padded board onto which they placed lengths of sheets or blankets before pulling down a matching padded arm and pulling a lever to release a blast of steam. Each sheet was moved through the press, folded and placed on a shelf to one side. Vicenta and the other girls then collected the finished laundry and delivered it to a storeroom to await collection. Alongside the steam presses another column of women used electric hand irons on fixed padded boards to press army uniforms and fold them neatly ready for collection.

The laborious job of pushing the trolleys up and down the laundry was made worse by the intense heat and humidity within the building. There wasn't much time for conversation between the women and what little passed between them was frequently drowned out by the din of washing machines and steam irons. It was midday before they stopped.

Over a lunch of *puchero* – a thin, greasy broth of vegetables and rough cuts of meat – Vicenta was introduced to some of the other women who had formed themselves into small cliques that seemed to represent their relative status and tasks. Vicenta joined the other "trolley girls" who, as relative newcomers to the laundry, seemed to be regarded as the lowest rank of workers. Conversation in Vicenta's group was guarded at first as the women appeared nervous of expressing an opinion about anything other than the weather. Gradually, however, the small talk developed into a more meaningful dialogue as some of the women discussed their homes and their families and their feelings about work. Vicenta was the only one in her group from the dormitory, the rest travelling to work daily and returning to their homes in the Alicante suburbs. The consensus of opinion was that Señor Alvarez was a fair boss so long as you arrived on time and did as you were told. To Vicenta's surprise their was no sign of resentment amongst the women, a couple even expressing the opinion that they were glad of the work and happy to do their duty for the New Spain.

A bell rang after half an hour and work resumed, continuing until the bell rang again at five in the evening when Vicenta was left to find her own way back to the dormitory. The streets of Alicante were just returning to life after the customary siesta. Shops and banks were re-opening and the pavements were thronged with people going about their business. Once more Vicenta was struck by the apparent normality of life as she negotiated her route back to the Auxilio Social. A sudden thought entered her head. No one was forcing her to return to the dormitory; there were no locks on the doors and no guards to check her in and out. If she wanted, she could just keep on walking and go wherever she pleased. But then reality dawned and she realised that, though there were no locks or bolts or bars on the windows, she was, for all intents and purposes, a prisoner with nowhere else to go.

Her spirits rose when Maite returned and recounted the events of her day. She had been assigned to work at a centre for young mothers established by the Sección Femenina in an old schoolroom not far from the city's town hall. Her job had been to arrange tables and chairs, make coffee and distribute literature to the women who attended in two sessions, morning and afternoon. At the end of each session she dispensed soap, disinfectant and de-lousing powder. Cushy work, Vicenta thought, comparing it to her own arduous shift at the laundry.

'I suppose someone has to help disseminate Falangist propaganda,' she said to Maite with a dismissive sneer. 'What was it? More lectures about obedient wives, dedicated mothers and diligent housekeepers?'

'And faithful servants of the Church,' Maite replied with a sneer of her own. 'What else would you expect?'

'I think I'd rather work in the laundry. At least it's honest work, even it does mean washing the filthy uniforms of Franco's troops.'

'I know what you mean,' Maite responded, 'but actually I was quite surprised.'

'What do you mean?'

'Well yes, there was the usual anti-feminist message, but there was also some good advice.'

'What, on how to sweep the floor or wash a man's soiled underpants?'

'Actually, no,' Maite continued. 'There was a lot of good advice about health and hygiene, childcare and nutrition.'

'I'll bet there was. And no doubt there was plenty of encouragement to procreate and bring forth the next generation of little fascists loyal to Franco and the Catholic Church.'

'My, my,' Maite jeered. 'Work in the laundry certainly doesn't agree with you, does it? You'd better be careful what you say around here.'

'I don't care. I just feel we are being used to help cement the Fascists' rule over our country and further the reactionary aims of the upper classes in the Sección Femenina.'

'You may be right,' Maite said, 'but the war is over and lost. There's no point in expecting a fight back, so if Spain is to emerge from these dark days it will be through the will of the people and not through the actions of a few disorganised rebels.'

'And what of people like my husband, unjustly incarcerated simply to strengthen Franco's hold on power? Are we just to abandon them?'

Maite took Vicenta's hand. 'You know I'm not saying that. I understand that you hate the forces that have taken Eduardo away from you. I know you will do everything you can to find him and get him released. But in the meantime you must not let this quest consume you or you will be left embittered and powerless. Just like you, I hate being manipulated by the anti-feminists, but all I'm saying is that there is some good in what they are trying to do. Child mortality rates in this country have been appalling for decades with most women preferring to call on the services of local quack midwives whose practices are often little removed from witchcraft and whose ignorance frequently causes more harm than good. If the Sección Femenina can change that by encouraging people to seek proper medical advice and follow basic principles of health, hygiene and child care, then I for one am in favour of that, even if their motives are disingenuous.'

Vicenta looked away and pouted.

Maite continued undaunted. 'And their support for the elderly and homeless fulfils an obvious need even though it goes hand in hand with their pious preaching. And I've heard that they are attempting to organise rudimentary education for all young people even in the remotest areas – something the last government signally failed to achieve.'

Vicenta snapped back. 'I've heard that as well. Girls are to be educated separately from boys and no doubt differently. They'll follow the examples of the fascists in Germany and Italy and try to rewrite history. They'll turn women into domestic slaves or factory fodder, whilst safeguarding the interests of the privileged and powerful. Birth control will be declared sinful and men will be the only ones deemed fit for political or professional positions. That's not education, that's social engineering.'

'You may be right Vicenta, but at least it's a start. Personally I don't think they will succeed. Spain's economy is a wreck right now and eventually it will dawn on the authorities that economic progress will never be achieved by subjugating half the population and imagining they will be content with domesticity alone.'

'I hope you are right Maite. I truly hope you are

right.'

Isobel's letter arrived a week later. She was pleased to discover that Vicenta was safe in Alicante and she even enthused about Vicenta's service with the Auxilio Social, deeming it to be an opportunity rather than an obligation. Clearly, Vicenta realised, the full impact of the Sección Femenina's ideological programme had yet to reach Benimarta. There was news of Francisco, Isobel's husband, who was now working as a driver for the Ministry of the Interior, transporting food supplies between Denia, Benissa and Alicante. Although Isobel never mentioned it, Vicenta knew that to obtain such a privileged position, Francisco must have joined the ranks of the blue shirts. There had been no word from Eduardo.

A twinge in her abdomen reminded her of the daunting problems she faced. She had told no one of her plight, not even Maite. Her morning sickness seemed to have passed, but as she felt her stomach, she realised her pregnancy was beginning to show. Fortunately her standard issue skirt and blue blouse both had a little room for expansion and her usual white pinafore could always be loosely tied to disguise her predicament.

At the end of another week's labour in the laundry Vicenta was exhausted. She could easily have slept for the whole weekend, but Maite announced that she and Ramón had organised a picnic for Sunday afternoon in the Canalejas park.

In watery sunshine they walked together along the sea front esplanade in the direction of the port, entering the park through gates flanked by sculptures of lions and dogs. Despite the chill breeze, the park was thronged with people strolling along the walkways between neatly tended flower beds and closely mown lawns. Ramón spread a blanket in the shade of an ancient fig tree.

Their picnic was a meagre repast of bread with wafer thin cured ham, a chunk of hard cheese, tomatoes and a few green olives. Ramón had brought some red wine in a label-less bottle which he said was from a friend's bodega. Maite supplied a wedge of stodgy cake made from pumpkins. Nearby there were several other family groups enjoying the winter sunshine and more sumptuous picnics with seemingly endless supplies of food and wine emerging from boxes and baskets. Well dressed women in tailored suits watched over children in their Sunday best. Some of the men wore military uniforms and others sported blue shirts with jodhpurs and knee length leather boots.

There seemed no suspicion between the various groups and it was as if, being Sunday, everyone wanted simply to enjoy the peace and calm of the park. But there was an arrogance about the more affluent groups who talked and laughed loudly, not caring if they were overheard. In contrast Vicenta, Ramón and Maite talked in hushed tones cautious not to draw attention to themselves.

Two small boys in scruffy clothes approached one of the more affluent groups seated just a short distance away. At first they were shooed away by one of the women with a dismissive wave of her hand. But one of the men, admonished her mockingly, calling the boys back. He wore a khaki jacket, baggy trousers and knee length canvas gaiters which were the uniform of the Spanish Foreign Legion together with the distinctive red tasselled side cap and black leather cross belt. An embroidered arm badge bore the Legion's insignia of a crossbow, rifle and axe centred with a royal crown and three red and yellow stripes on his sleeve denoted his rank as sergeant.

A conversation followed, inaudible to Vicenta and her friends. The boys were made to stand to attention and the Legionnaire uttered an instruction upon which the boys raised their right arms in unison in the fascist salute. The soldier walked round them prodding and poking and pulling at their ragged clothing. There was raucous laughter from the Legionnaire's friends as he rejoined them on their rug. Then they began throwing food in all directions – bread, bones, bits of fruit and cake. The boys scrambled around the grass, picking up the morsels and stuffing their mouths and their pockets before running off into the distance.

Watching the scene, Maite, Vicenta and Ramón became subdued. Each of them wanted to condemn the conceited behaviour they had witnessed but they all understood it would have been pointless, even dangerous, to have intervened. Vicenta was in a pensive mood, her thoughts with Eduardo, wondering where he might be and what he might be doing on this peaceful Sunday afternoon. Maite seemed to understand her cheerless mood and did not prompt or probe. Ramón, on the other hand was more cheerful and tried to engage Vicenta in conversation, remarking about the weather and the food. He was an attentive host, passing bread and liberally filling their wine cups. Vicenta humoured him with perfunctory comments, unwilling to engage in any meaningful conversation. More than once she thought she saw Ramón staring at her face, but he quickly lowered his eyes and glanced in another direction.

As the sun descended behind La Muntanya d'Alacant to the west of the park, the air chilled and the walkers and picnickers began to drift away. At the exit to the park Maite and Vicenta prepared to leave Ramón and return to the dormitory. Ramón gave Maite a brotherly peck on the cheek and turned toward Vicenta as if to do the same. Still lost in her own thoughts, Vicenta was oblivious to the gesture and offered her hand which Ramón shook gently before turning to leave. Only Maite noticed the look of disappointment of her brother's face.

Over the next few weeks Vicenta became accustomed to the routine at the laundry. It was hard, physical work, but it passed the time while she waited, still hoping for news of Eduardo. One day Señor Alvarez approached her to announce that she was to be moved from trolley duty to make way for a couple of new recruits. Instead she was to be trained to use one of the heavy presses. The work was less arduous, but repetitive and equally exhausting as the heat and steam from the press left her drained at the end of each day. Then one day, without warning, there was a sudden rush of work as a never ending stream of lorries arrived at the loading bay. All the girls were under instructions to give priority to the washing of uniforms, setting aside the bedding and blankets for later. In conversations during the short breaks between work there were rumours of an upcoming event; a military parade some said, others spoke of important visitors arriving in the city.

It was late on Thursday afternoon before all became clear when all the women of the Alicante Auxilio Social were summoned to a meeting in the Salon de Plenos of the town hall. Most of the assembled women were overawed by the baroque splendour of the council chamber with its high vaulted ceiling and impressive central chandelier. The antique chairs with their embossed red leather seats had been moved to one side so that the hundred or so women stood in the room's central aisle chatting in whispered tones in reverence to the grandeur of their surroundings. A hush descended as a pair of lavishly embroidered curtains at the side of the central podium parted and a group of smartly dressed women entered followed by a priest in a plain brown cassock.

Vicenta recognised the priest as Father Lorenzo the chaplain to the Alicante Auxilio Social who had interviewed her after her first visit to the soup kitchen. The group took their seats on the mahogany dais which was set against the backdrop of an enormous embroidered banner depicting the coat of arms of the fifteenth century Catholic Monarchs, Ferdinand and Isabella. At the centre of the group was a woman Vicenta recognised as Maria del Carmen López del Hierro. She was dressed in a heavy woollen two-piece grey suit with a calf length skirt and high buttoned jacket. Her dark wiry hair was parted from the left and pulled severely across her brow. The only embellishment to her otherwise austere appearance was a simple string of graduated pearls. In dead silence she rose to speak.

'Welcome ladies of the Alicante Auxilio Social. How good it is to see you all together and to reflect on the great work you carry out in the service of New Spain. I trust that you, too, will reflect on the privilege afforded to you by the Auxilio Social to learn and to benefit from your period of service with our organisation so that in due course you will be well equipped to take your place in society as mothers and homemakers ready to support your husbands and families in rebuilding our great country.

'Today marks a momentous occasion in our history; for today the body of our beloved Don José Antonio Primo de Rivera y Sáenz de Heredia, first Duke of Primo de Rivera and third Marquis of Estrella has been exhumed from the ignominious grave in our city where he was buried after his brutal and unjust execution by a republican firing squad on 20th November 1936.

'Tomorrow, the founder of the Falange and architect of our ultimate victory will begin the journey to his rightful resting place alongside the Kings and Queens of Spain in the San Lorenzo Monastery of El Escorial. And we have the privilege to be able to witness the beginning of this long journey as, over the next ten days, his coffin will be carried on the shoulders of patriots on its two hundred and eighty mile trek through the heartlands of Spain.

'At eight o'clock tomorrow we will gather together in the Avenida Oscar Espla to hail the funeral cortège and wish our heroic father Godspeed on his glorious voyage to join the divine immortals of our great country.

'Be sure your uniforms are clean and tidy and your pinafores crisply pressed. Polish your shoes, wash your hair and brush it neatly. Wear no make up for this is a solemn occasion and above all remember to salute our illustrious warrior. Don't be afraid to shed tears for our exalted champion for this is a day that henceforth will be celebrated by all true Spaniards.'

With that, the rest of the group stood and all left the room leaving the audience to depart in a growing chorus of whispers.

'Well, I for one will not be going to celebrate the funeral of the author of Spanish fascism,' Vicenta said as she left the town hall with Maite to return to the dormitory.

'You think you have a choice?' Maite remarked in response. 'Do you think your absence would not be noticed?'

That night the hillsides surrounding the city of Alicante glowed amber as beacon fires were lit and sustained until dawn broke.

The welcome warmth of the wintry sun gradually rising above the Mediterranean eventually reached the Avenida Oscar Espla where Vicenta and Maite and the rest of the Auxilio Social contingent had stood shivering for almost two hours. Father Lorenzo had organised the women into neat ranks from the edge of the pavement. Maria del Carmen had just arrived and passed between the ranks inspecting the women, straightening berets, buttoning jackets and pinning back loose strands of hair.

Alongside the women was a contingent of the Juvenile Falange; the boys in purple-blue shirts and long khaki trousers, the girls in knee length skirts and sailor style blouses with deep square collars. On the opposite side of the avenue the pavements were thronged with shabbily dressed people of all ages standing dozens deep and craning their necks to get a better view along the street in the direction of the city centre. Regular soldiers in brown greatcoats with rifles held across their chests stood on the street at intervals facing the crowds.

A buzz of excited conversation filled the air disguising a distant hum of engines which gradually grew to a crescendo as a squadron of ten Breguet light bombers descended from above the railway station and swooped low along the broad avenue before fanning out over the sea as they reached the port. The deafening roar of the engines as they passed low overhead caused some of the people to scream in fear as if reminded of the frequent aerial assaults conducted by these same aircraft at the peak of hostilities in 1938.

Suddenly the crowd became agitated as people pushed forward, some pointing up the length of the avenue toward the railway station in the distance. The sound of horses' hooves clipping on the cobbles began to echo between the tall buildings that flanked the Avenida Oscar

Espla as gradually a contingent of the Caballería Mora, the Moorish Cavalry, came into view. A file of almost identical black horses approached, mounted by cavalrymen in red shirts their black trousers with red side stripes tucked into polished black boots. Long white burnooses billowed behind them and their turbaned steel helmets glistened in the sun as did the tips of their lances each embellished with a yellow and red pennant.

Behind the cavalrymen a troop of twenty blue shirted Falange Español troops goose-stepped slowly, holding their pace to a slow march as their polished brown knee boots banged loudly on the surface of the road. Each wore a ceremonial silver dagger clipped to their trouser belts and their red berets bobbed up and down in unison.

Next came a group of priests, drably dressed in plain brown cassocks tied at the waist with a plain rope cord. Each one carried a wooden staff topped with a simple metal crucifix. Behind them a bishop shuffled in tiny steps his gold-topped crosier planted firmly with every other stride. In contrast to the priests, his uniform stood out with a white frock coat topped by a short red cape and cincture band adorned with a heavy silver cross. His stiffened silk mitre was heavily embroidered in gold and two fringed red lappets draped his back.

Finally came the coffin, draped in a simple black pall overlaid with the red flag of the Falange, its central black stripe bearing the yoke and arrows emblem. The coffin was mounted on two, ten metre long beams each hewn from a single piece of oak and borne by twenty khaki clad regular soldiers, five on each side in front and behind. They marched in perfect time taking steady short steps so as not to sway or jolt the coffin.

As the cortège approached the women of the Auxilio Social, the cavalrymen came to a sudden halt. Everyone nearby looked up the avenue to the coffin. The pall bearers now stood still with their feet together and their free arms clamped rigidly to their sides. In a carefully choreographed move twenty more soldiers, these dressed in grey-green serge, stepped forward, ten from each side, to place their shoulders beneath the beams and replace the army regulars who stepped smartly back to the kerb.

On the bishop's signal the procession advanced once more and as the coffin neared the women, right arms were suddenly flung forward, raised diagonally with palms pronated. A roar greeted the passing coffin as the cry, "Arriba España!" rang out repeatedly, echoing the final words of José Antonio Primo de Rivera as he faced the firing squad.

Maria del Carmen was the first to react raising her right arm and joining the rhythmic chanting. This prompted the other women of the

Auxilio Social to follow suit, saluting and calling out in unison. Reluctantly Maite followed their lead and raised her right arm as the coffin approached. Only Vicenta refused to join in, standing motionless and staring straight ahead. Maite noticed Maria del Carmen look in their direction and the soldier standing almost in front of them began to scrutinise the crowds on the pavement.

'For God's sake put your arm up,' Maite said to Vicenta, digging her in the ribs.

'I won't,' Vicenta replied.

'Do you want to get arrested? Just raise your bloody arm and say nothing.'

Begrudgingly Vicenta did as instructed and raised her right arm mouthing the words, 'Arriba España' until the coffin had passed. Behind the cortège the crowds rushed from the pavements and onto the street to form an orderly procession stretching back almost as far as the eye could see. The women from the Auxilio Social followed suit, breaking ranks to merge with the crowd. Maite and Vicenta were swept along with the tide of bodies and found themselves in the midst of the column shuffling along the avenue in a seething mass of people unable to extricate themselves.

Just ahead of them, and alongside the pallbearers, a man in a scruffy grey coat suddenly burst from the crowded pavement and strode toward the coffin. He was clutching a tattered flag of red, yellow and purple stripes – the flag of the second republic. Above the noise of the chanting crowds his voice, raw and hoarse could just be heard yelling, 'Abajo el Fascismo. Muerte a la Falange. Viva la Republic.'

As he neared the coffin, he threw the flag which landed partly across the back of the casket and draped over the heads of the first two pallbearers on the left hand side. Without breaking stride, the first soldier grabbed the flag and quickly threw it to the ground where it was trampled underfoot by the following marchers. Still the man advanced trying to grab the Falange Flag draped over the coffin. He almost succeeded before being grappled to the ground by one of the soldier guards lining the street. A second soldier rounded on the man helping to drag him to the side of the pavement and shoving the butt of his rifle into the man's face. Blood poured from his nose and he curled in a foetal position as the two soldiers kicked out at his head and his abdomen. Unbowed he continued to yell, 'Abajo Fascismo. Abajo Franco el dictador.'

From a few yards ahead a bearded man in a long black leather coat and grey fedora approached the melee in steady purposeful strides. On reaching the scene he gave a gruff instruction to the two soldiers who stopped their onslaught and pulled back. Calmly the man pulled a pistol from his coat pocket, placed the barrel against the man's temple and pulled the trigger. The gunshot was barely audible above the din of the clamouring crowds but a woman nearby screamed and provoked several others to do the same. The man in the leather coat issued another instruction to the soldiers before melting into the crowd. The two soldiers grabbed the protester's body by his feet and dragged him through the crowds and down a side street. The cortège continued unhindered, as did the relentless chanting, 'Arriba España, Viva Franco, Viva Falange.'

From her position just behind the moving cortège Vicenta witnessed the whole scene. Sickened, she demanded of Maite, 'We've got to get out of here.'

'We can't just walk off,' Maite responded. 'We'll be spotted.'

'I don't care. I'm not staying here.

'All right,' Maite said. 'Wait a moment. I'll pretend to faint and you can help me to the side of the street.' With that, she stumbled and appeared to go weak at the knees. Vicenta placed her arm around Maite's back and under her armpit, pretending to support her friend and assist her to the side of the road where Maite slumped to the ground. Amidst the excited crowd, no one seemed to notice them and they waited there for a few moments as the procession continued to move along the avenue. One of the soldiers approached them and asked what was wrong.

'My friend has fainted,' Vicenta said. 'She just needs a few moments to recover and she'll be fine.'

Spotting their uniforms, the soldier seemed to take pity on them. 'Perhaps you'd better get her out of here and back to the Auxilio Social,' he said.

'I think you are right,' Vicenta said, lifting Maite to her feet.

The soldier stepped into the crowd, still cheering on the pavement, and forced a way through so that Vicenta and Maite could follow. Once at the back of the pavement Vicenta eased Maite down to a sitting position and thanked the soldier.

'She'll be fine now. I'll make sure she gets home safely.'

'Make sure you do that,' the soldier instructed as he re-entered the crowd and resumed his position on the street.

Back in the dormitory Vicenta was fuming. 'What's happened to Spain? You saw that man murdered in public view and no one batted an eyelid. And those crowds, all they wanted to do was show their devotion to the author of Spanish fascism. How could they stand by and watch a peaceful protester gunned down?'

Maite was just as angry herself. 'You're a fool Vicenta and so was that man, whoever he was. Did he really think he could get away with such a futile gesture? Don't you realise what's happened to Spain? The war is over. Franco won and it's time to move on. You saw those people in the street. Most of them were there out of choice, no one forced them to be there; no one forced them to chant Franco's name.'

'Perhaps not, but perhaps they haven't seen their husbands or their families hauled off and imprisoned unjustly to rot somewhere in a stinking jail.'

'Are you really so stupid, Vicenta? Everyone suffered in the war. People lost fathers, sons and brothers, if not in battle then through disease or starvation. And now Spain is on its knees, most people just want an end to violence and death. They don't care who won, they just want to get on with their lives; work and put food on the table and clothes on their backs.'

'Even if that means accepting fascism and living under a tyrannical dictator?'

'Yes, even that. Not everyone is an idealist like you.'

Vicenta raged, her jaw set like stone. 'I'm no radical idealist, but I know what's right and what's wrong. You can kowtow to the blue shirts if you want, but while Eduardo remains incarcerated by those fascists pigs, I will use every last breath I have to find him and get him released; and if that means standing up to authority then that's what I will do.'

Maite could see the determination etched on Vicenta's face. She knew that it was time to make her friend face the truth. 'Vicenta, I admire your devotion to your husband, but surely you must realise that Eduardo is dead. Even in this war torn country you would have heard something from him by now if he were still alive.'

Vicenta raised her hands to cover here ears. 'Don't say that,' she yelled. 'I refuse to believe it. Eduardo is alive somewhere and I will not rest until I find him. He's alive I tell you.'

Maite calmed herself and slowly shook her head. Seeing the gesture, Vicenta rose to her feet and moved toward Maite, her arms flailing. Maite raised her own arms to protect herself and then grabbed Vicenta in a bear hug. Calmly she said, 'I wish I could offer you some hope, Vicenta, but I fear what I have said is a reality and there's no point in believing otherwise.'

Vicenta pulled away. 'Don't say that, I refuse to listen. I refuse to accept what you say.' Weeping hysterically she turned to walk away and suddenly shrieked, grabbing her abdomen and doubling up in pain.

Maite took her by the shoulders and led her to sit on the side of her bed. 'Vicenta, what's the matter with you? What happening?'

Vicenta uttered a low moan. 'Nothing,' she said, 'I'll be fine in a minute.' As she said this she howled again, her face racked with pain as she fell back on the bed and curled up, pulling her knees to her chest.

'I'm going to find a doctor,' Maite said, standing.

Vicenta grabbed Maite's wrist in a vice-like

grip. 'No. No doctors. I beg of you, no doctors.'

Vicenta's grip faltered and her arm fell away as she slumped backwards onto the bed. Her face was ashen and her brow beaded with sweat.

'Please, no doctors,' she murmured as her eyelids flickered and closed.

The glare of light reflecting off a bare white ceiling made Vicenta squint. Gradually she adjusted to the brightness and surveyed her surroundings. She found herself in a small stark room, the walls devoid of ornamentation save for a painting of the Madonna and Child, their heads illuminated by halos and surrounded by adoring angels. A vague figure hovered at her side dressed in a grey habit; a pure white wimple framed the face, drawn into folds beneath the chin. For a moment Vicenta wondered if this was an apparition; perhaps she had died and joined the angels. But then the smell of bleach and the feel of stiffly starched sheets gave her the realisation that she remained in the corporeal world. Panicked, she lifted the sheets to find she was dressed in a flimsy white bed shirt, buttoned up to her neck and extending well below her knees. Without looking she could feel she was without underwear and it made her feel naked and vulnerable. She clasped anxiously at her chest, relieved to find that Eduardo's ring and key still hung from the cord around her neck.

'Ah, you are back with us, my dear,' the nun

said, plumping up the pillow. 'For a while we feared we had lost you. My name is Sister Alicia, I've been watching over you for the past two days, and praying for you of course.'

Vicenta tried to lift her shoulders, but found herself enveloped by the tightly tucked sheets. The nun reinforced Vicenta's confinement by pressing down on her shoulders.'

'There, there, Vicenta,' she said. 'You must lie still and rest. You are very weak.'

Vicenta slumped back to her pillow.' Where am I?' she asked feeling helpless and confused.

'You are in the Hospital Santa Helena not far from your dormitory at the Auxilio Social. You were severely constipated, but we gave you an enema and that was quickly sorted out. You had a small blood clot as well, but everything is fine now and your baby is perfectly healthy. There's no reason why your pregnancy should not continue to full term if you rest and take care of yourself.'

Vicenta was still taking it all in. Her pregnancy had been discovered and with it the lies she had told when she arrived in Alicante. What would she say? What would happen to her if the Auxilio Social had discovered her predicament? Would they expel her and throw her onto the street? Where would she go? How would she cope?

'You have a visitor,' said Sister Alicia. 'She's been waiting here for two days. I'm sure she will be relieved to know you are finally awake. Lie still and I get her.'

The nun left the room and returned a moment later with Maite who immediately rushed to the bed to hold Vicenta and kiss her on the cheek.

'I've been so worried,' she said. 'You looked so ill when I called Sister Asunción. We both thought you might die. It was Sister Asunción who called the hospital and they brought you here by ambulance. I'm so happy to see you are all right.'

Vicenta looked beyond Maite to the nun and then glanced back to Maite. 'Thank you,' she said and then, 'Sister Alicia, do you think I could have a few moments in private with my friend.'

'Very well,' she replied. 'But just a few minutes and then you must rest.'

As soon as the door closed Maite sat on the side of the bed and gripped Vicenta's hand. 'I'm sorry. I know you said no doctors, but you looked so ill I really didn't have a choice.'

'I understand,' Vicenta replied. 'I'm sure you did what you felt was best and you were probably right. It's just…'

'I know. The baby. Why didn't you tell me you were pregnant?'

'I probably should have, but I just didn't know what to do for the best and I have been so focussed on finding Eduardo.'

'Does he know about the baby?'

'No. I only discovered I was pregnant after he was arrested and taken away.'

'No wonder you are so desperate to find him. But perhaps this is good news. Perhaps, knowing of your condition, the Auxilio Social will help you find him.'

Vicenta slumped back on her pillow. 'I very much doubt that. You see, I lied when I arrived here. I told them my husband died in 1937.'

'But surely they'll understand when you tell them the truth.'

Vicenta huffed. 'You really think so? When I tell them Eduardo was arrested and charged with sedition, you think they will move heaven and earth to find him? I very much doubt it. When they find out I lied to them they'll probably throw me out on the street.'

Maite drew back. 'Oh Vicenta, please don't say that, I couldn't bear it.'

The door flew open and Sister Alicia reappeared. 'That's enough for now Señora Giménez. Vicenta needs her rest. You can visit her again tomorrow.'

'But...'

'No buts, Señora. It's time for you to leave.'

Maite looked at Vicenta who nodded feebly. 'I'll be fine, Maite. I'll see you tomorrow.'

'If you're sure,' Maite said. 'You rest and I'll be back in the morning.'

Vicenta blinked her eyes in acknowledgement.

As soon as Maite left the room, Sister Alicia began fussing, straightening the sheets and smoothing Vicenta's hair.

'There's someone else who's been waiting to talk to you. Señora López del Hierro. If you feel up to it, I'll send a message to her now. If she's not busy she could be here in about half an hour.'

Vicenta said nothing, fighting the panic that was rising in her body. She wished she had never come to Alicante; never joined the Auxilio Social; never lied. More than anything she wished that Eduardo was alive and at her side. And then Maite's words came back to her, "Eduardo is dead." Could she be right? Had her mission really been a fanciful quest, doomed from the outset?

The door sprung open and Señora López del Hierro strode toward the bed. Sister Alicia followed carrying a wicker chair which she placed behind Maria del Carmen, plumping up the seat cushion as she did so.

'Thank you, Sister Alicia. That will be all for now,' she said dismissively as she sat in the chair and dragged it closer to the bed. 'Well, well, Vicenta, you've certainly been through a torrid time.'

'I'm feeling much better now, thank you.'

'I don't just mean your admission to hospital. I mean your whole journey to Alicante and your time here with us.'

Vicenta could feel her face reddening.

'How long did you think you could keep your pregnancy a secret?'

'I don't know. I didn't really think at all. I was

just desperate for help and when I found the Auxilio Social and they gave me work and a place to stay I was afraid to tell the truth in case I would be rejected.'

Maria del Carmen smiled benignly. 'My dear child. Do you think we are so cold hearted that we would reject a woman in her hour of need? Isn't that the very reason for our existence – to support women who have suffered through the troubles our country has faced and to help them become useful, productive members of society?'

Vicenta swallowed hard. 'I... I was embarrassed.'

'Ah, now we come to the nub of it.' Maria del Carmen said sternly. 'You told us you weren't married; that your husband died in 1937. Is that not so?'

'Yes,' Vicenta replied meekly.

'Yes, that he died or yes, that's what you told us?'

'Both,' Vicenta said, trying to sound convincing.

'I see. So you had a fling with a local lad and ended up getting yourself pregnant. You couldn't face the shame of it in your village so you decided to come to Alicante. Is that the top and bottom of it.'

'No,' Vicenta refuted a little more forcefully than she had intended.

'No? Then what?'

'I was raped.'

Maria del Carmen looked aghast. 'Raped you say. Did you report this to the police?'

Vicenta lowered her eyes. 'No, I couldn't report it, there was no point. He was a blue shirt.'

'Ah, I begin to understand. But did you talk to the man? You know men have lustful desires they sometimes find difficult to control. Perhaps he really liked you, but as so often with men, he couldn't find a way of expressing his feelings and simply got carried away. After all, Vicenta, you are an attractive young woman.'

Vicenta struggled to hold her rage. How could this stuck up old prune, probably a bitter old spinster, even dare to make excuses for such a vicious, cold hearted bastard as Juan-Martin Garcia?

'The man is married and before you say anything more, no, I didn't egg him on. Perhaps you can now understand why I couldn't stay in that village.'

Maria del Carmen scowled, unused to being spoken to in such strident tones.

'I suppose I'll have to leave the Auxilio Social now,' Vicenta said, adopting a more deferential demeanour.

'My dear, what must you think of us. There's no question of you leaving us now.'

Relieved as she was, Vicenta felt there was something rather ominous in Maria del Carmen's manner.

'How far has your pregnancy progressed?' she

asked.

'Around three months.'

'*Around* three months? Don't you know exactly?'

'Three months,' Vicenta affirmed. 'I was unconscious for a while after the attack and then with my journey to Alicante and everything else that has happened, I've rather lost track of time.'

Maria del Carmen lowered her eyes quizzically. 'Well then, given your condition, I don't think we can allow you to continue working in the laundry. You must rest here for a few more days and we'll see if we can find something less strenuous for you to do until the baby is due. Can you read and write?'

Vicenta looked confused. 'Yes, of course.'

'Good, then we'll see what we can do. When the time comes, you will have your baby here. We have good doctors and Sister Alicia is a trained midwife. You'll be in good hands. Now rest and I will see you again when you return to the dormitory.'

CHAPTER TEN

Vicenta's new assignment was to a literacy group, teaching girls aged between eleven and fourteen which was held in a small annexe to the church Parroquia del Beato Fransisco Blazquez. She taught two classes each day in the morning and afternoon each comprising between fifteen and twenty girls though attendance was erratic. Many of the girls were little more than street urchins and some came from orphanages run by the Auxilio Social. Their clothes were often dirty, tattered and worn, their hair invariably lank and greasy and sometimes riddled with lice. Even in the cold of winter and without any form of heating, Vicenta felt obliged to keep windows open to disperse the rank smell of unwashed clothes and bodies.

The equipment supplied was basic at best; rickety desks with broken hinges and chairs of varying sizes, often with broken backs or wobbly legs. A blackboard supplied was without an easel and rested on a table leaning against a wall. Reading materials were just as crude; a handful of battered children's books with broken spines and missing pages which the girls had to share sometimes one between three. Paper and pencils were always in short supply. The girls themselves were generally polite, well behaved and attentive, though at times Vicenta found her voice almost drowned out by a cacophony of coughs and sneezes.

Vicenta was appalled by the general standard of literacy. Many of the girls had little or no knowledge of the alphabet and some barely knew how to hold a pencil. Even in Benimarta, miles from the nearest big town or city, most children could read and write adequately by the age of eleven.

In spite of the privations, Vicenta loved her new assignment and despite the girls' unkempt appearance and dubious personal hygiene, she loved them as well. And her affections were generally returned by the girls themselves, especially the orphans who saw her as the nearest thing to a mother figure they had known, at least in recent times.

She was disturbed, however, by the fervent rantings of Father Lorenzo which he insisted must preface every lesson. He harangued each class with his unerring message of female inferiority and subservience, frequently backing up his pronouncements with biblical quotes and the pious preachings of dubious scholars and philosophers. Of greater concern was his insistence on lingering in the class during lessons, hovering over the girls as they sat at their desks and occasionally touching them on the head or shoulder. More than once she had felt compelled to intercede discreetly, placing herself between the priest and one of the girls or distracting his attention to draw him away. Her actions often provoked a glare of annoyance and she was sure he perceived the purpose of her interventions.

The redoubtable Maria del Carmen del López del Hierro seemed impressed with Vicenta's work when she visited the class, remarking on the enthusiasm of the girls and their orderly behaviour. Vicenta took the opportunity to plead for more books and other teaching materials. To her surprise, Maria del Carmen was very receptive. Buoyed, Vicenta took a chance and raised the subject of the girls' poor hygiene and tatty clothes. The next week a consignment of boxes arrived at the classroom containing fifty or more children's books; used but in good condition. There were pencils and crayons as well and a huge roll of white paper from a firm of printers which the children could cut into useable sheets for writing and drawing. The following day a van arrived and unloaded boxes of second hand children's clothing, much of it clearly from well-to-do homes. The boxes all bore printed labels reading, *'Donación de la Sección Femenina de la Falange Español.'* There was another heavy box with an identical label that contained bars of hard soap and packets of nit powder. A dozen nearly new desks arrived a few days later with a carpenter who set about repairing the chairs and some of the older desks.

With improved conditions and better equipment the girls' learning flourished. The classroom's malodorous atmosphere had disappeared and attendance levels were up. Except when Father Lorenzo was present, the classroom was full of laughter and exuberance. Vicenta felt she had found her vocation and threw herself into her work with gusto. Even so, never a day passed without her thoughts turning to Eduardo. The passage of time never dimmed her fervent hope and belief that he was alive somewhere, incarcerated in jail or forced to work in a labour camp.

As if as a reminder of the omnipresent menace of Franco's dictatorship, Maria del Carmen visited one day to announce an important event. A delegation from Madrid was due to arrive in Alicante in four weeks time, headed by the Minister for National Education, José Ibáñez Martín and accompanied by the Archbishop of Valencia Prudencio Melo y Alcalde. As part of the event, the delegation would be inspecting the services provided by the Auxilio Social and the itinerary included a half hour visit to Vicenta's class. To Vicenta's dismay Maria del Carmen had asked Father Lorenzo to oversee the programme for the visit to the school and he took to the task with his usual authoritarian fervour.

'Your girls can sing, I presume.'

'I suppose so,' Vicenta replied. 'I've heard one or two of them singing children's songs.'

'Good. We'll start with Cara al Sol, of course. But not the old battle tune. There's a new version by Velázquez. I heard it in church last week.

It's called Amanecer. More suitable to the female voice, I think, almost like a love ballad.'

Yes, but it's still the official hymn of the Falange Español, Vicenta thought. 'Isn't that a little ambitious for these young girls. After all, they have no musical training and I am not sure I am competent to teach them,' she said, hoping to forestall the idea.

'Of course you are not a competent musician,' the priest said dismissively. 'I'll arrange for Father Joachín to come over and give them lessons. He's master of music at the cathedral. A most able teacher, I'm sure. Four weeks should be plenty of time to get them in tune.'

Thwarted, Vicenta merely nodded her acceptance.

'And then something to demonstrate their reading ability, I think.' the priest continued.

Enthused at this prospect Vicenta, interrupted. 'Yes, what a good idea. They can read passages from their children's books and perhaps a few nursery rhymes.'

'Nonsense,' the priest interjected. 'Such frivolous trifles would be most unsuitable. Such an occasion demands something much more formal and sedate. Proverbs 31, I think. I'll select the texts myself and you can make sure the girls are word perfect by the time the Archbishop arrives.'

The weeks that followed saw a transformation in the small annexe that housed Vicenta's class.

Decorators arrived to scrape flaking paint off the drab beige walls and cover them with a pale canary yellow. The creaking, splintered floor boards were sanded and re-pinned and finished with a fresh coat of varnish. More of the rickety desks and chairs were repaired or replaced and the previously defunct cast iron estufa was brought back to life, fuelled from a neat pile of logs.

To Vicenta's dismay, the girls' crayon drawings were removed from the walls and replaced with religious prints and quotations from the Psalms.

Father Joachín was a kind and patient teacher and though Vicenta detested the theme of Cara al Sol she couldn't help but marvel at how the old priest transformed the class from a group of discordant warblers to a tight and tuneful ensemble. Ignorant of their exploitation, the girls enjoyed their musical tuition, especially when Father Joachín broke from the routine and taught them to sing a few traditional folk songs, though he was always careful to make sure Father Lorenzo was out of earshot. Less enjoyable was the learning by rote of the ten verses from Proverbs carefully selected by Father Lorenzo on the subject of The Virtuous Woman. Vicenta despaired at the subject matter almost as much as she despised the priest's harsh treatment and bitter criticism if any of the girls so much as stuttered when reading their allocated texts. Worst of all was the frequent patting and petting he used to show his approval of some of the girls when their reading was deemed to be acceptable.

Satisfied with his work, Father Lorenzo's final instruction to the girls on the day before the planned visit was to scrub their faces and wash and comb their hair before coming to school in the morning. He also instructed them to wear clean clothes with long sleeves and high buttoned necks.

Everyone seemed to have complied when they lined up for inspection an hour before the dignitaries were due to arrive. Vicenta, too, was subjected to the priest's close scrutiny as he cast his eyes over her freshly pressed blouse and apron. He curled his lip purposely as he made a point of noticing her distended abdomen. Though he made no comment, the gesture expressed his disgust more eloquently than mere words. Perhaps for that reason, if for no other, she was instructed to remain in the background and refrain from speaking to any of the visitors when they arrived.

The floor boards rattled with the sound of thumping boots and shoes as the girls stood in unison on Father Lorenzo's instruction as the entourage entered the room and traipsed across the floor to the row of chairs placed at the front of the classroom. Maria del Carmen led the column, dressed in one of her characteristically strait-laced tweed suits. Her grey speckled auburn hair was pulled from her face and neatly tucked beneath a broad rimmed green felt hat adorned by a single pheasant quill jutting at an angle from the beige silk hat band.

Archbishop Prudencio Melo y Alcalde was next in line, the soft leather soles of his gold braided episcopal sandals shuffling quietly across the floor. The sound of his feet was virtually inaudible, drowned out by the rustle of a billowing bright red satin cape that flowed down to his ankles with side slits through which his jacketed arms protruded. A matching red skull cap topped his bald pate and a heavy gold cross and chain rested centrally across his expansive chest.

José Ibáñez Martín, the Minister for National Education was the last of the bigwigs to take his seat, crossing his legs as he did so to allow the turn-ups of his baggy suit trousers to flop away from his polished toe capped shoes. A grey double breasted jacket was buttoned tightly around his portly frame and a tight fitting starched collar with tie appeared to pinch at the folds of his flabby neck. What was left of his thinning black hair was plastered close to his head and a carefully trimmed pencil moustache bedecked his tight mouth and thin lips. He peered sternly through a pair of thick-lensed spectacles set in perfectly round heavy black fames.

A retinue of anonymous functionaries was last to enter the hall and Father Lorenzo chaperoned them to a separate group of chairs located on the far side of the room adjacent to the roaring estufa.

After signalling for the girls to sit, Maria del Carmen gave a short speech of welcome to the Minister and the Archbishop. By her usual standards the remarks were calm and measured, devoid of political rhetoric or nationalist hyperbole. Perhaps, Vicenta thought, even the redoubtable Maria del Carmen López del Hierro was overawed by the occasion. No sooner had she returned to her seat than Father Joachín sprang into life, clapping his hands and summoning the girls to rise again, standing to attention behind their desks.

Casting a wide gaze across the class, he rose momentarily to his tiptoes and then wafted his hands wide apart before bringing them together and lifting them upwards. Falteringly at first, the girls' voices burst forth, quickly finding their pitch and harmony and settling into the rhythmic flow of the song following every sway of Father Joachín's body and every motion of his arms.

Vicenta had to concede that the song was mellow and melodious, even moving. The Archbishop appeared lost in the performance, closing his eyes and cocking his head to one side as if to pick out each and every note. Maria del Carmen allowed her body to sway gently in time to the cadence of the tune. Only the Minister appeared unmoved, staring expressionless at some distant point in the back of the hall. As the song reached a gentle crescendo, perhaps he alone recognised the incongruity of a group of young girls singing the words of the traditional battle hymn.

Volverá a reír la primavera, que por cielo, tierra y mar espera. (Spring will laugh again, which we await by air, land and sea.)

¡Arriba escuadras a vencer, que en España empieza a amanacer! (Onwards squadrons to victory, that a new day dawns in Spain!)

A quiet ripple of polite applause was led by Maria del Carmen as the girls were instructed to sit. Then Father Lorenzo moved to stand in front of the class, announcing that some of the pupils would now read from prepared texts taken from Proverbs 31.

First he called the name of Almira, a twelve year old orphan with mousey brown hair cropped in a short wispy fringe. She rose from her seat clutching a sheet of paper which quivered in her trembling hands. Hesitantly she began to read.

'A Virtuous Woman serves God with all of her heart, mind, and soul. She seeks His will for her life and follows His ways.'

Next it was the turn of Lenora, a frail ten year old with short curly black hair, reading through a pair of wire framed spectacles.

'A Virtuous Woman respects her husband. She does him good all the days of her life. She is trustworthy and a helpmeet.'

And so it continued as Father Lorenzo called

upon eight more girls to read their practised script.

'A Virtuous Woman teaches her children the ways of her Father in heaven. She nurtures her children with the love of Christ, disciplines them with care and wisdom, and trains them in the way they should go.'

'A Virtuous Woman cares for her body. She prepares healthy food for her family.'

'A Virtuous Woman serves her husband, her family, her friends, and her neighbors with a gentle and loving spirit. She is charitable.'

'A Virtuous Woman seeks her husband's approval before making purchases and spends money wisely. She is careful to purchase quality items which her family needs.'

'A Virtuous Woman works willingly with her hands. She sings praises to God and does not grumble while completing her tasks.'

'A Virtuous Woman is a homemaker. She creates an inviting atmosphere of warmth and love for her family and guests. She uses hospitality to minister to those around her.'

'A Virtuous Woman uses her time wisely. She works diligently to complete her daily tasks. She does not spend time dwelling on those things that do not please the Lord.'

'A Virtuous Woman is a woman of worth and beauty. She has the inner beauty that only comes from Christ. She uses her creativity and sense of style to create beauty in her life and the lives of her loved ones.'

Satisfied, father Lorenzo stepped aside and looked toward the dignitaries as if expecting applause. He was greeted with silence. Maria del Carmen looked flustered and began to rise from her chair as if to fill the void. Before she could speak, the Minister rose to his feet.

'Thank you girls,' he said, strolling before the front row of desks. 'You read as well as you sing. That was excellent. Now tell me. How do your like coming to school?'

He gazed across the whole class, but the girls seemed frozen in their seats. Pausing at the end of the row, he tapped the shoulder of Consuela, at fourteen, the oldest in the class.

Consuela shot to her feet. 'I like school very much, sir,' she said and immediately sat down.

A look of consternation gripped Maria del Carmen's face as she glanced across to Father Lorenzo who appeared equally perturbed.

Next the Minister moved between the desks and hovered at the side of Estella one of the youngest in the class. 'And what is your name?' he asked.

'My name is Estella,' she replied, standing and then bobbing in a half curtsy.

'And tell me, Estella, what do you like best about school?'

Without hesitation the young girl replied. 'I like our teacher, Señora Reig. We all like Señora Reig, sir.'

Turning to the podium, the Minister caught the eye of Maria del Carmen. 'Are we not to meet the girls' teacher? Is Señora Reig with us?'

At the side of the room Father Lorenzo shot to his feet. 'Perhaps the Minister would like…'

Before he could finish Maria del Carmen interjected. 'Señora Reig is here at the back of the hall. Vicenta, please come forward.'

Alarmed, Vicenta remained in her seat, not knowing what to do.

'Come along, Señora Reig,' the Minister said. 'I'd like to meet the teacher of these well behaved little girls.'

Vicenta stood and walked along the side of the hall until she was face to face with José Ibáñez Martín. If he noticed her expectant state he did not immediately comment.

'I am pleased to meet you Señora Reig,' the Minister said offering his hand.

Vicenta took the proffered hand and shook it briefly, wondering if she should curtsy, but remaining rigidly upright.

'Your class does you great credit.'

'Thank you,' she replied. 'It's a pleasure to teach them.'

'But tell me,' the Minister continued, 'are all your lessons so serious and dour?'

Vicenta noticed Father Lorenzo flash her a dark scowl.

'Not at all, sir. For much of the time our lessons are full of smiles and laughter. Many of the girls have had little in the way of schooling and they are all very keen to learn. But of course there has to be a balance between pleasurable learning and disciplined tuition. It is finding the right balance that is the key to making progress.'

Suddenly the Archbishop, who to that point had appeared disinterested in the conversation, stirred. 'My sheep hear my voice, and I know them, and they follow me,' he said, quoting from the Gospel of John. 'Is that what you are trying to say?'

Vicenta looked bemused as she did not recognize the quotation or its pertinence to what she had said. 'I'm not sure if the metaphor is entirely apt,' she said, cautious not to appear argumentative. 'I simply believe that if you know your children and if they know you, then it is easier to encourage them to learn.'

The Archbishop responded to Vicenta's comment with a gentle nod. 'I suspect that is exactly what Our Lord was trying to say.'

A thin smile crossed the face of Maria del Carmen, contrasting sharply with the grimace that distorted Father Lorenzo's countenance.

One of the functionaries stood and stepped toward the central podium. 'Your Grace, Minister, I fear we are running behind schedule. We should perhaps move on.'

CHAPTER ELEVEN

After the deemed success of the dignitaries' visit Maria del Carmen took more of an interest in Vicenta's class. Both the Minister and the Archbishop had commented favourably on what they had seen and this meant that Vicenta's requests for more books and writing materials met with a positive response. However, her subtle attempts to reduce father Lorenzo's input to classes met with stubborn resistance. Whenever she could, Vicenta tried to undermine his message with her own guidance on freedom, individuality and independence.

One of her biggest regrets was that she could not break the absolute rule that the girls' education must end on their fourteenth birthday so that they could be put to work. And this was how she lost Consuela, one of her brightest pupils who showed more than enough potential to progress to higher education given the chance. She was even more downcast to hear that Consuela had been assigned to work in the Hospital Santa Helena where Vicenta had been taken when her pregnancy had been discovered. Consuela's job, it emerged was as a cleaner, scrubbing floors and emptying bed pans.

Vicenta's friend, Maite continued her work at the centre for young mothers and the two women often engaged in a discourse about their respective roles. Both enjoyed their work but shared their frustrations about the overarching influence of Catholic and Falange principles that imposed a rigid doctrine of anti-feminism. They socialised when there was time, visiting the City's art galleries and museums and occasionally eating out together in some of the cheaper bars and restaurants. They managed once to go to the cinema to watch *La Diligencia*, a Spanish version of John Ford's *Stagecoach* staring John Wayne. Though they both enjoyed the movie, the occasion was marred by a Falange propaganda film that preceded the main feature and showed endless clips of General Franco being feted by saluting supporters wherever he went.

One Saturday evening Maite announced they were going to a local dancehall. Vicenta, now heavily pregnant, was reluctant at first but allowed herself to be persuaded and spent most of the evening dancing with Maite's brother Ramón. It was the first time she had seen him in a jacket and tie. The collar of his shirt was slightly frayed and uncomfortably tight, but with his slicked back hair and shiny shoes, he still cut quite a dash. He was a good dancer as well, light footed and precise. Taking Vicenta in a formal hold around her waist and gently clasping her left hand he led Vicenta through unfamiliar steps without once treading on her feet. He was attentive as well, allowing her to rest at intervals and bringing her water when she

asked.

'You know he's in love with you,' Maite suddenly announced when she and Vicenta sat briefly in an alcove at the side of the dance floor.

'Don't say that,' Vicenta said, quite clearly irked at the suggestion.

'Why not?' Maite continued. 'He's quite handsome don't you think? Some people would consider him quite a catch.'

'You know why not.'

'Because of Eduardo? I thought you had accepted it was time to move on.'

'Then you thought wrong, Maite. I can't "move on" as you put it. I made a pact when last I was with Eduardo; a pact that we would always be bound together. I cannot simply nullify that pact; not until I know what has happened to Eduardo.'

'And if that never happens, what then? Maite said, a touch of irritation in her voice. 'Are you going to waste your life? You're going to have a baby soon. Ramón knows that and he's willing to take on that responsibility because he loves you. In the circumstances I thought you would have jumped at the chance.'

'You just don't understand, do you? I'm in love with Eduardo. He's my husband in case you've forgotten. I can't just ignore that fact even if I wanted to. I like Ramón, he's a kind and thoughtful man, but I don't love him and he can never be a father to my child.'

'I just thought…'

'Then don't think. I'd like to go now and I don't want to talk about this again.'

That night Vicenta's sleep was disturbed by shifting images she could not control or shut out. One minute she was lying, breathless in Eduardo's arms as they basked in the afterglow of slow sexual fulfillment; the next moment Juan-Martin Garcia's foul breath and guttural moans pervaded her subconscious as he thrust his hips, slamming her into the alley wall. Ramón appeared on bended knee declaring his love and promising to care for her and her unborn child.

Six weeks later Vicenta was summoned to the office of Maria del Carmen at the feeding centre still housed in the old department store where they had first met. Her classes with the young girls had continued uneventfully, apart from an occasional spat with Father Lorenzo, but even his domineering presence failed to dampen her enthusiasm for her work. So she was puzzled to be called in and wondered if Father Lorenzo had finally tired of her attempts to undermine his doctrinal preachings on the subject of domesticity and unquestioning obedience to the Church.

She was relieved when Maria del Carmen finally arrived, unaccompanied, after keeping her waiting in the office for almost ten minutes. Wearing a soft pink knitted twinset adorned with a heavy gold chain, she strode purposefully across the office and took her seat at the desk in front of Vicenta. Her hair, normally combed tightly to her head and with a severe parting, was this time falling in soft rumpled curls. Her whole appearance gave Vicenta an impression of a more benign being, quite different from the authoritarian façade to which she had become accustomed.

'Thank you so much for coming in,' Maria del Carmen said, pulling her seat closer to the desk.

I didn't think I had a choice, Vicenta thought.

'I expect you are wondering why I asked you to meet me.'

'I was a little puzzled, yes, not to say nervous.'

Maria del Carmen smiled, a fuller, friendlier smile than Vicenta had ever seen on the face of the Secretary of the Auxilio Social.

'There's no need to be nervous,' said Maria del Carmen, reaching into the leather briefcase she had placed on one side of the desk and extracting a large manila envelope.

Despite the previous assurance, Vicenta gulped hard wondering what the envelope contained.

Maria del Carmen continued, 'It is now six months since you first joined the Auxilio Social and that means you have fulfilled your obligation as decreed by the new government.' She reached into the envelope and extracted some papers. 'That means you are entitled to these.' She slid the papers across the desk. 'There's a certificate there recognizing your service and a full travel permit. More importantly there's an identity card officially stamped by the Guardia Civil. Look after them, they are important documents.'

Vicenta picked up the papers and looked at each one in turn. Stuttering, she spoke, 'Thank you. I… I hadn't expected this. To be honest I didn't even realize I had been here for six months. I… I don't know what to say.'

'There's nothing to say. You've earned the right to these documents and the privileges that go with them.'

'Privileges?'

'Yes, it means you are fully accredited as having completed your time with the Auxilio Social and free to travel wherever you want without hindrance.'

'Does that mean I have to leave the Auxilio Social? What about my class?'

'My dear, you don't *have* to do anything you don't want to. You can stay or leave, it's up to you. Have you thought what you might like to do?'

'This has come as a bit of a surprise. I really don't know what I might do.' Vicenta thought for a moment and then spoke again. 'I'd be reluctant to leave my girls though. I've really enjoyed teaching them and I think they like me as well.'

Maria del Carmen leant back in her chair and smiled again.

'That's what I hoped you would say, Vicenta. We'd be happy for you to carry on your work with the class if that's what you want.'

'Thank you, I'd like that.'

Maria del Carmen sat forward once more. 'But have you thought about the longer term?'

Vicenta looked bemused. 'The longer term, I'm not sure I know what you mean.'

'The whole education system in Spain is in a mess. It lacks structure and organisation. The Government has great plans, but their delivery depends on good teachers and since the war these have been in short supply. From what we've seen you have the potential to become a full time professional teacher. How would that suit you?'

Vicenta tried hard to hide her scepticism. Much as she enjoyed teaching the rudiments of literacy to her group of otherwise uneducated young girls, she could not abide the thought of becoming a part of the new regime's attempts to re-write history. She knew already that the government planned to re-Catholicize education and use it as a propaganda tool. Girls and boys were to be educated separately and with different curricula. Secular and progressive teachers were being purged and the Church was intent on making education a purely authoritarian experience aimed at bringing students into submission and conformity.

'I'd have to think about that,' Vicenta said after a pause.

'I really think you should,' Maria del Carmen said, scrutinizing Vicenta carefully. 'Of course there's one small problem.' She nodded at Vicenta's bulging abdomen.

Instinctively Vicenta placed a hand on her belly.

'When is your baby due?'

'In about fives weeks.'

'And have you thought about what you might do afterwards?'

Vicenta was becoming concerned about the direction the conversation was taking and she was not sure she wanted to discuss this topic with anyone, least of all the Secretary of the Auxilio Social.

'No, I haven't thought about it,' she said defensibly.

'Then you must,' Maria del Carmen said stridently. 'Life in Spain for a single mother would be very difficult indeed. No husband, no work and no means of support. You would become a burden on the state at a time when the state is ill equipped to help. You would be condemning yourself and your child to a life of poverty and deprivation. Worse than that you would be wasting the talents you undoubtedly have.'

Vicenta fully understood the import of Maria del Carmen's prompting, but did not respond.

'Given your circumstances you should give serious consideration to the alternatives. Spain lost a great many young men and women during the war. That means there are a great many grieving parents out there who would be grateful for the opportunity to take on a young baby and give it all the advantages of a stable home.'

Especially if they are good Catholics or Falangists, Vicenta thought, though she did not care to argue the point.

'As you suggest, I will give it some thought.'

'I really think you should,' Maria del Carmen said in a tone that sounded more like an instruction than a suggestion.

'I will,' Vicenta replied meekly, knowing that now was not the time to argue.

Sensing Vicenta's reticence, Maria del Carmen brought the conversation to a summary conclusion. 'Make sure you do,' she said, rising from her seat and striding toward the door.

Unwelcome as it was, Maria del Carmen's directive forced Vicenta to confront an issue which she had hitherto purposely avoided. Now it was time to face the reality of her situation. Spain was heading in a direction she abhorred and yet, by the evidence of her own eyes, the people, weary from the hardships of war and cowed by the forces of repression, were in no mood to resist. Perhaps she, too, should accept the way things were and find a way to accept the current situation and make a life for herself. But what of Eduardo? Vicenta knew that thousands of political prisoners had disappeared and probably died. The old guard at Albatera prison had told her how prisoners had been shot or died of disease or malnutrition. Then again, the evil prison clerk, Silvestre Moreno, had told that that Eduardo had never been registered at the prison. Maite was convinced that Eduardo must be dead but Vicenta still refused, absolutely, to accept this. But blind faith, she knew, would not bring Eduardo back and she had reluctantly grown to realize that there was nothing more she could do to find him – except hope and pray. And now, with her baby due in a few weeks time she knew she had to plan for the future. Touching her abdomen she thought about her baby. Here, living and growing inside her body was a small human being, part of her flesh and blood. Eduardo's absence meant she would have to bring the baby into this world and nurture it alone. Without his support she knew it would be a struggle for her and the baby to survive. Perhaps Maria del Carmen was right, there were other people willing and more able than herself to take on the task of bringing up a child. At that moment Vicenta felt the baby move within her womb. And at that same moment Vicenta understood the bond between mother and child had already been formed – an unbreakable bond that would endure whatever hardships the world might present.

CHAPTER TWELVE

Maite, too, received her papers that week. She was given the opportunity to continue her work at the centre for young mothers, but declined, preferring instead to take a job at a local bakery. It was menial work and poorly paid, but it was free of the political propaganda that was part of the daily routine at the centre.

Vicenta continued to teach the girls in her class though now she was paid a small wage. She had said nothing more to Maria del Carmen and she knew that this could only be a short term engagement – until the baby was born.

Free of their obligations to the Auxilio Social, the two women decided to pool their resources and rent an apartment to free themselves of the austere stringency of life in the dormitory. In spite of the basic facilities and the drabness of the rooms, not to mention the ingrained grime, Vicenta and Maite were excited to occupy their tiny one bedroom flat. After the constraints of life in the dormitory, this was like regaining their freedom and they set about cleaning and furnishing the place with gusto. Everything they bought was used and tatty, but it mattered not to them. Ramón chipped in with a few items he said had "fallen off the back of a lorry" though Vicenta suspected he had bought them himself.

As her due date approached, Vicenta found her work more and more tiring. She thought about standing down, but that would have meant simply sitting around waiting for the event to happen, so she plodded on, never letting her enthusiasm wane.

One Tuesday afternoon, after her class had been dismissed, Vicenta set about her usual task of tidying the classroom, collecting up paper and crayons, stacking books and cleaning the blackboard. Satisfied that everything was in order, she walked to the door and looked back at the room with its neat rows of desks and chairs and paused to think how difficult it would be to leave all this behind when her baby was born. She set aside the thought and closed the door stepping out into the corridor that linked the annexe to the main church. As her shoes clipped along the hard stone floor she noticed a dim light emitting from the small frosted glass window set in a wooden door at the far end of the corridor. As she approached she thought she heard the muffled tone of a girl crying inside the small room which was used as a store for cleaning materials and equipment and normally kept locked. Pausing outside the door, the crying became louder and more hysterical and then a shrill voice rang out.

'No, please. Please don't make me.'

Alarmed, Vicenta grabbed the door knob, twisted it and thrust the door open wide. In the dim light all she could see was the black silhouette of a man arched over the corner of the room with one arm leaning against the wall.

'Please, no, I can't,' the young girl pleaded from behind the man's silhouette.

'You have to. It is God's will,' a gruff voice demanded.

Adjusting her focus, Vicenta saw two bare legs with black shoes and socks emerging from a black cassock that had been pulled up around the man's waist.

Realising what was happening Vicenta shrieked.

'Father Lorenzo, you dirty bastard, what the hell do you think you are doing?'

Startled, the priest turned toward her, his penis, held in his right hand, dripping a thread of semen. Behind him Vicenta recognized Estella, one of her youngest pupils aged just nine. She was crouched, cowering in the corner. Her hair was ruffled about her head, her eyes wide open in panic and the profuse tears that streaked her ruddy face mingled with blobs of semen that dribbled from her chin and onto her blouse.

In a fury Vicenta lunged across the room and lashed out at the priest. Before he could react, Vicenta had gouged his face with her fingernails and shoved him to one side so that he stumbled against the back wall. His cassock dropped to cover his legs as he used both hands to regain his balance. Recovering, he wiped his face with his right hand and pulled it away to see a thick smear of blood.

'You bitch,' he yelled thrusting forward and shoving Vicenta against the side wall. He raised his right fist to aim a blow at her face but she lifted her left arm to block the blow.

'Get away from me you pervert,' she yelled, flailing both her arms to keep him at bay.

The priest raised his own arms to protect himself from Vicenta's onslaught and managed to grab her in a bear hug, turning her body and slamming her face against the wall.

'Get off me you brute,' she screamed, struggling to release his grip and using her weight to lean away from the wall. 'You filthy bastard,' she yelled, 'I'll report you for this.'

The priest released his bear hug then used all his strength to shove Vicenta back into the wall. Her abdomen hit first flattening her womb and causing her to yell in pain and fear. Then her face slammed into the wall, crushing her nose and she tasted a salty trickle of blood ooze into her mouth. Dazed, her body crumpled and she slithered to her knees.

'You fucking whore,' Father Lorenzo sneered. 'You'll report me will you?' He stepped forward and leaned over. Fearing he might strike her again, Vicenta pulled her knees up to her chest and covered her face with her arms.

Snarling, the priest continued his rant. 'And now you are about to give birth to a bastard. What were you paid for selling your body you fucking slut? You say a word about this and I'll make sure everyone knows exactly what you are.'

Straightening, he stepped back and then swung his right foot at Vicenta's cowering body. Seeing the blow coming, she fell to her side and the kick caught her full in the back.

'Just remember, if you know what's good for you and that bastard baby of yours, keep your fucking mouth shut,' he yelled before turning and walking out of the room, slamming the door behind him.

It took a moment or two for Vicenta to recover her senses. She was aroused by the sound of Estella whimpering in the corner, her body heaving with each sob. Vicenta's first thought was to go to the girl and comfort her, but as she tried to stand she was paralyzed by an excruciating pain in her abdomen. She straightened her body in an effort to stretch out and ease the pain, but it had no effect. She placed a hand on her womb which was hard, almost solid, quite different from before. Suddenly the pain stopped completely and she felt her stomach muscles relax as well. Relieved, she allowed herself to rest for a moment but then felt a warm sticky sensation between her legs. Lifting her skirt she placed her hand between her legs and pulled it away to see it smeared with a pink, jelly-like substance. At that moment the pain in her abdomen returned, more intense than before and she realized she was going into labour.

The sheet pulled up to her chin was moist from her sweat and smelled musty. As she breathed deeply, the mustiness was replaced with a strong scent of bleach and disinfectant which made her feel nauseous.

The familiar figure of Sister Alicia hovered at the side of the bed and placed a soft hand on her shoulder.

'Ah, Vicenta,' the Sister said. 'You've had a scare, but everything is fine, there's no need to worry.'

'But I felt some blood,' Vicenta said.

'It was just a show of mucus,' the Sister said. 'Quite normal. And you had a couple of short contractions, but your baby is not ready to join us just yet. All the same it's as well you are here in the hospital where we can keep an eye on you. You have young Estella to thank for that. When she found you she ran outside and stopped a woman in the street. That's how you got here.'

'Estella, how is she?' Vicenta asked cautiously.

'Estella? She's fine, why wouldn't she be?' said Sister Alicia. 'Now just sit up a moment while I straighten your pillow. It won't be long now.' As Vicenta sat, she realized she was wearing only a cotton bed gown and clutching her neck she discovered that the cord holding Eduardo's ring and key was missing.

'My clothes?' she said. 'Where are my clothes?'

'Don't fret, Sister Alicia said. 'We've put all

your things away for safekeeping. They'll be returned to you when you are ready to leave. I just have to pop out for some water and fresh towels, but don't worry I'll be back shortly.'

Vicenta's head was spinning, running through events at the classroom. The image of poor Estella came into her head, cowering and bewildered in the corner of the room, her face streaked with tears and seminal fluid. She had Estella to thank for calling help and she feared for the poor girl and wondered what would happen to her now.

The contractions were becoming more frequent and lasting longer. Sister Alicia had raised and separated Vicenta's knees covering them with a sheet for the sake of modesty. A nurse in a pale green uniform had joined the Sister though she had not been introduced.

'I think baby is ready to join us now,' the Sister said. 'When the next contraction starts you need to push. Push hard but don't hold your breath. Can you do that?'

Already panting, Vicenta nodded.

A sudden gush of liquid hit the rubber sheet placed between Vicenta's feet and some of it splattered the floor beneath the bed.

'It's nothing to worry about. Your waters have just broken. It won't be long now,' said Sister Alicia. Turning to the nurse and motioning to the floor she added, 'Get someone to clean that up will you, we don't want to slip and fall.'

The nurse left the room and returned a minute or so later with a young woman dressed in a plain brown house coat, her hair pulled up and covered with a red head scarf. Vicenta recognized her immediately as Consuela, the girl who had left her class just a few weeks before. She was carrying a galvanized bucket and a mop.

'Clean that up will you and be quick about it,' ordered Sister Alicia.

Consuela recognized Vicenta and she acknowledged the girl's faint smile with one of her own. Consuela wrung out the mop and began to wipe the floor at the side of the bed. The nurse had stepped to one side and was fiddling with a pile of towels on a shelf at the end of the room. Sister Alicia meanwhile was busy looking for signs of the baby's head.

After a brief glance around the room, whilst still pushing the mop, Consuela moved her face close to Vicenta's and whispered in her ear.

'Don't let them take your baby away.'

Startled, all Vicenta could say was, 'What?'

'I said, don't let them take your baby away.'

'Haven't you finished yet?' Sister Alicia barked.

'Yes Sister,' Consuela said.

'Then leave us, now.'

It was two hours later that Sister Alicia announced, 'You're doing fine Vicenta. I can see the baby's head. Just a couple more pushes and we'll be done.

Vicenta was nearing exhaustion, her whole body ached and she was soaked with sweat. One final push and the baby emerged.

'You have a baby boy,' Sister Alicia said, holding the infant above Vicenta's face.

Messy, covered in white greasy vernix and spattered with blood, the baby began to bawl. Vicenta looked up at the child, its tiny face distorted by the effort of crying. She raised her hands to reach for the baby, but Sister Alicia withdrew. 'We have to cut the umbilical cord,' she said and then nurse needs to clean him up.'

'Please, let me hold him,' Vicenta pleaded.

'All in good time,' the Sister said. 'First you need to push out the placenta. Can you do that for me?'

A gentle push and the placenta was released.

Vicenta watched the nurse wipe the baby with a clean towel and wrap it in a blanket. His bawling was strong and incessant.

'I want to hold him,' Vicenta demanded.

'Let nurse clean you up first,' said Sister Alicia, standing and taking the baby from the nurse.

As the nurse wiped Vicenta's thighs and legs, Sister Alicia rocked the baby back and forth. Suddenly she announced, 'I'm very concerned. Your baby is not breathing properly; the lips are turning blue. I need to get him in an incubator immediately.'

'No don't take him away, I forbid it,' Vicenta demanded.

'You're just being hysterical,' the Sister said. 'He needs to be in the incubator. Stepping toward the door Sister Alicia added, 'You must rest now. Nurse will give you something to help you sleep.'

As soon as the nurse's back was turned, Vicenta spat out the tablets she had pretended to swallow.

'Just sleep now,' the nurse said. 'I'll be back in a little while.'

Alone in the room, Vicenta could hear nothing except the trample of feet in the corridor outside and faintly, in the distance, the muffled sound of a baby crying. She wondered if it was her baby and longed to go to it. She swung her body from under the sheets, placed her feet on the ground and attempted to stand. She was wearing nothing but a flimsy gown, buttoned to the bottom and damp with sweat. She looked for some shoes or slippers, but could see nothing; there wasn't even a cupboard in the room where she might look. The stone floor was freezing cold and as she took a couple of hesitant steps toward the door her legs gave way and she crumpled, clutching at the side of the bed.

The door opened and the nurse entered. 'What on earth are you doing? Get back in bed immediately.' She lifted Vicenta back on to the bed and tightly tucked the sheets. 'I thought you would have been asleep by now,' she said suspiciously.'

'I just want to see my baby.' Vicenta said.

'All in good time,' the nurse said matter-offactly. 'Your baby is very poorly. He's in the incubator and Sister Alicia is with him, so he is in God's hands now.'

'But I want to see him. Why won't you let me go to him?'

'You're not strong enough. It would be too distressing. Now just do as you are told and stay here. Sister Alicia will be along as soon as there is any news.'

As the nurse left the room and the door closed Vicenta heard a faint click and realized it had been locked.

Through the silent hours of darkness Vicenta fought against sleep. All she could think about was her baby and though she had seen him only for a fleeting moment, every single feature of his scrunched up face was etched on her memory. Over and over Consuela's words came back into her head. *Don't let them take your baby away.*

As dawn broke and the bars at the single small window cast shadows across the floor of the room, the hospital began to come to life. Once more, footsteps could be heard in the corridor accompanied by the squeal of trolley wheels coming and going. Vicenta listened hard for the sound of crying, but could hear nothing.

A key rattled in the door lock and the handle turned. Sister Alicia entered with another woman in a nun's habit, this one blue in contrast to the Sister's grey. With solemn faces both women shuffled toward the bed. Vicenta lifted her head and tried to lift her body, but the Sister pressed firmly on her shoulders to prevent her from rising.

With no obvious signs of emotion, Sister Alicia spoke, 'This is Reverend Mother Inocencia. I'm afraid we have some bad news for you Vicenta.'

Without preamble the Reverend Mother said, 'Your baby has died.'

'No, that can't be. I don't believe you.' Vicenta screamed.

'You must calm down, Vicenta, said Sister Alicia. 'I know this is a terrible shock for you, but becoming hysterical will not help.'

The Reverend Mother spoke again, 'Your baby had fluid in his lungs. The condition is known as wet lung. It is not uncommon and most babies recover quite quickly. We gave him oxygen and a gentle massage to stimulate his breathing, but I'm sorry to tell you that this failed. His lungs never functioned properly and this led to suffocation.'

'But I heard him cry,' Vicenta said.

'That means nothing,' Reverend Mother said dismissively.

'Where is he? I want to see him,' Vicenta said, again trying to lift herself from the pillow.

Sister Alicia reinforced her thrust. 'I'm afraid that won't be possible.'

'What do you mean? Surely I can see him. I... I need to see him,' Vicenta said. And then after thinking added, 'There will be a funeral to arrange and he'll have to be buried.'

'That's out of the question,' the Reverend Mother said. 'Harsh as this may sound, the truth is that your baby never had a life. He was never baptized and so a funeral is out of the question. All we can do is trust in God's mercy and pray for his salvation.'

'I demand to see my baby. It's my right.'

The Reverend Mother's face distorted to a deep scowl. 'Don't talk to me about rights young lady. If God has seen fit to punish your immoral actions, you have no rights. You cannot question the Will of God. Let that be an end to this matter. We have disposed of the baby's body already. You will have to pray for God's forgiveness and find a way to atone for your sins. You may rest here until the end of today and then you must leave.' Turning to Sister Alicia the Reverend Mother said, 'Come Sister. Our work here is done.' The two nuns turned and left the room without locking the door.

Vicenta was distraught. She could not believe her baby was dead; she had seen it only briefly and heard it cry, but now it was gone. She thrust her head into the pillow and sobbed uncontrollably. She was so immersed in her grief and anxiety that she failed to hear the door to her room open or the sound of approaching footsteps. When a hand touched her shoulder she jerked round from the pillow to peer into the face of

Consuela.

'What are you doing here?' Vicenta asked abruptly.

'I've been told to bring you these,' Consuela replied placing a tattered cardboard box on the bed. 'It's your clothes and shoes.'

Vicenta grabbed the box and rummaged quickly through the contents. She was relieved to find Eduardo's ring and key still attached to the cord and lifted it to tie around her neck.

'They say you'll be leaving today,' Consuela said.

'They've told me I have to leave today. I don't think I have any choice in the matter.'

Consuela lowered her eyes and spoke hesitantly, 'But your baby…'

Vicenta lurched forward grabbing Consuela by her shoulders. 'What do you know about my baby?' she demanded.

Consuela pulled back. 'I… I can't tell you anything.'

'Consuela, when I saw you yesterday you said to me, "Don't let them take your baby away." What did you mean by that.'

'I shouldn't have said that, I'm sorry.'

'Don't be sorry, Consuela. They say my baby died, but if you know anything about my baby, you have to tell me. Please, I beg of you.'

Consuela raised her face to look directly into Vicenta's eyes. 'I don't think your baby is dead.'

'What? What do you mean?'

'It's happened before. They say a baby has died, but it's not true. The baby is given away.'

'Given away? What do you mean?'

'People come here to see the Sisters and later I've seen them go away with new born babies taken from mothers who have been told their babies have died.'

'What sort of people?'

'I don't know who they are. They are obviously well-to-do people. I've seen them come in wearing fancy clothes and they leave in smart cars taking a baby with them.'

'But how do you know the babies are not theirs?'

'Do you think I am stupid? The women are not pregnant; they've never been pregnant. They just turn up one day and leave with a baby. And at the same time when I'm sent to clean rooms, I've met mothers like you who have been told their babies have died.'

'Well, babies do sometimes die,' Vicenta said, trying to understand what Consuela was saying.

'Not this many?'

'How many are you talking about?'

'I can't say exactly. Some of the mothers don't want to talk, but others are obviously upset and they tell me what has happened. They say their babies have died and nearly always it is the same thing – breathing problems. Their babies are taken to an incubator and then they are told they have died.'

Vicenta looked incredulous, 'How many babies are you talking about?'

'I don't really know. It's possible that some of the babies actually died, but there are too many. I've heard the same story at least a dozen times since I came to work here.'

Vicenta thought for a moment. 'But you've only been here a couple of months, haven't you?'

'Just over two months. That's what I mean, there are just too many. And another thing, nearly all the mothers who have been through this are unmarried, or if they are married their husbands are in prison.'

'How do you know all this?'

'Because most of these mothers are very upset. They are left alone here for a couple of days thinking their babies have died. They have no one to talk to, so they talk to me when I go in to clean the rooms.'

Vicenta's head was spinning. What if her baby boy had not died? The Sisters at the hospital knew of her circumstances; Reverend Mother Inocencia had said as much when she ranted about Vicenta's immoral activities. What if her baby was still alive and about to be given away to some rich couple? Her mind went into overdrive. What if the Sisters were involved in a conspiracy to take perfectly healthy babies away from unmarried mothers or mothers whose husbands had been imprisoned as republicans, leftists or communists? What if the people who took the babies were deemed to be good Catholics or Falangists? No. This just wasn't possible. Suddenly Vicenta thought of her own child.

'Do you know what has happened to my baby?' she pleaded.

'No, I can't be sure,' Consuelo said. 'I can't even be sure he is still alive.'

Vicenta leaned forward holding Consuela by the shoulders again and looking directly into her face.

'This is very important, Consuela. I need you to think carefully. Do you know what happens to the babies after their mothers have been told they have died?'

'I can't be certain, but I think they may be taken to a special room on the second floor.'

'What makes you think that?'

'Well, there's a room up there at the end of the corridor. I've seen the Sisters and nurses going in and out, but it's always kept locked. I've cleaned the corridor outside, but I've never been inside. Sometimes I've heard babies crying inside the room.'

'But that's not so unusual. This is a maternity hospital after all.'

'Yes, but the maternity wards are all on this floor. The second floor is all men's surgical wards.'

Vicenta's heart leapt with a sudden faint hope.

'Consuela, I need your help.' Vicenta said excitedly. 'Now listen to me carefully.'

CHAPTER THIRTEEN

Consuela had done as she had been instructed and it was four thirty in the afternoon when Maite arrived. Vicenta was already dressed in her old clothes and sitting on the edge of the bed. They had fifteen minutes to kill and spent the time discussing their plan. Just as they were about to leave the room the door opened and Sister Alicia entered and looked suspiciously at Maite.

'My friend has come to take me home,' Vicenta said, trying to preempt the Sister's enquiry.

'Good,' the Sister said. 'I'm glad you are well enough to leave. It would do you no good to dwell on your grief in this place. I'll show you out if you like.'

'Thank you,' Vicenta said. 'We'll be fine and I'd just like to spend a moment or two here before I leave. You see my only memory of my baby is in this room and doubtless I shall never return, so perhaps I can say a short prayer before I go.'

'I understand,' the Sister said, but don't take too long. It doesn't do to wallow in sadness, and sentimentality will do you no good. We all need to get on with our lives and learn the lessons from our past indiscretions. I will leave you now. May God go with you.'

As Sister Alicia left the room Maite said, 'We need to hurry.'

'I know, but give the Sister a moment to leave the corridor.'

After waiting a minute or so, Vicenta and Maite left the room and turned right toward the staircase at the end of the corridor. They paused for a moment and instead of descending they climbed the stairs to the second floor, emerging through a set of swing doors. Getting her bearings from Consuela's directions, Vicenta knew they were at the far end of the corridor from the room they were looking for. Gingerly they walked along the corridor praying no one would see them. As they neared the room they saw the short alcove Consuela had described which led to a bathroom and toilets. They slipped into the alcove and waited. Vicenta was panting, clearly out of breath. She looked pale and her skin was clammy.

'Are you all right?' Maite asked.

'I'll be fine. I just need to catch my breath.'

Moments later Maite slipped her head around the corner and looked back toward the staircase from which they had just emerged.

'Here's Ramón now,' she whispered, followed by, 'Shit! There's someone coming out of the ward. It looks like a food trolley.'

'Ah,' they heard Ramón say to the woman pushing the trolley. 'I wonder if you can help me. I'm here to see my father on the ward, but I've been driving for a long time and I need to use the toilet first.'

'Just down there on the right,' the woman said, barely stopping as she pushed her trolley toward the lift by the staircase.

Ramón continued down the corridor and joined the women in the alcove, puffing his cheeks in a sigh of relief.

'Thank you so much, Ramón,' Vicenta said, kissing him softly on the cheek.

'There's no need for thanks. Now let's get on with this before anyone else comes along. You two stay here.' Ramón slipped out of the alcove and moved to the adjacent door. He paused to listen at the door but heard nothing. 'Are you sure this is the right room?' he called back.

'That's what Consuela said,' Vicenta answered.

Ramón tried the handle. 'It's locked, as we expected.' He removed a small crowbar from the inside pocket of his jacket. 'One of the advantages of being a blacksmith – tools of the trade,' he said.

Ramón wedged the crowbar between the door and the jamb, banging it in with the palm of his hand. He levered the crowbar outwards and there was a sound of splintering wood. He banged the crowbar a little further then levered again. The door sprang open with a loud crack as the strike plate on the inside of the frame broke away with a large splinter of wood.

'We're in,' he said summoning Vicenta and Maite to join him. They all scrambled inside the room and closed the door behind them.

It was a small room just six metres long and half as wide with a single small window at the far end which provided a dim light. The walls and ceiling were painted in plain magnolia and a central row of three electric lights were switched off. Against the left hand wall stood a row of four simple metal cots with side bars that extended at the sides above the level of the thin mattresses resting in the centre of each cot. An absence of bedding showed that two of the cots were empty, but the other two, at the far end of the room, both contained pillows and blankets.

'I'll stay here by the door,' Ramón said. 'Vicenta, go and take a look.'

Vicenta was supporting herself against the wall at the side of the door, still panting heavily. Maite thought Vicenta was about to faint and took her arm.

'Come on, Vicenta,' Maite said. 'Hold on to my arm.'

Vicenta walked unsteadily down the side of the room toward the first occupied cot and leaned over to take a look. The baby in the cot was lying on its side and all Vicenta could see was the back of its head.

'Is that your baby?' Maite said.

'I can't see him,' Vicenta replied, 'I don't know.'

'Come round this side and take a closer look,' Maite said.

They rounded the cot and Vicenta crouched

down to be at eye level with the child who was gurgling softly in its sleep.

'That's not him,' Vicenta said, standing.

Taking Maite's hand, Vicenta approached the next cot and again leaned forward. This time the baby was lying on its back staring up at the ceiling. The baby's face was puffy and a little blotchy and the head was covered with a sprinkling of downy brown hair. Vicenta gazed into the baby's blue-grey eyes and knew immediately.

'It's him,' she said as her legs buckled and she slumped to her knees.

Maite grabbed Vicenta under the armpits and lifted her to her feet. 'Hold on to the side of the cot,' she said. 'Are you sure?'

'Do you think I wouldn't know my own child,' Vicenta said tersely.

Maite ignored Vicenta's irritable tone. 'All right, Vicenta, stay there and I'll lift him out.' She reached over and loosened the blue blanket covering the baby's body then lifted him from the cot and wrapped the blanket beneath him. Immediately he began to cry, a loud piercing bawl.

'Can't you keep him quiet?' Ramón called out from the far end of the room. 'We can't leave this room with him making that din.'

'Give him to me,' Vicenta said, releasing her grip on the cot and holding out her arms. Maite handed the baby to Vicenta who cuddled it gently against her chest and rocked him from side to side. 'Shush,' she murmured softly, blowing softly against the baby's mouth. Almost immediately the baby stopped crying and seemed to smile back at Vicenta.

'Come on,' Ramón said. 'Time to leave.'

As the two women joined Ramón at the door, he took a peek outside. Satisfied the corridor was clear he whispered, 'Maite, you go first and wait for us at the stairwell.'

Maite did as instructed and walked, unhurriedly toward the stairs, reaching them just a few seconds later.

'Are you ready, Vicenta?' Ramón asked.

Vicenta nodded.

As they walked down the corridor Ramón supported Vicenta with an arm around her back, careful not to hurry her. They were halfway down the corridor when they were halted by the sound of the lift coming to a stop next to the stairwell. Maite retreated a couple of steps down the stairs as the concertina gate slid open, rattling on its rails.

Ramón felt Vicenta begin to buckle and strengthened his grip around her waist. 'You can do this Vicenta,' he said calmly, 'just keep on walking.'

As they neared the lift a nurse emerged carrying a cardboard folder under her arm. Startled by Ramón and Vicenta, she gave them a quizzical look.

'Ah, nurse,' Ramón said, 'I wonder if you can

help us. My wife and I are looking for the maternity ward. We have an appointment with the paediatrician, but we seem to have lost our way.'

'You're on the wrong floor,' the nurse said, stepping sideways to take a look at the baby cradled in Vicenta's arms. '*Que bonito*,' she said unable to resist the temptation of stroking the baby's face with her finger. 'Is it a boy or a girl?'

Ramón could feel Vicenta's body quivering. 'It's a boy,' he said, 'our first.'

The nurse looked away from the child and stared at Vicenta who responded with a weak smile.

'Are you all right?' The nurse asked. 'You look a little flushed.'

'I'm fine thank you,' Vicenta said in a wavering voice.

'You'll have to excuse my wife,' Ramón said. 'She's still quite weak after the birth and our baby has had some breathing difficulties. That's why we're here to see the paediatrician.'

The nurse stepped back.

'Oh, I'm sorry, I'm holding you up. You need the first floor, one down. Here, why don't you take the lift?' She reached out and slid open the concertina gate, closing it behind them once they had entered. 'Just press one.'

'Thank you,' Ramón said as the lift began to descend.

They reached the ground floor a few moments later and emerged into the lobby just inside the hospital entrance. Maite reached the lobby a couple of seconds later having sprinted down two flights of stairs. She did not join Ramón and Vicenta who were now paused just outside the lift. Instead Maite walked over to the small reception window on the left hand side of the lobby behind which sat a smartly dressed lady tapping noisily on a typewriter. As Maite engaged the receptionist in conversation, Ramón and Vicenta slipped past, heading for the exit.

Outside the entrance doors, Ramón and Vicenta stood at the top of a short flight of stone steps leading down to the pavement and the road which was busy with traffic. The early evening sun was shining directly in their faces and made Vicenta squint. Instinctively she tugged the blanket a little higher to shield her son's eyes from the bright light. Staring into the baby's face, he seemed just to gaze back at Vicenta with a look of innocence. Maite now joined them at the top of the steps and placed a reassuring arm around Vicenta's shoulders.

'Are you all right, Vicenta?' she asked.

'I'll be fine. Just give me a moment.'

'We need to get to the truck,' Ramón said. 'It's just up there on the right and parked around the corner. Do you think you can make it?'

'Well, we can't stay here can we,' Vicenta said. 'Let's go.'

As Vicenta began to descend the steps she looked up the street to her right in the direction they were about to turn. Suddenly she was stopped dead in her tracks as she spotted a nun heading from that direction toward the hospital entrance. The nun's blue habit was billowing in the breeze and her head was bowed looking down at the pavement. Vicenta did not need to see the nun's face to recognize her.

'What's the matter?' Maite asked, concerned at Vicenta's sudden hesitation.

For a moment Vicenta appeared frozen to the spot and Maite thought she might be about to faint.

Without warning, Vicenta straightened and thrust her baby into Maite's arms. 'Don't say anything,' Vicenta said. 'Take the baby now and go with Ramón to the truck. I'll meet you on the corner.'

Surprised, Maite took hold of the baby awkwardly and cradled him in her arms. 'But Vicenta...' she said.

'Please, just do as I ask. I need you to walk down the street like a normal couple. Maite, you need to hide your face with your shawl. Whatever you do, don't stop to talk to anyone.'

Maite and Ramón did as instructed, turning right at the base of the steps and walking side by side along the pavement. After about twenty metres they were level with the nun and moved to the inside to pass. The nun raised her head briefly and glanced over at the couple for a split second as they passed and continued up the street. Vicenta watched from the hospital steps, relieved to see that the nun did not break her stride. She thought momentarily about retreating back inside the hospital, but before she could make up her mind the nun looked up at her and their eyes met. Vicenta could feel her heart thumping in her chest and her legs wobbled. She took a deep breath and moved slowly down the last couple of steps and on to the pavement. She thought of turning left in the opposite direction away from the nun, but before she could decide a voice rang out.

'Vicenta, is that you?' Reverend Mother Inocencia called.

Vicenta simply stopped and confronted her.

'You're leaving us then?' Mother Inocencia said.

Trying hard to hold on to her emotions, Vicenta spoke. 'Yes, there's no point in moping about in hospital. It's time to go home.'

The nun placed a hand on Vicenta's arm and looked at her with a sardonic smile. 'I'm sure you are right, dear,' she said. 'It does no good to dwell on tragedy or question the ways of the Lord. Perhaps this has been a blessing in disguise. Home is the best place for you now. You must rest and recover, then move on.'

Vicenta almost spat in the nun's face. 'I'll try to do that,' she said straining every muscle in her face to avoid sneering. 'Now, if you'll excuse me I have a bus to catch.'

Vicenta stepped to one side and walked away not daring to look back at the nun. Had she done so she would have seen Reverend Mother Inocencia's face distort with a contemptuous smirk as she climbed the steps and entered the doors of the hospital.

Maite handed the baby back to Vicenta as soon as she closed the door of the truck. She looked into her child's face and stroked it gently with her finger. The baby looked back at Vicenta and his tiny face scrunched into a beguiling smile. Vicenta forced herself to smile back. *If only you knew*, she thought. *This is just the start of a perilous journey and who knows where it will take us?*

It was too risky to go back to their flat so they headed for Ramón's small apartment on the outskirts of the city. Vicenta thanked Maite and Ramón for their help and while she breast fed the child they discussed what they should do next. By now the nuns must surely have discovered that the baby had been removed and it wouldn't take a detective to realize who had taken him. Maite thought the nuns wouldn't dare to try and get the baby back, given how they had lied about the child's death. Vicenta disagreed. She recalled Father Lorenzo had called her a whore; it would be easy for him to denounce Vicenta as an unfit mother and have her arrested so they could take the baby away. And with Vicenta out of the way, they could cover up the scandal of how other babies had been taken from their mothers. In fact, the best way to hide their sordid secret would be for Vicenta to disappear permanently. Vicenta had no doubt this could easily be arranged given the influence of the nuns and Father Lorenzo. It would have the added advantage of making sure Vicenta could say nothing about Father Lorenzo's sexual proclivities.

They could hide out somewhere in Alicante, but if the authorities were determined, a mother and new-born child would be easy to find. Despite Maite's concern, Vicenta determined that she must leave Alicante. But where could she go? In these straitened times it would be difficult for a single mother to survive and care for her child. Wherever she went she would run the risk of being questioned and, were she ever to seek help or support from the authorities, she would run the risk again of being separated from her child. They had to think of another plan and decided to sleep on it. Ramón offered his bed to Vicenta, but she declined and asked instead to sleep on the small sofa; she didn't expect to get much sleep any way, what with the trauma of the day's events and the demands of the new baby. Maite was persuaded to make use of her brother's bed and Ramón said he would sleep on the bedroom floor. As they prepared to retire, Maite turned to Vicenta and spoke, 'Have you decided on a name for your baby?'

'I have,' Vicenta replied. 'I will call him Renato.

It means reborn.'

Vicenta knew she had to leave Alicante; to stay would mean almost certain detection and arrest. But where could she go? Even with the travel documents she had obtained by virtue of her time with the Auxilio Social, she doubted she could simply turn up in some other town or village without questions being asked. And then where would she stay? She had just a few pesetas to her name and no means of earning more to support herself, especially with the demands of a new born baby.

By morning Vicenta had slept for just an hour or so as she lay on the sofa nursing Renato and mulling over their future. At some point in the night she had formulated a plan. It was fraught with danger and she knew it might not work, but she could see no alternative. It would give her and Renato a roof over their heads and, if her plan worked, it would protect her from the possibility of being denounced and losing her child. It was a desperate measure, but she could think of nothing else.

Ramón and Maite emerged from the bedroom surprised to see Vicenta dressed and alert. Before she could say anything, Maite spoke.

'Vicenta, Ramón has an idea. I know it may sound hazardous, rash even, but we have talked it over and it could work.' She turned to Ramón.

Ramón coughed nervously. 'If you'll let me, I

would be willing to pose as your husband, or at least as the father of the child. We could leave Alicante together and move to another town anywhere, wherever you choose. I have a little money and we could find somewhere to stay, set up home together. I could find a job – blacksmiths are always in demand – and hopefully we could just blend into the background and no one would be any the wiser. If we could see out a few months this way and allow things to die down, the authorities would surely stop looking and we would be safe.'

Vicenta looked into Ramón's anxious face and was struck by his sincerity. He was a handsome man, honest and trustworthy and in any other circumstances she would have been flattered by his proposal and convinced as to its practicability. But she was married, married to Eduardo, and no matter how faint the hope of finding him again, she could not countenance the idea that he was dead. Besides, she knew how great a sacrifice Ramón would be making – giving up his job, his home and his family here in Alicante – and for what? For a hazardous venture that could lead him into serious trouble with the risk he might be denounced and arrested. As she knew all too well, anyone who just turned up as strangers in a different town would be viewed with suspicion. The tentacles of Franco's new dictatorship spread throughout Spain and wherever they surfaced there would be Falangists waiting to ask questions. Much as she appreciated Ramón's earnest offer of help, she knew that the only way to survive was to place herself in a position where her presence would be accepted and where she might receive a degree of immunity from suspicion and scrutiny.

Vicenta stepped over to Ramón, placed a hand on his arm and held his gaze.

'You are a good man, Ramón, and I am grateful for your offer. But it would be asking too much of you.' She saw his eyes dim, hooded with concern.

'But what will you do?' Maite implored, anxiety etched on her face.

Vicenta looked up at Ramón and touched his face with the back of her hand. 'I would however like your help in another way, if that is all right.'

'Anything,' Ramón said, 'you only need to ask.'

CHAPTER FOURTEEN

The journey to Benimarta took two days and two nights, including a stop over in Benissa at the offices of Mora and Blasco, Lawyers.

Throughout the journey, Ramón had held his feelings in check. He was far from convinced that Vicenta's plan was workable, let alone safe, but she was adamant and determined to press ahead. Ramón had brought food for the journey and they ate at the roadside to avoid stopping at any of the towns or villages through which they passed. They slept side by side on a waterproof oilskin beneath Ramón's truck and Vicenta cuddled Renato in a heavy blanket to ward off the chill and the damp of the summer nights.

As they approached Benimarta, Ramón tried one last time to get Vicenta to think again. His concern for her was genuine, she knew, but what she did not realise was that his greater fear was that he might never see her again. Throughout the journey he had thought he might express his feelings and tell her he was in love with her and would do anything to protect her and the child. But he understood her devotion to her husband. He also knew that to express his belief that Eduardo was dead – whether from starvation or summary execution like so many other political detainees – would serve no purpose except to undermine Vicenta's absolute belief that she would one day be reunited with her husband. To do that, he realised would be to undermine her will to live and that was something he could not countenance, especially at this desperate time in her life.

They parted, at Vicenta's insistence, on the outskirts of Benimarta. Ramón had wanted to go with her to the village, but she steadfastly rejected the idea. Her plan was perilous enough as it was without taking the risk that Ramón might suffer by being accused of assisting someone who might still be regarded as a subversive. She thanked him profusely and then hugged him tightly and kissed his cheek before turning away to walk toward the village. Had he called back to her, she might well have wavered, for at that moment her heart was full of trepidation; not just in fear of what lay ahead, but also in distress at the hurt she knew she had caused to a man whom she had grown to trust and admire. Determined not to weaken, she forced herself to trudge up the hill toward the village her mind awash with fear and trepidation at what lay ahead.

Ramón stood silently, watching through tear-filled eyes as the forlorn figure with a baby in one arm and a battered old suitcase tucked under the other, slowly disappeared into the distance. His heart ached at the thought of leaving her, but he was bolstered by his admiration for a woman the likes of whom he knew he would never meet again. He made a silent vow that this would not be the last time he would see her.

Vicenta found the old town house very much as she had left it in the autumn. A few more tiles had slipped from the roof and a fresh layer of plaster and rubble had fallen behind the front door. The ashes from the fire she had set when last she slept in the house lay undisturbed in the hearth. The mustiness she had sensed on her last visit had disappeared thanks to the dry heat of the summer and the ample ventilation provided by the many broken windows. After a few gurgles and rattles a steady trickle of brackish water emerged from the kitchen tap and she was relieved to wash her hands and splash her face to remove the grime of her journey.

The few sticks of furniture she had found on her last visit remained dotted around the room – a rickety armchair, a low table, two upright chairs and a dusty sofa. In a corner of the kitchen she found a sturdy wooden crate with slatted sides which she determined would make a crib for Renato. Having clung to her baby for most of the journey, Vicenta was relieved to have somewhere safe to lay him down, even if it was just a box lined with a blanket.

As dusk fell, she found a rag to dust off the furniture and then beat the dust from the sofa.

The cushions were badly faded and worn at the edges, but the stuffing was surprisingly firm. Exhausted, she sat and lifted her feet to stretch out on the sofa and with minutes she had fallen into a deep dreamless sleep.

Renato's hungry cries awoke her some hours later, but he was quickly assuaged once attached to her breast and soon he was gurgling cheerfully. He seemed such a happy and contented child and Vicenta couldn't help wondering what his life would hold; what adversity he would face and, hopefully, what joys he would behold. Surely the fear and oppression that epitomised Franco's new Spain would one day give way to a restoration of justice and freedom from which all Spaniards would emerge stronger, wiser and more eager to defend. She only hoped that she would survive to see Renato enjoy such liberty and fulfill his destiny – whatever that may be.

The first faint glow of morning was just beginning to emerge when Vicenta was disturbed by a frantic banging on the front door of the house. Thoughtfully, she had wedged one of the chairs behind the door before falling asleep and now she could see the chair chattering against the rough stone floor under the strain of someone pushing against the door. Her first thought was to grab Renato and clutch him close to her chest.

'Go away, whoever you are,' she yelled, almost screaming in panic.

A voice boomed out from the other side of the

door. 'Vicenta is that you? It's Isobel.'

Vicenta immediately calmed at the sound of her sister's voice and stepped over to remove the chair. For a few brief moments the sisters stood in disbelieving silence before Isobel moved forward to embrace Vicenta. It was only when she clutched Vicenta in her arms that Isobel realised the baby was between them. She had known that Vicenta was pregnant but still she stood back, aghast.

'Vicenta,' she shrieked, 'is this your child?'

Pushing back the blanket to reveal the baby's face, Vicenta turned his body toward Isobel and said, 'Renato, meet your aunt Isobel.'

Isobel took the baby in her arms and cuddled him close, caressing his face with her finger. 'When... when was he born? When did you get here?'

'Just five days ago. We arrived here yesterday evening,' Vicenta answered. 'How did you know I was here?'

'One of the old women at the washhouse said she had seen someone enter the house last night. I was worried it might be robbers – not that there's anything here worth stealing, but I had to come over and check. I can't believe it's you. But what on earth brings you back here now? Nothing has changed here since you left and you must know it will be dangerous if you are discovered.'

'Sit down, Isobel, and I will explain.'

For the next hour Isobel sat rapt as Vicenta detailed the events that had taken place in Alicante. She gasped in horror when Vicenta told how the nuns at the hospital had tried to deceive her into believing her baby had died. Isobel sat open-mouthed as Vicenta explained how they had effectively kidnapped Renato from the hospital.

'I don't believe it,' Isobel said. 'How could anyone, let alone a Christian nun, contemplate something so evil?'

'I'm sorry to say, Isobel, that this is the way things are in Spain. The Church is all too willing to act hand in glove with new dictatorship. To them, I was seen as an unfit person to raise a child. Not just because I was alone, without the father, but because I was seen as a subversive, a leftist. They would have given my baby to supporters of the new regime confident that they would bring him up to be a good fascist.'

At the mention of the child's father, Isobel asked dolefully, 'Is there any news of Eduardo?'

'None.'

'You don't think he's…?'

'Please, Isobel don't say it. Oh, I know it's a possibility, but I can't allow myself to think it.'

Isobel lowered her eyes. She could see the determination in Vicenta's face, but she couldn't help thinking that after so long without any news or information whatsoever, her sister was clutching at straws.

'So now you are back here in Benimarta, but I don't understand. How do you plan to survive?'

Vicenta placed Renato in his makeshift crib then sat at Isobel's side and began to explain. When she had finished she could tell from the look of incredulity on Isobel's face that she had serious misgivings about what lay ahead.

'Will you help me?' Vicenta said.

'You know I would do anything to help you, Vicenta, but are you sure? It's just so...'

'Risky, I know, but it's the only way I can think of to keep Renato safe. My main concern is that you should not put yourself in peril, so all I ask is that you pass on the message, nothing more. If it all goes wrong then at least you will know the truth. But you must promise me that whatever happens you will not try to intervene.'

With a fearful sadness etched in her voice, Isobel said, 'I promise.'

Later that afternoon the door to the old house burst open and flew back on its ancient hinges sending a cloud of dust billowing in the sunlight that permeated the room through the west facing windows. Vicenta stood at the sink in the kitchen rinsing through a square of toweling nappy she had just changed and then wringing it out by twisting it in her hands. She had been expecting the visitor, but even so she jumped in surprise at the abrupt entrance and turned to face him.

'So it's true,' he said gruffly, 'the filthy whore has returned.'

Vicenta caught her breath and swallowed hard forcing herself to take a couple of steps forward and advance toward him. Silhouetted against the open door, she could easily recognise the bulky frame of her visitor, the wild wiry hair and the head that appeared too small for the mass of his body. And exaggerated in the shadow she saw the distortion in the symmetry of his profile caused by a lop-sided set of ear lobes, one much more pronounced than the other.

'Yes, I'm back,' she said, forcing every sinew to subdue the fear and loathing she felt and trying to sound determined and resolute.

With a mocking sneer the man spoke again, 'I thought we'd seen the last of you. What makes you think you are welcome here?'

'I have nowhere else to go.'

'I'd have thought anywhere would be better and safer than here, given your circumstances.'

'My circumstances?'

'Do I really need to spell it out?' He fingered his disfigured earlobe. 'You're the wife of a known subversive, a leftist, a political agitator. I could have you arrested for that alone; imprisoned, incarcerated. With any luck, we might get rid of you permanently. Which reminds me, is there any news of that husband of yours? Last I heard you'd gone off to look for him in Alicante.'

Vicenta resisted the temptation to spit in his face, gouge his eyes out – or worse. Instead she simply lowered her eyes and shook her head almost imperceptibly.

'No?' he said. 'Didn't think so. Thousands have died in those prison camps from what I hear. If the typhoid didn't get him he probably starved to death. Or perhaps he was executed; after all, he was deemed an enemy of the state. Whatever happened, he probably got what he deserved.' His mouth distorted to a thin sneering smile.

Vicenta so wanted to attack him; tell him that Eduardo had been wrongly accused; that he had been denounced for no other reason than jealousy and greed; that Eduardo was twice the man this evil apology for a human being would ever be. But instead she bit her lip and remained silent.

Juan-Martin Garcia was enjoying Vicenta's discomfort, glowering intently as if contemplating how he might exact his revenge on this feeble excuse for a woman.

'You know,' he said at last, 'I quite enjoyed our last encounter.' He took a step forward then turned to shove the door closed. 'Perhaps we could carry on where we left off. Only this time,' he fingered his earlobe once again, 'perhaps you might be more willing to oblige. I reckon you owe me.'

He took another step forward and Vicenta cringed, folding her arms across her chest, staring straight into his face and grimacing.

I'd rather die, she was about to say when the tense silence was interrupted by a barely audible whimper from Renato lying in his crib on the floor behind the sofa. The whimper quickly increased in volume to a piercing bawl.

Instinctively Vicenta stepped back behind the sofa, lifted her baby from the crib and clutched him tightly to her chest.

Suddenly bemused, Garcia stopped in his tracks before he regained his composure and curled his lips scornfully.

'Well, well, well,' he said, 'I see you have not come alone. And whose little bastard have we here?'

Vicenta tensed and swallowed hard. Her breathing was rapid and she could feel her heart pounding in her chest. She increased her already vice-like protective grip on Renato and then spoke in a faltering voice.

'He's yours Juan-Martin. You are the father of this child.'

The shock on his face was plainly visible as his mouth gaped and his eyes widened. Bewilderment was quickly replaced by rage as a purple hue transformed his swarthy face and his expression disfigured to a look of hostility.

'You're lying you bitch,' he bellowed, outrage etched in his voice.

'It's true, Juan-Martin. I wish to God it weren't, but this is your child, your son. Think about it. It was November when you… when you raped me. It's August now and the boy is just a week old.'

Garcia opened his mouth to speak, but paused

as if confused and contemplating the possibilities.

'It can't be. You're lying,' he said, with less conviction that he would have liked.

'Do you think I don't know my own body?' Vicenta scoffed. 'Do you think I haven't lived through the last nine months loathing the very thought that this baby is the outcome of your base behavior? There were times when I wished the sullied seed within me would die. I even contemplated getting rid of the child, but even the back street butchers have shut up shop since the war. I even thought of suicide. But deep down I knew that though this child was conceived in hatred and violence, it was still my own flesh and blood. And now that he is born I intend to do everything in my power to see that he survives. And if that means forcing you to accept your responsibilities then so be it.'

'Responsibilities?' Garcia said incredulously. 'Do you really think I'm going to accept this child as mine?'

Vicenta now summoned up every last ounce of courage, knowing that this was make or break. Quivering, she stepped forward again and thrust the child toward Garcia, pulling back the blanket to reveal Renato's face.

'Look at him, Juan-Martin. His name is Renato. You can deny it all you want, but the fact is he is your son; your own flesh and blood. He has a life of his own now and like it or not his future depends on you.'

Garcia gazed down at the baby's face, scrunched up and distorted as he continued to bawl. Vicenta looked for signs of emotion on Garcia's face but instead found only a look of bewilderment.

'What... what is it you want of me?' he said quietly.

'You've been married how long? More than ten years and you have no children do you? Until now.'

Garcia erupted, 'Don't you dare bring my wife into this. If you are thinking of telling her about this, then think again. You seem to forget, I have influence in this village. I could have you arrested in a moment and see to it that you disappear permanently. So don't think you are going to blackmail me into accepting responsibility for this child.'

Vicenta gulped another deep breath. 'I'm not trying to blackmail you Juan-Martin. Your wife need never know about Renato, if that is what you want. All I seek is a secure future for myself and Renato here in this village and for that, I need your help – or at least I need to know that you will not stand in my way.'

'Ha! Why the hell should I help you? Why, I might just get you out of the way and keep the child. I might even adopt him. I could say he's an orphan in need of a good home with a family loyal to the government. Yes, that's it. The benevolent Juan-Martin Garcia, pillar of this community, takes pity on a poor orphan child and brings him up as his own son. A neat solution all round, don't you think?'

Still trembling, Vicenta replied, 'I know you too well, Juan-Martin. I thought you might come up with such a plan. It would indeed be a neat solution – you could get rid of me and keep your son. That's what you would want after all, isn't it? To keep your son, your own flesh and blood. But there's a problem.'

'Oh?'

'After you have invested your time and energies in nurturing your son, bringing him up as the apple of your eye, guiding him and molding him in your own likeness with your values and ambitions, he would turn out to despise you; to reject you and everything you stand for.'

Garcia frowned, 'And how do you work that out?'

Vicenta squared her shoulders and looked straight into Garcia's eyes. 'Before I came back here, I stopped off at a firm of lawyers in Benissa. I have left with them a sworn statement of my circumstances, including details of how Renato was conceived. Believe me I have not left out a single detail of the horrible sordid episode. I have added that in the event that I were to disappear and be unable to be a mother to Renato then it would be because you arranged it that way. All this is set out in black and white and unless I am around to stop it, all these details will be revealed to Renato on his eighteenth birthday or before, should anything untoward happen to me.'

Garcia was at first dumbstruck but then recovered his composure to respond with ire. 'What a conniving little bitch you are, Vicenta Ripoll. What exactly is it that you want?'

Slowly, carefully Vicenta outlined her demands. She would be allowed to remain with Renato in Benimarta secure in the knowledge that she would not be arrested or denounced. She wanted simply to be free to live her own life and bring up Renato as her son. She wanted no money or favours from Garcia save to be free of suspicion and discrimination. Garcia would be allowed contact with the child and able to watch him mature, but he would not be acknowledged as Renato's father, at least not before his eighteenth birthday. If, at that time, Renato had grown into a mature adult, and if Garcia so desired, Vicenta would destroy her sworn statement and even acknowledge Garcia as Renato's father without mentioning the circumstances of his conception. Until that time Renato would be told that his father had died during the civil war.

'I'll leave you to think about it, while I feed the child,' Vicenta said before moving to the kitchen.

'Of course there's an easier solution to this problem,' Garcia announced when Vicenta returned.

'Oh, and what's that?'

'I could get rid of both of you.'
'I don't think you would do that, Juan-Martin.'
'And why not?'
'Because Renato is your son.'

PART TWO

CHAPTER FIFTEEN

With the less than snappy slogan "Sol y Playa" Pedro Zaragoza Orts sought to attract visitors from Northern Europe to the village of which he was Mayor. He had already arranged to pump water over a distance of ten miles to meet the demand from the hotels and guest houses that were beginning to emerge around the tiny fishing port of Benidorm. It was mainly the British who responded to Zaragoza's exhortations and with them came the ubiquitous bikini.

Egged on by conservatives and the Catholic Church, who remained central to the government, Franco had banned the bikini. A sight which was commonplace on beaches in the rest of Europe was viewed in Spain as indicative of the growth of liberal ideas and anti-Catholic sentiments.

But in 1953, working on the principle that you cannot stand in the way of progress, Zaragoza authorised the wearing of bikinis on the beaches of Benidorm. There was uproar; Officers of the Guardia Civil scuffled with scantily clad girls and the local archbishop threatened to excommunicate Zaragoza.

Undaunted, Zaragoza set off early one morning on his Vespa motor scooter heading for Madrid and seeking an audience with the Generalissimo himself. Nine hours later, with a grimy face and his clothes spattered in motor oil, Zaragoza met Franco personally. The patronage, not only of El Caudillo, but also of his wife, Carmen Polo, was secured. The excommunication process was dropped and the bikini stayed.

Symbolically at least, it was seen by some people as a defining moment. Tourists had out-faced the Catholic Church, and they brought with them, not just money, but the fresh air of democracy and the seeds of change.

Such progress was hard to discern in Benimarta where life continued pretty much unchanged from the early years of Franco's victory. Unemployment was rife and economic progress had stalled. Food remained in short supply with many essential items only available through the flourishing black market. There were rumblings of discontent, but Franco's hold on power had been strengthened by the outbreak of the Cold War and Spain's strategic position in the Mediterranean. The country's status as a bulwark against the further spread of communism helped secure economic support from the USA in exchange for the presence on Spanish soil of American air and naval bases. Membership of NATO followed and Franco even opened talks to join the newly formed European Economic Community, though these failed when the rest of the EEC members refused to negotiate with the Spanish dictator.

Though the Falange had been renamed Movimiento Nacional, Spain remained an anachronism. Franco insisted on retaining power, political opponents continued to be executed, political parties were banned and women's suffrage was non-existent. Indeed, women remained second class citizens requiring their husbands' permission to take a job, open a bank account or travel any significant distance. And on becoming married, a woman would forfeit control of all her property and anything she came to own during the marriage. Divorce was outlawed and contraception was illegal.

Reny gulped down the last of the puchero Vicenta had prepared, not minding the grease floating in blobs on the watery broth flavoured with nothing more than a few vegetables and a couple of meat bones. Despite the paucity of his diet he was a strapping lad approaching five foot eight as his seventeenth birthday drew near. His straight dark hair was greased and swept back at the sides then pushed forward at the front to form a quiff in the style of an American singer called Elvis Presley whose picture Reny had seen in a magazine.

Barely a day went by without Vicenta reflecting on the past. The old house had seen some repairs thanks to a little help from a few friends in the village who had been made aware that Vicenta was no longer "persona non grata". Even Francisco, Isobel's husband, had lent a begrudging hand. At least now the roof was watertight and the broken windows had new glass. The first floor bedrooms were still out of commission as the staircase remained unsafe, but Vicenta had arranged a screened off section of the main living room to form a bedroom for Reny. Vicenta herself still slept on the old sofa and an old laundry room had been fitted with a toilet and makeshift shower. It was all very basic, but given the hardships facing most people in the village, Vicenta was content.

Maite had visited occasionally, travelling in Ramón's truck which was generally loaded with bits of furniture and building materials that he thought might be of use. Ramón, who had never married, was always thoughtful and attentive though he never expressed his feelings beyond genuine concern for Vicenta's welfare and an interest in Reny's progress.

Reny had performed well at school. He was not exactly a model pupil and his teachers had commented more than once that he was inclined to be argumentative in class. Vicenta always promised to curb his quarrelsome inclinations though secretly she was pleased he had a mind of his own. Indeed it was something she had encouraged as a counterbalance to the doctrinaire education prescribed by the state and overseen by the local priest which saw boys and girls taught separately and quite differently. There had also been frowns of disapproval when Reny occasionally lapsed into speaking Valenciano instead of the Castiliano which had been deemed the only acceptable language of Spain. Again this was something Vicenta had encouraged at home as one of the few ways she could rebel against the dictates of the State. Since most of the villagers did exactly the same, she knew her defiance was unlikely to attract attention.

When he finished the meal Reny wiped his mouth and stood to leave.

'Where are you going?' Vicenta asked.

'I'm meeting Uncle Juan-Martin,' Reny replied. 'He has some tomatoes that are almost finished and he wants me to help him pull the plants. He's promised me a box if I help him. They'll mostly be green, but they'll ripen if you put them on the windowsill.'

It always rankled that Reny called him Uncle Juan-Martin. It was something Garcia had suggested without Vicenta's approval when Reny was much younger. She had made it plain that Garcia was not his real uncle, but she had not felt able to forbid the boy using the sobriquet. The fact was Garcia had befriended the boy, taking him hunting and showing him the rudiments of farming. He had even taught Reny how to operate a mula mechanica and allowed him to drive the contraption when he took produce to market. Reny seemed happy in Garcia's company and, so far as Vicenta could discern, Garcia had never attempted to make more of the relationship. Reluctantly Vicenta even accepted that without Garcia's help, or at least his compliance, she would have struggled to put food on the table. Above all, Vicenta was grateful for the fact that Garcia had stuck to his end of the bargain and kept his distance from her.

However, one problem loomed on the horizon. Garcia had hinted to Reny that he might support him so that he could continue his education at the university in Valencia. Reny was excited at the prospect, but Vicenta knew that higher education was the preserve of middle class, right wing conservatives. She did not wish to jeopardise his future by denying him the opportunity to go to university, but she feared that, ensconced in such an environment and no doubt indoctrinated by the Catholics who controlled the curricula, she might lose him to the very forces she had railed against for most of her life. More than anything, she knew that Reny's eighteenth birthday was not far away and she was concerned that Garcia might be manoeuvring himself into a position where she would be forced to acknowledge his paternity – something she dreaded above all else. This was made all the more possible since Garcia's wife had died from breast cancer the year before.

'Don't you have homework to do?' Vicenta called out to Reny's back.

'I'll do it later,' he said as he skipped out of the house.

Reny returned two hours later, breathless and excited.

'You should have seen it Mama; it was chaos. A tourist bus from Benidorm had taken a wrong turn in the village and ended up in Calle Denia. You know how narrow it is and the bus got trapped at the dogleg half way down. It couldn't go forward or backward so it was stuck there for nearly forty minutes. You should have seen the faces of the tourists when they were forced to get off. They were mainly English, I think, and there were two girls in bikini tops. Honestly Mama, I've never seen such a sight. I talked to one of the girls and she seemed very friendly, not the least bit embarrassed. She wasn't like any of the local girls I've met, but I don't think she understood much that I said.'

Vicenta frowned. 'And what did she say to you?'

'She asked me if I'd ever been to Benidorm, I think.'

'And what did you say?'

'I told her I'd never been there. Do you think we could go one day? I love to see what it's like – it sounds so… different.'

'Different, you say? Is that the place or the girls you are talking about?'

Reny flushed. 'Well… both I suppose.'

'So what happened to the bus?'

'The bus… oh well, after half an hour Uncle Juan-Martin came on his tractor and they towed it out backwards. I helped some of the villagers push it from the front, but even so it scraped along the walls and the front mudguard was ripped off. But it was okay to drive, so the tourists just got back on and it left. To think though, Mama, tourists in our little village.'

'Tourists indeed. Whatever next?'

The answer to Vicenta's question came clear a few weeks later when an estate agent's board appeared outside an old village house just off the main square in Calle San Cosme. The place had been empty and derelict for years, but it sold in a matter of days and before long, refurbishment began. A mountain of building materials appeared outside the house and an army of local tradesmen, some of whom had not worked for a decade or more, set about transforming the place. Villagers gathered to watch as an avocado bathroom suite was shoehorned through the front door. New wooden cupboards arrived for the kitchen with formica worktops and a stainless steel sink. There was even a white, upright refrigerator. One day a large van arrived with a logo on the side that read: "Lewis's of Manchester." Curtains, carpets, light fittings and furniture were unloaded under the watchful eye of the neighbours some of whom gasped in amazement at the sight of a chromium framed dining table with a red plastic top and four matching chairs.

Word spread that the new occupants had arrived late one night in a brand new Ford Anglia 105E Deluxe. It was spearmint green with a white roof and white wall tyres and attracted an admiring group of young boys, Reny included, anxious to peer through the windows to see the red leather seats, the dashboard radio, and the white plastic steering wheel.

Curtains twitched as Alan and Deborah Wright of Didsbury in south Manchester strode hand in hand in the direction of the village square late the next morning, heading for Bar Rincon. Their arrival was greeted with startled silence quickly followed by a hubbub of chattering as the locals assessed the two foreigners who looked completely out of place amongst the drably dressed regulars.

'You should have seen them,' Isobel said to Vicenta later that afternoon, babbling in excitement. 'He looked so smart in a dark blue blazer with shiny brass buttons and a pair of baggy pleated trousers. He had a pair of those two tone brogue shoes, you know, like Fred Astaire wears, and one of those bright silk things, a cravat I think it's called, round his neck. And he smoked a pipe.'

'I don't suppose you noticed the colour of his socks,' Vicenta asked, poking fun at her sister.

Isobel paused as if to think. 'You're teasing me,'

Isobel replied before pressing on undeterred. 'Oh, but you should have seen her; so sleek and elegant. She had one of those knee length full taffeta skirts with box pleats. It was beige and pulled in at the waist by a tiny belt – I've never seen such a slim waistline. And she must have been wearing one of those bullet bras – it made her breasts look like... well, like pointed cones. She had a little red polka dot handkerchief tied round the neck of her white blouse. And her hair, it was cropped like a boy's hair with a short fringe. I tell you, Vicenta, she looked just like Audrey Hepburn in Roman Holiday.'

'And what else, did you find out about our visitors?' Vicenta asked with a hint of sarcasm which Isobel failed to notice.

'Well, he's a car salesman from England and she works as a secretary. Apparently they've bought the old house in Calle San Cosme as a holiday home. They'll be visiting two or three times a year. Can you imagine that – a home just for holidays? They must be very rich, I think, because they only stayed in Bar Rincon for half an hour and had a couple of drinks and when they went he left a tip of fifty pesetas. Imagine that, fifty pesetas, that's a day's pay in this village – if you can find work that is.'

The arrival of Benimarta's first foreign owners prompted a fierce debate in the village. There were those who viewed these interlopers as a threat, bringing with them strange ideas and outrageous behaviour that would inevitably corrupt impressionable young people. Others were more sanguine, seeing the foreigners as a source of work and extra income. There were others still who didn't care much one way or the other, but who were all too willing to take advantage of the opportunity to sell an old house that previously had no value and which had stood empty for years.

Within weeks of the Wright's arrival, four more "Se Vende" boards appeared in the village and the spirit of free enterprise blossomed. Jose Alvaro, the owner of Bar Rincon, had signs painted in imperfect English and planted on the main approaches to the village. Silvestre Batista a local vine grower somehow persuaded coach drivers to interrupt their trips for a short stop at his dusty old bodega on the edge of the village. And on spotting the coaches, other locals rushed out to sell all manner of homespun products. Spain's burgeoning tourist economy had well and truly arrived in Benimarta and even the ruling syndicate seemed unable, or unwilling, to stop it.

Two months after the arrival of Benimarta's first foreign invaders, Vicenta received a visit from Maximo Ballester the former Mayor of Benimarta and Eduardo's cousin. It wasn't the first time Vicenta had seen him since her return, in fact they had met on several occasions, but he had always seemed anxious to keep his distance. It was as if he was carrying a burden of guilt for having cooperated with the Falange in the immediate aftermath of the war and remaining silent as the people of the village were cowed by the repressive forces of Franco's new order. Perhaps because of this he had never once asked Vicenta about Eduardo. Now, however, things were at last beginning to change. After years of stagnation, crippling inflation and mass migration from rural areas, Spain was virtually bankrupt and the economy was on its knees. So dire was the situation that Franco, who once dreamed of a great African empire, had been forced to grant independence to Spanish Morocco. An ageing Franco was forced to abandon the dogmatic forces of the Falange and hand over the management of the economy, and to some extent the government, to a group of expert technocrats. This was not the start of liberalisation or democratisation, but even the Catholic technocrats of Opus Dei recognised that continued subjugation and high levels of corruption were holding back economic development and growth. Subtle as these changes were, people became emboldened, less willing to conform and more willing to speak their minds.

Perhaps it was this new self confidence that led Maximo Ballester to Vicenta's door, expressing his regret at Eduardo's disappearance.

'What do you suppose happened to him?' he

tentatively enquired.

'I really don't know,' Vicenta said. 'Perhaps I will never know.'

'Do you think he's...' He paused and changed tack. 'He might still be alive?'

'After all this time, I doubt that very much, but still... deep inside there's a part of me that clings to a faint hope. If I ever lost that, I doubt I could survive.' Vicenta took a deep breath and swallowed hard to hold back the tears that were welling in her eyes. 'But you didn't come here just to ask about Eduardo after all this time.'

Maximo shifted his eyes away from Vicenta as if not wanting to witness her anguish. Nervously he spoke again. 'You are right, but my reason for coming does have something to do with Eduardo.' He turned his head to see the look of surprise on her face.

'There's something you need to know, Vicenta; something others would not want you to know.'

'Oh,' Vicenta said with a sense of hopeful curiosity.

'As I said, it is not about Eduardo himself but... well, it's about Casa Pepita.'

'What about Casa Pepita?'

'You know it's been empty these last ten years since the Guardia Civil moved out to the new headquarters in Jalon? They left it in a bit of a state by all accounts.'

'I've seen that for myself,' Vicenta said abruptly.

'Last year the government issued a decree dealing with abandoned property. It's one of the measures they've introduced to get the economy moving. You see after the war there was so much property left unoccupied and untended when people died, moved away or just disappeared. More often than not the original ownership was never registered and as the owners cannot be traced the property is just sitting there going to rack and ruin. Now the government wants to bring it back into use.'

Vicenta was growing impatient. 'So what has this to do with Casa Pepita?'

'Well, under the government's decree anyone who can show they have the intention, and the funding, to bring one of these properties back into use, can make a claim to take ownership the property. If the claim is allowed to stand, and there is no counter claim, then an order will be granted and they can register themselves as the new owners and take it over.'

With a growing sense of unease, Vicenta began to see where the conversation was heading.

'And someone has made such a claim in respect of Casa Pepita?' she asked.

'I'm sorry, but yes. An official claim was lodged ten weeks ago alongside plans to convert it into a guest house.'

Vicenta blanched. 'But this can't be right. Casa Pepita belongs to Eduardo and I know his ownership was properly registered. I won't let this happen. There must be something I can do to stop this. Why haven't I been told before now?'

Maximo looked shamefaced. 'I'm sorry, Vicenta, but I... I wasn't sure what to do and I'm not sure there is anything you can do in any case.'

'What do you mean, nothing I can do? I must have some rights. There must be a way to stop this happening.'

'Perhaps, but it's going to be difficult and time is very short.'

'Short? What do you mean?'

'As I said the claim was lodged ten weeks ago. A notice was supposedly posted on the wall of Casa Pepita, but it was deliberately hidden away from view and in any event it probably blew away after a couple of days. Another notice was pinned on the board in the town hall at the same time, but I know for a fact it was hidden away amongst lots of other notices so that no one would see it. And anyway, who goes in the town hall these days apart from syndicate members and their functionaries? The notice period expires in two weeks and then the provincial court in Alicante will almost certainly grant the order.'

Vicenta's face set as if in stone, her eyes flared and she spoke through gritted teeth. 'I will not allow this to happen,' she said as she started pacing the room. 'There must be a way to stop it.'

Maximo shuddered in the face of Vicenta's despair. He understood the anger and frustration she must be feeling, but he could also sense her determination. He did not want to raise false hope for he knew the situation was desperate, but out of loyalty to his cousin he also knew he must try to help.

'Sit down, Vicenta, and let's talk this through. It may be difficult, but let's see what might be done.'

Vicenta wanted to race up the street and bash on the doors of the town hall until someone listened and stopped this outrage. Reluctantly, however, she was persuaded to sit on the sofa that was her bed whilst Maximo drew up a straight backed chair to sit opposite.

'You say there are papers?'

Suddenly Vicenta's eyed widened. 'Yes… Yes there's an escritura and a copy of the registration document from the land registry. And I think there's a copy of Julio's will – he left everything to Eduardo his only child.'

'And do you have these documents?'

Vicenta's thoughts returned to last time she saw Eduardo and his final words. Instinctively she clutched her throat to feel the thin gold ring attached to a cord around her neck and next to it the small brass key.

'No, but I know where they are.'

'And you can get them?'

'I will if I have to,' she said, her jaw set in resolve.

Maximo could sense Vicenta's tenacity, but he

knew he must keep her hopes in check.

'I'm sorry to tell you Vicenta, but there's another problem. Even if you had the documents, the only person who could oppose the claim would be Eduardo himself.'

'But Eduardo's not here and there's no proof he is dead.'

'I understand that but, after an absence of more than seventeen years the courts are likely to presume he is dead. It's been done before.'

'But I'm his wife. I'll contest the claim myself.'

Maximo hooded his eyes. 'I think you know as well as I do, Vicenta, women have very few rights in respect of property and without documentary proof that the house has passed to you, I doubt the courts would accept any claim you make. In fact, in Eduardo's absence and the presumption that he is dead, the only person who might legitimately make a counter claim would be a male heir or a male relative.'

Vicenta suddenly perked up. 'But you're his cousin aren't you Maximo?'

'You're right of course, but I'm Eduardo's cousin on his mother's side – my mother was the sister of Julio's wife, Pepita. As such, I am not regarded as a male blood relative in the eyes of the law.'

Vicenta sank back in the sofa and bowed her head as if in resignation though in fact her mind was buzzing with a mixture of anger and apprehension. Maximo sat in silence sharing her despondency.

'You haven't told me who has made this outrageous claim,' Vicenta said, looking up to catch Maximo as he averted his eyes.

'It is Juan-Martin Garcia.'

Vicenta knew exactly what she had to do.

Even at two in the morning the humidity was oppressive and Vicenta was sweating profusely as she approached Casa Pepita. A thin crescent moon did little to illuminate the dark streets of Benimarta which slumbered in silence against a background of crickets chirping in the distant campo. She knew better than to approach the house via the front gates. Apart from being highly visible, the gates were locked and chained with a heavy padlock. Instead she slipped down the back alleys, thankfully devoid of street lights, to a small gate in the walled garden at the rear of the house. In her time at the house this gate had never been locked and she just hoped nothing had changed. She paused at the corner of the garden wall feeling her pulse quicken. The rear of the house was overlooked by the back rooms of a row of houses that fronted onto Calle Dalt. All the houses appeared to be cast in total darkness with the exception of a dim light emitting from the louvred shutters of a bedroom window in the centre of the row.

She shuffled slowly along the wall feeling her way to the recessed gate. She paused again to catch her breath and felt for the cast iron ring that turned the latch on the inside of the solid wooden gate. Grabbing it with both hands she began to twist the ring, but it refused to budge. For a moment she thought of abandoning her mission, but quickly realised that was not an option. She took a deep breath, lifted the ring again and used the palms of both hands to rotate it anti-clockwise. Again it refused to move until suddenly, and with a loud clank, the latch on the inside of the gate lifted from its catch. Vicenta froze and glanced at the overlooking houses waiting a minute or so to check they remained in darkness. Now her head was pounding and she gulped another deep breath. Satisfied that no one had heard the noise from the latch, she leant her shoulder against the gate and began to push. There was movement, just an inch or two, and then the gate became fast as it dragged along the paved footpath within. She realised the gate must have sagged on its hinges and took hold of the ring latch once again, this time lifting as she pushed. Gradually the gate moved inwards until there was a space of a foot or so through which she was able to squeeze, closing the gate behind her.

Ahead, at the end of a terracotta pathway she could just make out the outline of Casa Pepita with its twin chimney stacks rising above the apex of the roof. Much of the pathway was overgrown with vegetation, but it did not inhibit her progress as she picked her way toward the rear of the house. A waft of warm air filled her nostrils with the fragrance of night scented jasmine that caused her to remember the long summer evenings she had spent in the garden with Eduardo in the days when it was neatly tended and full of exotic plants.

She reached the rear wall of the house and found the solid wooden door that in her time was always locked and bolted on the inside. A hefty shove confirmed this was still the case. Carefully and with her back to the wall she shuffled sideways always keeping an eye on the houses overlooking the garden.

She reached the second of three rear windows all covered with hinged wooden shutters. She knew they were held fast with a small brass swivel latch located on the inside. Taking the heavy screwdriver from her trouser pocket she wedged it between the two shutters and banged it firmly with the heel of her right hand. Levering the screwdriver to one side, she was worried that the inner catch would break with a crack, but the frame had rotted over the years and it gave way almost silently allowing Vicenta to open the shutters outwards. The glazed windows behind were equally dilapidated and easily prised open. After climbing inside, Vicenta pulled the shutters together then struck a match to light a small length of wax candle. She was in the formal dining room that had once housed a long oak table with chairs for twelve. Now the space was empty save for a couple of wooden crates and a small pile of logs to the side of the ornate fire place. The paintings that had once graced the walls were long gone, leaving dusty outlines on the panelled walls. Bare wires dangled from holes where once there had been a matching set of four elaborate wall lamps. Her destination, the library, lay ahead through a recessed door at the far end of the room. As she picked her way slowly in that direction her footsteps disturbed flecks of dust that floated in the air highlighted by the flickering light of the candle.

The door to the library was already ajar and moved silently on its hinges allowing Vicenta to enter. Focusing on the marble fireplace at the far end of the room, she failed to notice the fallen bookcase at her feet. Her toe stubbed against the side of the shelf and she fell forward landing heavily on her front and banging her elbow on the floor. The candle fell from her grip and she was suddenly plunged into total darkness. She gulped a breath and forced herself to swallow hard as she adjusted her body to a kneeling position and began to fumble across the floor feeling for the candle. It was then she realised the floor was littered with old books that must have tumbled from the fallen bookcase. Padding and patting the floor, she succeeded only in raising a cloud of dust that almost choked her as she inhaled. She stopped floundering and felt for the matches in her pocket. Striking a light, she found the candle a few feet in front of her and set it aflame. Now she could see that all the freestanding bookcases had been toppled forward, their contents strewn across the floor in what appeared to be a deliberate act of vandalism. Anxiously she moved her gaze to the fireplace, relieved to see that the bookcases on either side were still in place, fixed to the walls. The books they once contained had been thrust to the floor and lay in irregular piles with pages open and spines split. But the shelving was still in place. What was it Eduardo had said? The third shelf of the left hand bookcase. Placing the candle on the shelf Vicenta studied the back panel, looking for a handle or something to grip. She saw nothing but a flat piece of wood. Pressing gently with the palms of her hands she attempted to slide the panel to the left, away from the chimney breast. It moved almost imperceptibly, but lifted in the grooved slots at the top and bottom and stuck fast. She tried again, this time maintaining an even pressure and slowly the panel slid away to reveal a small metal door with a tiny keyhole. With a growing sense of apprehension she took the key from the cord around her neck and placed it in the lock, turning it gently to feel the latch slide away. She lifted the candle from the shelf and peered inside the space. With utter relief she viewed the single bundle of papers tied together by a length of tape, knotted at the top.

She placed the bundle under her arm then retraced her steps through the cluttered library into the empty dining room, out through the window, down the weed infested pathway and out through the gate which she pulled shut behind her.

The church bell struck three muffled chimes as she weaved her way back through the empty streets, peering around every corner to check there was no one about. She was on the last leg, still clutching the bundle of papers beneath her arm, when a figure emerged from a doorway on the left hand side of the street. Instinctively she thrust her body against the adjacent wall hoping she would not be noticed. The figure paused, struck a match and lit a cigarette then coughed and spat out a gobbet phlegm before shuffling off in the opposite direction.

Panting rapidly and damp with sweat Vicenta finally reached her own house. Reny was still sleeping soundly in his screened-off bedroom space. She pulled back a chair and sat at the small dining table in the middle of the room. By candlelight, she carefully untied the knot in the tape and began leafing through the papers. The escritura (deeds) for Casa Pepita comprised twelve pages stitched together with pink ribbon. Vicenta quickly turned to the last page to see the signature of Eduardo's father, Julio, above an official Notary's rubber stamp and the date 1927. Beneath the escritura she found several architects' drawings of the house and a collection of bills which she pushed to one side. The next document was hand written in copperplate script and clearly headed "Testamento de Julio Ripoll." In the dim light it was difficult for her to read the precise contents, but she could easily recognise Julio's signature on the final page alongside that of an abogado whose name she could not decipher. It was dated April 1926. There was no will for Eduardo though she was not sure he had ever made one. The final document bore the official logo of the Ministerio de Hacienda and was headed "Registro Catastral." It showed the registration of Casa Pepita together with its plot and the size of the construction.

Everything Vicenta hoped for and needed was there. Now her next step was clear. She always knew this day would come, but the prospect filled her with dread and the very thought of it caused her heart to flutter. However, she knew it was something she could not avoid or defer.

CHAPTER SIXTEEN

The village school had long since closed and it would be a further month before it opened its doors again. In the relentless heat of late summer it was customary for the young people of the village to stay up late. Sleep was difficult and it seemed pointless to retire early only to curse the climate and dampen the bedclothes. Vicenta was used to this and so Reny's absence at two in the morning was unremarkable. So, too, was the fact that at ten in the morning he lay motionless in his bed, oblivious to the deliberate rattling of pans and clanking of plates with which Vicenta tried to rouse him. He shuffled and turned issuing a loud yawn that Vicenta took as her cue.

'Ah, so you're awake at last, sleepyhead. Your breakfast is ready. Hurry now, wash your face and clean your teeth. I have something to tell you.'

Breakfast was a day old bocadillo, sliced, drizzled with olive oil and smeared with the juice of a cut tomato. As Reny sat at the table, Vicenta could not resist the temptation to straighten his uncombed hair. He retaliated by raising a hand to ruffle it again with a tut of irritation.

'You said you had something to tell me,' he said, crunching the bocadillo and washing it down with a swig of strong coffee.

'Finish your breakfast first.'

Vicenta took a seat on the opposite side of the table and gazed at Reny as he continued to eat and drink. Times had been tough, though no tougher than for most of her neighbours. Through it all she had marvelled at Reny's gradual development from infant to boy to teenager and now to the verge of manhood. He had never been a demonstrative child, but a smile, a touch or an occasional hug reinforced the bond Vicenta knew existed between them. True he was no angel, but she liked his rebellious streak and he seemed, instinctively, to know where to call a halt without the need for rancour or recrimination. Now, however, she was about to test his character in a way that no child ought reasonably to endure. She had been rehearsing her words all night trying to convince herself he would understand and forgive. Now, as she looked into his eyes, she paled at the consequences of what she was about to do.

'Well,' Reny said, pushing his coffee cup to one side.

Vicenta took a deep breath and exhaled, puffing her cheeks and swallowing hard. She caught his eyes and he seemed to lock on to her gaze as she began to speak.

'Reny, what I am about to tell you will affect you for the rest of your life; it will undermine much of what you have learned and believed to this point in your life and it will cause you to question my behaviour and the decisions I have taken. I ask only that you listen to what I have to say, always remembering that the things I have done have always been with you in mind – as a way of securing your future and ensuring that I have been at your side as a mother and with a mother's love.'

Reny's brow creased in puzzlement, but still he held her gaze.

Vicenta took encouragement from his silence. She unfolded the paper she had clutched in her hand and pressed it flat to the table.

'This letter was written in 1940, just a few days after you were born. It was always my intention that you would read it one day, perhaps when you were a little older. But circumstances have occurred that force me to show it to you now. I'll explain more about that later, but for now I'd like you to read it in full without forming any opinions or asking any questions until you have reached the end.

Vicenta pushed the paper across the table and stared intently at Reny as he lowered his head to read it.

August 1940
Benissa.

My Dearest Renato,

There are two circumstances in which you may be reading this letter. The first is that you have come of age, in which case I will have achieved my ultimate ambition of guiding you safely through your early years, nurturing your character and personality and enabling you to achieve whatever you may strive for. The second is that, for whatever reason, I have not been able to be at your side as your mother and mentor. I pray that it is the former.

You will have been told that your father died during the civil war that ravaged this country from 1936 until 1939. I must now tell you that this was an untruth – a convenient story to avoid awkward questions that might otherwise arise and for reasons that will become apparent as you read this letter.

The true story begins in the days before you were conceived. Your father, Eduardo, and I were just beginning our lives together when the inglorious civil war came to an end. It was a war that placed father against son, brother against brother, but we were lucky that we survived that time without direct involvement in the conflict. Your father was a well respected journalist and understood the dangers of those times. He was always careful not to appear to support one side or the other. But when the conflict ended and the forces of Fascism emerged triumphant everything changed. The new government engaged in a wholesale purge of all those who were perceived to be a threat to the new regime. People were denounced unfairly, arrested unjustly and imprisoned without trial.

Your father was one such victim and he was arrested and imprisoned in Benimarta on 22nd November 1939. It was three days before I was able to see him in prison; he was disheartened and reconciled to his fate, but he was not afraid.

On the way home from visiting Eduardo I was attacked in the street, beaten and violently raped. When, a few days later, I recovered from this ordeal, I tried to see Eduardo again only to be told he had been removed from Benimarta and sent to prison in Alicante. I was distraught, my future in Benimarta was precarious as the wife of an alleged dissident and so I determined I would travel to Alicante to find Eduardo and secure his release.

My time in Alicante was fraught with danger, but I managed to visit the prison in Albatera to which I believed Eduardo had been assigned. By then, the prison had been closed, but I talked to a former guard who described to me the atrocious conditions which the prisoners had endured – many died of disease, starvation, even summary execution. Despite all my efforts, I never found Eduardo. After many months in Alicante I began to imagine Eduardo, like many thousands of others, had died or been killed, but a part of me still refuses to accept this as a reality.

It was on my way to Alicante that I realised I was pregnant. I was determined to continue my journey to try and find Eduardo, but on arriving in the city I had nowhere to stay and no way of supporting myself. It was for this reason I joined the Auxilio Social. I did not support the aims of this organisation or its philosophies, but for all that they gave me a roof over my head, put food on the table and ultimately legitimised my existence by giving me official papers and travel documents.

With no news of Eduardo and no reason to return

to Benimarta, I might well have stayed on in Alicante were it not for the events surrounding your birth. At full term in my pregnancy I was admitted to a maternity ward run by the Auxilio Social and a group of Catholic nuns. Within minutes of your birth you were taken from me by one of the nuns who told me you were unwell and needed special attention. A few hours later the nun and a Mother Superior returned to tell me you had died. It was the worst moment of my life.

Soon after this, I learned that the Catholic nuns had adopted the practice of removing babies from what they deemed "unsuitable mothers" (in my case, the wife of an arrested dissident) under the pretence that the children had died and in order that they could be farmed out for adoption by families loyal to the regime. It was only by chance that I discovered this information and only by good fortune and the help of some loyal friends that I was able to find you and effectively kidnap you from the hospital.

After being deceived into believing you had died, I was overjoyed and vowed there and then that I would do whatever was necessary to secure your future safety and well being. However, I could not remain in Alicante for fear the authorities would find me and take you away again. I thought of moving away to some other town, but with nowhere to live and no means of support, this would have been impracticable. So, as I write this letter my only option is to return to Benimarta and this is what I plan to do. I know this will be fraught with danger – I might easily be denounced and arrested and you might easily be taken away from me again. I am determined not to let this happen.

To return to Benimarta free from the threat of arrest, I need the backing and support of someone in authority who can legitimatise my presence in the village and enable me to live without fear and raise you as my child. Such a person exists in Benimarta – his name is Juan-Martin Garcia and he is a member of the ruling Falange syndicate. But Garcia is no friend of mine, indeed it was this man who unjustly denounced your father and had him imprisoned and then transported to Alicante. But I have a hold over Garcia, or at least I hope I do, for it was this man who raped me that night in Benimarta. My plan is to try and convince Garcia that he is your father and in this way, hoping he believes me, to secure our future. If I am believed, and Garcia agrees to help, I will insist that he is never acknowledged publicly as your father though inevitably he will expect to play a part in your life.

I know this is a perilous venture and by the time you read this letter I might not be around to explain more, in which case my plan will have failed. In whatever circumstances this letter reaches you, I hope and pray you will forgive my lies and deceptions always believing that everything I have done, or tried to do, has been with the single motive of wanting to be your mother and bring you up as my child and the child of your father, Eduardo.

One question will inevitably arise. How can you be sure Eduardo is your true father? In answer all I can say is that I cherish the joyous moment of your conception just two days before Eduardo was arrested. I felt his presence in my body throughout my pregnancy. And from the moment I looked into your eyes, just seconds after you were born, my faith was affirmed.

Please believe me, dear Renato, I love you and always will.

Your mother,
Vicenta Ripoll.

Reny pushed the letter to one side and looked up at his mother. Her eyes were moist and her expression full of anguish. She could only imagine the confusion and distress that must be running through his mind. What she had not imagined was the anger with which he reacted and which distorted his expression to one of outright rage.

'I don't believe this,' Reny burst forth. 'You're saying Uncle Juan-Martin raped you. That you lied to him and told him he was my father and that my father didn't die in the war but was arrested as some kind of dissident.'

'He's not your uncle, I've always told you that,' Vicenta snapped, realising it was not that fact that was the cause of Reny's indignation. She reached across the table to hold his hand, but he withdrew, sitting upright against the back of his chair.

'I know that,' he retorted, 'but you're now telling me that all this time he has believed I am his son. And now you say you lied to him, and to me. How can I believe anything you say?'

Vicenta was overwrought. She knew Reny would be upset and she had prepared to ease his confusion and explain more, but confronted by his anger she began to question whether she had been right to reveal the truth at this time and in this way. Her anxiety was heightened when Reny suddenly jerked upright, flinging his chair to the ground and striding intently toward the door.

'Reny, where are you going? You don't understand. Times were very different then. Everything I did was for you. Please let me explain.'

Her pleadings fell on deaf ears as Reny departed the house slamming the door behind him and leaving Vicenta distraught.

Could it possibly be that everything she had strived to achieve had come to nothing? Perhaps she had been wrong to expect him to understand. Her deceitful actions had always seemed justified in her mind; motivated by desperation and her determination to hold on to her son. Foolishly she had believed Reny would understand her rationale, but now she realised he had never lived through those times; never known the sheer hopelessness that had driven her to take such extreme steps to protect their future. Now she had just dismantled the foundations upon which Reny had built his life and left him floundering in confusion and anger at being told the unwanted truth. And for what? Just to stop Garcia getting his hands on Casa Pepita. A crumbling pile of stone and rubble was surely not worth the risk of losing her son. A sudden dread made her flinch. Would Reny run to Juan-Martin Garcia? He was, after all, the nearest thing to a father figure Reny had ever known. What lies, what distortions might Garcia evince to turn Reny against her? Might Garcia even convince Reny that he was his true father? The thought was too terrible to bear. Vicenta dropped her head to her arms and wept uncontrollably.

These thoughts and worse pervaded Vicenta's every moment through the rest of the day as she waited for Reny to return. When darkness fell, sleep evaded her as a vision of Garcia's face seeped into her subconscious mind. Mingling with his crazed eyes and a face distorted with perverted pleasure as he thrust his body against hers, Vicenta saw another, more terrifying image; a sneering, smiling Garcia was looking back over his shoulder as he strode into the distance with Reny skipping blithely at his side.

'Francisco found him around midnight last night,' said Isobel pushing a bedraggled Reny through the door. His face was drawn and pale and he lowered his bloodshot eyes to the floor as Vicenta rushed to hug him. He did not reciprocate Vicenta's over exuberant embrace, but when he allowed his head to rest on her shoulder and whispered the words, 'I'm sorry Mama,' her heart leapt.

'He was slumped against the fountain in the

square, drunk, I think, and he'd been sick,' Isobel continued. 'Francisco offered to bring him here, but he was adamant he wouldn't come, so Francisco brought him to our house. He was very confused and gabbling about all kinds of things that didn't make sense. After Francisco went to bed, I made a pot of coffee and... well, we've been up all night and had a real heart to heart. I think he understands things a little better now, but you still have some explaining to do – to me as well as to Reny.'

'I know,' Vicenta said, releasing Reny from her vice-like clinch. 'But for now I think he needs some sleep.' She stepped over to Isobel and hugged her gently, kissing her cheek. 'Thank you sister,' she said. 'I've been frantic with worry. I'll explain everything later.'

Though her body was racked with tiredness Vicenta sat beside Reny's bed never loosening her grip on his hand even when she slipped into a fitful sleep of her own.

Refreshed and showered, but with his hair still fighting its own battle for freedom, Reny emerged to sit at the dining table and gulp down a glass of orange juice before chomping ravenously on a bocadillo filled with sliced chorizo.

'You didn't even tell Aunt Isobel that Gracia wasn't my father,' he said at last, carefully nibbling the flesh from the stone of a plump green olive.

'No, I've never told anyone. I created the lie and

I just had to stick with it – until now.'

'Of course, Aunt Isobel knew about how Garcia... how he attacked you. She told me how she nursed you through your injuries afterwards and how you had to leave her house because she would be in trouble for helping you if anyone found out. I never realised things were so bad in those days, but Aunt Isobel has told me all about it. Why didn't you tell me what it was like back then?'

Vicenta looked slightly embarrassed. 'I... I didn't want to burden you with the hatred I have learned to live with. Spain is slowly moving away from those dark days and one day the truth will be told.'

'She told me you bit his ear off when he... when he raped you.'

Vicenta was shocked that he knew about this.

'I...'

'Serves him right I say, the nasty bastard.'

Vicenta didn't hold with swearing, but just this once let it go.

'So you believe what I set out in that letter – about being raped by Garcia?'

'After talking to Aunt Isobel, yes. There's no doubt in my mind.'

'And do you understand why I lied to convince him he was your father?'

'I didn't at first, but now I can see how you had no choice, especially after what happened at the hospital, though I still find it hard to believe that a group of nuns could be so wicked.'

'Believe me, Reny, if I had not lived through it myself, I would never have believed such a thing could have happened. But my biggest regret is not telling you the truth about your father, Eduardo. You do believe he is your father don't you?'

'I know you have misled me about some things, I can see now why you did that, but I don't believe you would lie to me about my father. And anyway, Aunt Isobel says she knew from the first moment she set eyes on me. I'm just surprised Uncle... Garcia was taken in.'

'He believed it because he wanted to, but women have a way of knowing these things.'

'There's one thing I don't understand though. Why did you decide to tell me now after all these years?'

Vicenta reached across the table and took hold of Reny's hand. This time he did not flinch.

'The letter which you read was a safeguard that if anything happened to me, you would one day know the truth. As time has passed I have thought on many occasions that perhaps the truth should stay hidden and you should be left to live your life free of the bitterness and hatred I have learned to live with. But last week something changed. To explain this I need to tell you about my last moments with Eduardo.'

Vicenta released Reny's hand and sat back in her chair gathering her thoughts.

'When I last saw Eduardo he had been in prison here in Benimarta for three days. I saw him in his cell where he had obviously been beaten. He had committed no crime, that much was clear, but in those times all it took was a denunciation from someone in power and you could be arrested – no charges, no trial, nothing. The person who denounced your father was Juan-Martin Garcia.'

'But why would he do such a thing?' Reny asked.

'You may well ask. Before the war Eduardo and Garcia were friends; not close friends and they never shared the same political beliefs, but whereas Eduardo stayed neutral, Garcia joined the Nationalists and fought in the war. I don't think he saw much action, but like many of his compatriots, when Franco's forces won the war they returned home with a sense that the country belonged to them and that those who had opposed them must be weeded out and eradicated.'

'But you said father remained neutral?'

'That's true, never doubt that. But when people like Garcia took over they used their power to suit there own ends, expropriating land and property and lining their own pockets. Garcia was an ordinary man, a farmer, and he owned a small parcel of land on the outskirts of the village. Eduardo was relatively wealthy because he was a professional and he had inherited a house and substantial lands from his father, Julio, who died in 1930. Garcia was jealous – and greedy – he tried to use his new found power to take that property from Eduardo.'

'But surely he couldn't just steal it?'

'Well, possibly not. But when your father was in prison Garcia tried to force him to sign over ownership in return for his release.'

'So why didn't father just do as Garcia wanted if it would have secured his freedom?'

'Your father knew it was not that simple. If he had signed the papers and been released he could, in time, have contested Garcia's ownership. Remember no one knew how long the regime would last. So Garcia needed Eduardo out of the way. That's why Eduardo refused to sign the papers. Then, after Garcia... after he raped me, I tried to see Eduardo again at the prison. But he had been taken away the night before. The guard told me that three men had presented papers in the middle of the night that allegedly consigned Eduardo to prison in Alicante. They took him away in a truck and that's the last I ever heard. And, Reny, you need to know this – Juan-Martin Garcia was one of the three men who took him away.'

Reny looked thoughtful, as if trying to take all this in.

'But you still haven't explained why you have decided to tell me all this now.'

Vicenta swallowed hard and continued.

'You know the grand old house on Calle de

Denia, it's called Casa Pepita?'

'Yes, I know the place. It used to the the headquarters of the Guardia Civil.'

'That's true. But Casa Pepita belongs to your father. I never told you about it because it would raise too many questions and in any event the place is so vast and dilapidated that no one had the money to do anything with it. But all that changed last week when I heard that Garcia had applied for an order to take ownership of the place and convert it into a guest house. His claim is based on the contention that Casa Pepita has been abandoned and that the owner cannot be traced.'

'Can that happen?'

'Under the present law, yes it could. You see even though there is no evidence that your father is dead, after such a long time his death could be presumed in law. As his wife, the law says I have no right to the property. So the only person who could contest Garcia's claim would be a male relative or heir.'

Reny blinked and frowned as the import of the statement hit him.

'So you are saying that I could contest this claim of Garcia's and claim ownership of Casa Pepita? And that's why you decided to tell me all this now?'

'I thought about it very carefully, Reny. I even wondered if it might be best just to stay quiet and let Garcia take over the place. But I just couldn't do that. It would mean that Garcia would achieve by stealth what he failed to do by threatening your father. So you see we have to stop him.'

'But don't we need papers, documents, proof of some kind?'

Vicenta took encouragement from Reny's inquisitiveness.

'Yes, we need papers. The last time I saw Eduardo in the prison, he gave me a key to a secret compartment in the library at Casa Pepita – it was as if he always knew such a moment would come. Two nights ago I crept into Casa Pepita and recovered all the documents – deeds, registrations and a copy of Julio's will. They prove beyond doubt that the house belongs to Eduardo.'

'But if my father is presumed dead, how does that help?'

'In Spanish law, if Eduardo is dead, or presumed dead, then all his property automatically reverts to you as his son.'

'I see,' said Reny, his shoulders slumping under the weight of the revelations.

Vicenta allowed him a moment to recover then pressed on.

'But we have a problem, Reny, or two problems in fact.'

Reny raised his eyebrows. 'Oh?'

'We have only ten days to contest Garcia's claim.'

'And the second problem?'

'We have no way of proving you are Eduardo's

son.'

'Blood testing is a possibility,' said Maximo when he visited Vicenta and Reny the next morning. 'I've made some enquiries and it seems we would need a court order to force Garcia to take the test and in any event the current tests only have a 40% exclusion rate. In other words the tests don't prove who the father actually is, they just show who could not be the father in 40% of cases.'

Vicenta sighed, frustrated at the lack of progress. She knew with absolute certainty that Eduardo was Reny's father and yet she could not find a way to prove it. And then a sudden thought struck her.

'Maximo,' she said, 'we are approaching this from the wrong direction. It is Garcia who is trying to prove that the house has been abandoned and has no rightful owner. If we contest that claim, by stating Reny is the owner by virtue of being Eduardo's son, then surely it will be up to him to prove otherwise. I know he could claim that Reny is his son as he has been led to believe, but then it would be up to him to prove it.'

'I don't know,' Maximo said. 'What you say sounds right, but I'm not an expert in the law.'

'And nor is Garcia,' Vicenta said, her mind churning over the embryo of an idea.

'What's this?' Garcia demanded when he picked up the manilla envelope Vicenta had placed on the table.

His house, near the centre of the village, was cast in semi darkness; the shutters closed to exclude the sunlight and the stifling heat that otherwise would have permeated the building's cool interior. In the gloom Vicenta could just make out Garcia's swarthy face, his brow creased with confusion at the unexpected visit. She had long since set aside the odium she felt toward the man who had assaulted her so brutally, but even with the passage of time and the protection his patronage had afforded, forgiveness was not in her heart. Even so, she knew that what she was about to do would deal the man a devastating blow and rip away everything he had believed for almost eighteen years. A part of her might easily have revelled in revenge exacted at last from the man who had changed the course of her life in so many ways. Yet she had no sense of reprisal; more a feeling of trepidation at what was about to unfold.

'Read it,' she said tersely.

She watched in silence as Garcia ripped open the envelope and began to read its contents. His eyes narrowed and the furrows in his brow deepened as his face grew red with anger.

'This cannot be,' he blurted out at last, throwing the papers onto the table between them. 'The boy is my son, you told me yourself and I have watched over him all these years. Now you claim he is Eduardo's son and heir to his property. This is just a trick to stop me getting my hands on Casa Pepita.'

'You're right. I am doing this to stop you getting hold of Casa Pepita, but it's no trick. You are a fool, Juan-Martin. Renato was never your son. I told you that because it was the only way I could remain in this village in safety. You believed it because you wanted to; because you're a vain blockhead who never fathered children of his own. If things had been left as they were I might have settled for that and remained silent. But you couldn't stop at that, could you? No, even after all this time you are not content with having consigned Eduardo to his almost certain death, now you want to achieve what you always wanted – to take over his land and property. That's why I have told Reny the truth; about his father, about how you tried to force Eduardo to sign over the house and how you raped me. Yes, he knows everything about his "uncle" Juan-Martin Garcia and what's more, he believes it – all of it.'

Garcia was panting rapidly. His face, already flushed, turned crimson and his eyes bulged. He snatched the papers from the table and scrunched them into a ball throwing it toward Vicenta who let it hit her face and fall to the ground, all the time maintaining her steely glare and refusing to flinch.

'I'll contest this,' he bellowed. 'You can say all you want, but the boy is my son. And after what I've done for you and the boy I deserve the house and I'll have it if it's the last thing I do.'

'Fine,' Vicenta said, struggling against the tide of fear rising in her body, causing her stomach to churn and her hands to shake. 'If you still believe Reny is your son, then you'll have to prove it – in court. And I'll be there to give my side of the story – every last gory detail including how you lost half your ear. Of course, you could take a chance and have a blood test, but you'd be wasting your time. You see, I know the truth with absolute certainty. I've known it since the moment Reny was born.'

Garcia's shoulders seemed to sag and his face softened.

'How could you do this to me?' he said quietly. 'After all I've done for you and Reny.'

'Do you really need to ask?' Vicenta said, turning on her heels and striding out of the house.

Two days later Garcia's claim to take over Casa Pepita was withdrawn.

PART THREE

CHAPTER SEVENTEEN

Church bells rang out to mark the beginning of a week long period of official mourning. For many people it turned into a week long fiesta as bottles of cava which had been chilled for several days were finally popped and the celebrations began in earnest. Franco had lingered near to death for weeks and his demise had been wrongly reported on several occasions before the actual event occurred just after midnight on 20th November 1975. Such was the uncertainty about his impending death that for weeks after, one American network regularly started its bulletins with the by-line – "Breaking news, Generalissimo Francisco Franco is *still* dead."

Two days after the death of El Caudillo, Prince Juan Carlos, whom Franco had chosen as his successor in 1969, became king – Spain's first ruling monarch since 1931. Despite being groomed by Franco, Juan Carlos immediately began to dismantle the organs of the dictatorship and implement a transition to democracy. Elections followed in June 1977 and a new Spanish constitution was adopted after a referendum in December 1978. But the transition was not without its problems as the political forces of both the right and left sought to avoid having to deal with the legacy of Francoism. The result was *el pacto de olvido* (the pact of forgetting) which sought to ensure that difficult questions about the past were conveniently set aside for fear of undermining "national reconciliation." It meant that responsibility for the civil war and the repression that followed was not to be placed at the door of any individual or political group. Many saw it as a means of brushing Franco's crimes under the carpet, though in reality no political pact could erase the collective memories of a generation.

The corks popped at Casa Pepita as well. Vicenta looked out proudly at the gathering of friends and family as she strolled around the immaculate gardens of the house. Reny's wife, Leonora, whom he had met whilst studying architecture at university, fussed anxiously around their six year old daughter, Alisa, who seemed put out by the attention being paid to her eight year old brother Roberto whose First Communion they were celebrating that day. Dressed in a pretty white cotton dress fringed with lace and with her fine blond hair set in ringlets around her chubby face, Alisa bore a subtle resemblance to Vicenta, her grandmother. Roberto, looked uncomfortable, trussed up in a tightly buttoned tweed jacket over grey flannel shorts and knee length woollen socks. His black lace-up shoes, shiny and polished at the beginning of the day, were already scuffed and dusty, the result of his energetic romp chasing a couple of other boys around the garden. His straight dark hair, brushed flat with a side parting before the communion service was now an unruly mop having assumed its natural attitude. As he stood uncomfortably at his father's side, fidgeting fretfully to loosen his tie, Vicenta was once again struck by Roberto's uncanny resemblance to his grandfather, Eduardo. If any lingering doubts remained about Reny's parentage, one glimpse at Roberto would have dispelled them.

Vicenta's old friend Maite stood to one side with Armando, her husband of twelve years and their twin daughters, Candida and Carisa who clung either side of their uncle Ramón. Despite a greying at the temples and a furrowed complexion Ramón had maintained his rugged good looks. He and Vicenta had exchanged numerous letters over the years and Ramón had visited Benimarta on a regular basis, not least because he and Maite were Godparents to both Roberto and Alisa. Now a successful entrepreneur, having expanded his blacksmith's business, Ramón had paid for Reny's passage through university. Their correspondence and conversations had always been warm and friendly and a fondness had developed between them. Occasionally Ramón had hinted at a more intimate relationship, but Vicenta always seemed reticent and Ramón sensed that as long as Eduardo's fate remained a mystery, Vicenta was unwilling to release herself from the ties that still, after all these years, bound her to her husband.

Casa Pepita itself looked splendid, recently refurbished and totally redecorated at considerable cost thanks to Reny's significant success as a professional architect with smart offices on Denia's grand boulevard, the Marquesa de Campo. The tourist boom had spread from Benidorm to the whole of the Costa Blanca and when not designing hotels, Reny was busy with developers anxious to move inland and meet the burgeoning demand for holiday homes from wealthy clients in northern Europe.

Reny's wife, Leonora, was a qualified teacher who, Vicenta was pleased to note, railed against the doctrinaire education which, though still prevalent in many state schools, was beginning to moderate as the influence of the Catholic Church waned. She was a handsome woman with an aquiline nose and high cheek bones though these sharp features were softened by her sultry brown eyes and naturally pouting lips. Leonora would have been happy for Vicenta to live with them at Casa Pepita and Reny had even produced plans to convert the library into a self contained apartment. But much as Vicenta loved the house and was happy to see it brought back to life, it contained too many memories of her life with Eduardo and so she remained in the old town house which, like Casa Pepita, had been completely refurbished and modernised.

Economically, Spain remained on its knees, crippled by high unemployment, rocketing oil prices and plummeting productivity. The growth of tourism and the boom in construction, especially in the Costas were the only bright lights in an otherwise gloomy scenario. The election of a new centrist government in 1977 did little to improve matters since the political classes were largely preoccupied with the process of democratisation at the expense of economic policy. The Falange Española had been virtually disbanded having received less than one quarter of one percent of the votes in the general election. But this was not the death of right wing conservatism as many of Franco's supporters transformed themselves into the so called Popular Alliance. And much to Vicenta's chagrin it was the Popular Alliance that had taken control of Benimarta's municipal government. Cleverly they had distanced themselves from anyone previously connected with the old Falange syndicate that had governed the village through Franco's era. But the old guard were still there, albeit in the background, and still pulling strings – including Juan-Martin Garcia.

Just days after celebrating Roberto's First Communion the village was abuzz with a frenzy of rumour and speculation. A bulldozer working on the foundations of a new development of holiday homes on the outskirts of the village had accidentally strayed beyond the boundaries of the site and unearthed human remains buried at the bottom of a shallow ditch. Work had been halted immediately and the site sealed off.

When Vicenta heard the news her heart sank and she seemed, instinctively, to know the significance of the gruesome discovery. Without hesitation she marched determinedly from her house to the site. The bulldozer rested silently at the side of the ditch leaning forward with its giant blade raised from the ground. A hastily erected canvas screen pinned to metal poles hammered into the ground, shielded the whole of the site from prying eyes. A workman, whom Vicenta presumed to be the driver of the bulldozer, stood to one side looking bewildered as he pulled on the stub of a cigarette and flicked the remnant to the ground. As Vicenta drew closer to the compound she was confronted by a green-uniformed officer of the Guardia Civil with a semi automatic rifle slung across his chest.

'I want to see the body,' she demanded as she stood eyeball to eyeball with the officer.

'No one goes in,' he replied tersely.

Undeterred, Vicenta moved forward pushing the guard to one side. 'I demand to see the body,' she said.

As the guard regained his balance he snatched

at her arm and pulled her up short. 'No one enters,' he said.

Vicenta wrestled to free herself from the guard's grip and moved forward once again. The guard stepped sideways and blocked her path. As she raised her arms to push him to one side the guard stepped back a pace, removed the rifle and thrust the butt into her stomach.

'I said, no one goes in. Now move away,' he ordered.

Vicenta doubled up in pain and fell to her knees, prompting the driver of the bulldozer to come to her aid. He leant forward and placed his hands under her armpits lifting her to her feet.

'I think you'd better back off lady,' he said, attempting to steer her away from the confrontation.

The guard remained firmly in his place with the rifle pointed in her direction. 'Come away now,' the driver said, ushering her away.

Vicenta turned to glare at the officer. 'On whose authority do you deny me access to this land?'

'On the authority of the Mayor,' the guard replied nonchalantly.

Reluctantly Vicenta backed away then shrugged off the driver. 'Are you the one who unearthed the body?' she asked.

The driver looked sheepish but replied with a nod of his head.

'Tell me, what did you see?' she implored.

I... I'm not sure I should say anything.'

Vicenta turned and grabbed the man by the collar of his jacket.

'Damn you,' she yelled. 'Tell me what you saw.'

Reluctantly the man spoke. 'All I can tell you is that the body was curled up on its side. It was a man, I would guess judging from the remains of the clothing – a shirt, trousers and boots... and not very old, I'd say – the body that is. I've seen ancient bones before and these were definitely not ancient.'

Vicenta released her grip on the man's collar and her shoulders slumped. 'Thank you,' she said almost in a whisper.

'There's one other thing,' the driver said hesitantly. 'The man's hands were tied behind his back.'

Vicenta's despair suddenly turned to rage as she turned once again to challenge the guard. She was stopped in her tracks by Maximo who engulfed her in his arms and pulled her, weeping, to his chest.

'You'd better come away now, Vicenta,' he said in a sympathetic tone.

'It's Eduardo,' she said, sobbing uncontrollably in Maximo's enveloping embrace. 'I know it is.'

In a bedroom at Casa Pepita, Vicenta succumbed to sleep only when exhaustion overwhelmed her. It was a sleep bedevilled with nightmares and broken abruptly when she uttered an almost bestial scream. 'Eduardo. I failed you Eduardo.'

Reny was quick to clasp her in his arms and offer reassurance. 'It's all right Mama,' he said. 'You're safe here.'

Vicenta shrugged him away. 'You don't understand, Reny. It's Eduardo, your father. They're going to take him away again and cover the whole thing up. I can't let that happen.' She swung her legs to one side and planted them on the floor attempting to stand.

Reny grabbed her shoulders and held her in place.

'Don't worry, Mama,' he said, 'It's all taken care of. Sleep now and we'll talk in the morning.'

Wearily she allowed herself to be lifted back to her bed though sleep evaded her as it would for many days to come.

Maximo entered the house just after eleven the next morning. Vicenta looked haggard with tousled hair and bloodshot eyes. Reny had coaxed her into eating a small madeleine cake and sipping a cup of strong black coffee. As Maximo sat on the opposite side of the table her eyes seemed to implore him to ease her pain. This he could not do.

'We have applied to the Mayor for an order of exhumation,' Maximo said, 'but he has refused to grant it. And without a formal exhumation there can be no post mortem and no formal identification of the body.'

'On what grounds can he do this?' Vicenta

asked.

'He claims that an exhumation would be contrary to the *pacto de olvido* and therefore contrary to the new constitution; that, he says, would simply reopen old wounds and damage national reconciliation which the pact was designed to secure.'

'Can he do this?'

'He can, but we can appeal to a judge.'

'Appeals, judges – that will all take time. Everyone knows the judges are the lackeys of Franco's old regime. What chance have we got with them? By the time they've finished pontificating, the body will have been removed and the evidence will have been destroyed.'

'That's not going to happen, Vicenta,' said Maximo. 'We've organised a vigil at the site and the press have been notified. There's considerable interest in the discovery – from the independent newspapers at least. If anyone tries to move anything from that site we'll know about it.'

Reny intervened. 'Maximo, you say a judge can overrule the Mayor and grant an order for exhumation?'

'That's right,' Maximo replied, 'but finding a judge who would be willing to do that may be difficult in these sensitive times.'

Reny looked thoughtful. 'There's a judge I know who may be able to help. I've worked with him on a couple of cases over land disputes. He's an independent thinker and certainly not one of Franco's lackeys. His name is Javier Hernandez and he works from the provincial court in Denia not far from my office. I'll see if we can speak with him.'

Javier Hernandez was anything but the archetypal lawyer. His office in a back street of Denia was cluttered with papers and files covering every inch of his desk and an adjacent table. There wasn't a single law book to be seen amongst the debris. His appearance, too, was anachronistic – his lower face was covered with several days' stubble and his head was topped with a mop of curly black hair that hung almost to his shoulders. In jeans and an open neck black shirt, he looked anything but a lawyer, let alone a judge.

He sat at the table and pushed away the remnants of what could have been breakfast or lunch then brushed a pile of crumbs into the palm of his hand before tipping them into a wicker waste paper basket.

Reny, Maximo and Vicenta sat opposite and peered over the cascade of paper as he turned the pages of a folder and scratched his chin. Finally he spoke.

'From the details you have sent me, I think you could have a case to overrule the Mayor's denial of an order for exhumation. Whilst the Mayor has local jurisdiction in such cases, all actions of a local administration are subject to the scrutiny of the provincial courts. Although the Mayor may be technically correct in siting the *pacto de olvido*, I think we can draw a distinction in this case. You see, the purpose of the pact was to effectively draw a line under the actions of the State in the period up to and after the Civil War. In effect it's an amnesty for all crimes committed in that period by both sides – Republican as well as Nationalist. But what we have here is something different. There's no suggestion that the deceased – if you'll forgive me that term – was the victim of any action by the state or any of its agents. In fact there is evidence to suggest that what we are dealing with here is a simple case of murder, unless that is anyone can come up with documents to suggest that the victim had committed or been charged with some heinous crime.'

'Eduardo was entirely innocent,' Vicenta interrupted. Reny took her arm and tried to calm her as the judge continued.

'I hear what you say Mrs Ripoll, but we are not dealing here with guilt or innocence, just the circumstances of the victim's death. And in this case I think it could be argued that justice demands at the very least that the body is exhumed in order to determine the identity of the victim and the cause of his death.'

'So you'll grant the order,' Vicenta said hopefully.

'I can't simply grant such an order here and

now, there are procedures to be followed and there will have to be a formal hearing in court. But in principle, yes, I think such an order could be granted.'

'Thank you,' Vicenta said.

The judge leant back in his chair and adopted a stern expression.

'I must warn you, however, that the process is not entirely straight forward – or certain. You see, I am a judge in the provincial court and all my decisions are subject to appeal in the Superior Court in Valencia. Given the sensitivity of cases such as this, and the – how can I put this? – the political affiliations of some of my superiors, there is every possibility that my judgement could be overruled within days.'

'So we'd be back to square one?' Reny said with more than a hint of exasperation.

'Not necessarily,' the judge said. 'It will be tricky and you would need to be well prepared, but there is a way we might make at least some progress before the weight of political interference comes crashing down upon us.'

Vicenta took heart from the judge's use of the term "us". 'Can I ask, sir, why you are doing this?'

The judge's eyes hooded and his voice lowered almost to a whisper. 'My father, Joachin, supported the Republicans during the war. He was arrested and executed by firing squad in 1940 along with eight other men from our village. They were all buried in a communal grave on the outskirts of our village, so at least my mother had somewhere to place flowers and grieve. Then, in 1959 the bodies, along with many more from other towns and villages, were removed, without permission of the families, and taken on Franco's orders to be placed in a huge crypt at Franco's grand masterpiece in El Escorial, the Valle de los Caídos (the valley of the fallen). They were entombed alongside Nationalist soldiers in what Franco thought would be a memorial to all those who died in the war. And now Franco himself has been laid to rest in this mausoleum and the place has become a Francoist shrine. I cannot tell you how much it pains my mother to know that her husband's remains lie in a crypt alongside his enemies that forms part of a monument to the man who was ultimately responsible for his death. No one has ever answered for my father's death and I doubt they ever will.'

'I'm sorry,' Vicenta murmured.

The judge brought himself back from his own sadness and once again adopted his habitual authoritative tone.

'There's one final thing about which I should caution you. I know, Mrs Ripoll, that you are convinced the body is that of your husband, but proving his identity may not be that simple after almost forty years.'

Before they left, Hernandez outlined the steps they must take to gain any advantage from an order for the exhumation of the body.

Since the order denying exhumation had been granted by the Mayor of Benimarta, he had to be given notice of any appeal against that order. The minimum period of notice was three days, but the law was vague and the judge suggested that the notice be delivered to the town hall late on a Friday evening as the town hall was about to close. The notice would need to be stamped in officially to prove receipt. This could be done by the clerk on duty at the time and with any luck it would then sit unnoticed in the town hall over the weekend. A hearing for the appeal would be scheduled for eight in the morning on the following Monday and an order for exhumation would be granted. From then on it would be a race against time before the Mayor of Benimarta, or more likely someone from the Popular Alliance, sought to annul the order in the Superior Court. For that reason Vicenta and her colleagues would need to have everything in place so that the order could be executed immediately after it was granted. This would need undertakers to be on hand together with a priest and transport to remove the body to a mortuary. A pathologist would then need to be on stand by to carry out an autopsy immediately the body arrived. When the autopsy was complete and the pathologist had written his report it had to be taken immediately to a Notary to be copied and certified. Once issued and certified the pathologist's report could not be hidden or destroyed, even if the Superior

Court overruled the order for exhumation.

It seemed so outrageous to have to go through such a clandestine process, but Reny and Maximo followed their instructions to the letter, though not without difficulty. The undertakers were arranged though they were unaware of the exact circumstances of the task to which they had been assigned. Finding a priest was also problematic, but Maximo knew of an old cleric from a neighbouring village who had always rebelled against the worst extremes of fascism. He was in his eighties and Maximo thought he would relish a last chance to rectify at least one injustice before he died. Hernandez suggested the pathologist himself – another man with a grievance against the old regime since his own father had died in a labour camp in 1942.

The following Monday, to everyone's surprise, having granted the order for exhumation, Judge Hernandez insisted on travelling to the site to personally supervise its execution.

The Guardia Civil officer was at first obdurate, even raising his rifle when confronted by the judge and his entourage which included Vicenta, Maximo and Reny. His protestations that he needed to consult his superiors were overruled by the judge who, conveniently, had arrived in his flowing black gown complete with a frilled white bib and his badge of office.

As the tarpaulin covering the body was removed Vicenta almost fainted, but was held firm by Reny and Maximo standing on either side. A few remnants of clothing clung to the skeletal bones of the torso and Vicenta thought she recognised them as the clothing Eduardo had worn when last she had seen him. The boots, which remained almost intact, seemed familiar to her, but they were just common boots worn by almost everyone. It was only when her eyes rested on the empty sockets of the bleached skull that Vicenta knew for certain. Even without the flesh that once gave life and form to the body, she knew she was viewing the remains of her husband. Tears puddled on her eyelids and began to cascade down her cheeks and fall to the ground. Her focus moved to the hands, balled into fists and tied firm with a short length rope, and her sorrow turned immediately anger.

The priest moved forward to the side of the ditch and spoke quietly and reverently.

'Oh Lord, As the mortal remains of our departed brother are taken to another place of rest we put our trust in You. May those who bear responsibility for this process show care and compassion and be given wisdom and skill, and may the journey's end be reached safe in Your presence. Amen.'

He moved away and the two undertakers began the process of lifting the remains from the shallow ditch. Reny and Maximo ushered Vicenta away.

It was almost midday on Tuesday when Reny returned to Vicenta's house with a notarised copy of the pathologist's report. And he had other news. The Superior Court in Valencia had met in an emergency session to consider an appeal against the exhumation order issued by Judge Hernandez. The appeal had been lodged in the name of the Mayor of Benimarta and the Judge had annulled the original order on the grounds that it breached both the letter and the spirit of the *pacto de olvido*.

'Never mind that,' Vicenta said. 'What does the pathologist's report say?'

Reny looked apprehensive as he withdrew a sheath of paper from a white envelope.

'I'll spare you the details, Mama,' he said, 'but the main findings are that the body is that of a male aged between twenty-five and thirty-five years old with dark brown hair and approximately 1.80 metres tall.' He swallowed hard and continued. 'The cause of death was a single gunshot to the back of the head fired at very close range. The pathologist has recovered the bullet which was lodged in the back of the forehead.'

Reny paused and looked at his mother who appeared devoid of emotion.

'Are you all right, Mama?' he asked.

'Please carry on,' she said impassively.

'The pathologist says that at this stage he cannot reach any conclusions as to the identity of the body beyond the features he has described. He has taken a mould of the teeth and if dental records are available it may be possible to match these. He also says that there is a new technique called DNA testing which matches a person's genetic code, but the technique is very new and not available in Spain as yet.'

'So we cannot say definitively that this is Eduardo's body?' Maximo questioned.

Vicenta interrupted abruptly. 'I don't need proof – it's Eduardo and it's clear that he was murdered.'

'But without evidence it will be difficult to…'

'Difficult to what..?' Vicenta snapped, 'Difficult to prove that he was taken from his cell and shot in cold blood. And we all know who shot him, don't we?'

Vicenta's declaration met with stunned silence.

'There's one other thing, Mama,' Reny said, reaching into his pocket. 'The pathologist gave me this. It was found clasped in the right hand.'

He reached forward and dropped something into Vicenta's open palm – a thin gold chain threaded through a gold crucifix.

Vicenta looked into her palm then clutched her hand to her breast as she wept.

'Mama,' Reny enquired, 'are you all right?'

'I'd like you all to leave now,' she said. 'I need some time on my own.'

Alone with her thoughts, Vicenta lived

through her last moments with Eduardo, fondling the thin gold ring and key that were strung around her neck and fiddling with the chain and crucifix she had given to Eduardo when she had last seen him in the jail in Benimarta all those years ago. Desolation and despair engulfed her as she imagined the lost years she had lived through; years that should have been filled with joy and love and laughter and perhaps more children. Gradually her despondency turned to anger as she contemplated the possibility that no one would answer for the crime and that justice would be denied her. She knew then what she must do.

It was almost midnight when Vicenta found what she was looking for in a cabinet beneath the stairs. She left the house and strode determinedly up the hill to the centre of the village keeping her arms close to her side and ignoring a passing greeting from an old man returning from Bar Rincon. She paused outside the solid wooden door, took a deep breath and turned the handle. The door opened silently into an inner vestibule at the end of which a dim flickering light filtered from a living room that reverberated with the harsh tones of a television turned to almost full volume.

Closing the door behind her, Vicenta moved across the vestibule and hovered in the open doorway taking in the scene. She could see the top of a head protruding above the back of a padded armchair facing the television screen. She could just make out the sound of gentle repetitive snoring. Slowly, purposefully, she moved across the room and pushed the button to turn off the television. In the sudden silence the man in the chair stopped snoring and stirred. Rubbing his eyes to restore his focus he began to rise.

'What the hell are you doing here?' he challenged.

Vicenta stepped forward and planted her feet apart then raised the barrel of the shotgun and shoved it into the man's chest forcing him back into his seat.

'Stay where you are, Garcia,' she demanded in a voice that reverberated with gruff determination.

'What... what do you want?'

'To be honest, I'm not sure what I want,' Vicenta said. 'What would you call it? Revenge, retribution satisfaction – justice perhaps?'

'What are you talking about?'

'Oh, I think you know that already. You denounced my husband for no other reason than your own jealousy and greed. And when he wouldn't give you what you wanted you took him from his cell in the middle of the night, murdered him and dumped his body in a ditch, but not before you beat me and raped me. And to think, you have lived comfortably in this village ever since pretending to be an upright citizen. Have you any idea what it's been like for me all these years wondering, not knowing what had happened to Eduardo, raising his son without him whilst all the time his brutalised body lay not five minutes walk from this house?'

'I... I'm sorry, Vicenta,' Garcia blubbered.

'Sorry? Don't tell me you're sorry. The only thing you are sorry about is that you have been found out. Sorry that you might finally face justice.'

'But those were different times,' he pleaded. 'The war... it brutalised everybody... on both sides. Things were done that everyone regrets. Hundreds, thousands of people died like Eduardo... it was just the way things were. It's history now. Even the government recognises that it's time to bury the past and move on.'

Vicenta's eyes bulged and the veins in her neck stood out.

'Ha,' she sneered. 'The *pacto de olvido*.' Still holding the shotgun firm she raised her right arm, bare to the elbow. 'You see this, Garcia.' She thrust her arm forward. 'As long as there is blood running in my veins I will never forget what you did, and the people of Spain will never forget the crimes that were committed against them.'

Fear etched Garcia's face as he listened to Vicenta's wild-eyed rant.

'What... what are you going to do?'

Vicenta resumed her grip on the shotgun with both hands and took a step back.

'Stand up,' she barked.

Garcia did as he was ordered and Vicenta moved behind him.

'Now kneel,' she commanded.

'But you can't...'

'Shut up and kneel,' she repeated, kicking Garcia in the back of his legs and causing him to slump to his knees. 'Now, up straight and put your hands behind your back.

'You can't do this,' Garcia wailed.

'You don't think so?' she shoved the barrel of the shotgun against the back of Garcia's head. 'Well, you are about to find out.' Her voice was low and calm and indignant.

Garcia's whole body was shaking. 'Please...' was all he could whimper before the blast of the gun echoed around the room. He fell forward and his head crashed against the floor. As he rolled sideways a dark stain spread through the front of his trousers and formed a puddle on the floor. He looked up, blinking, to see a shower of dust drifting down from a crater in the ceiling peppered with pellet holes. He began to bawl and snivel like a child.

'You have no idea how much pleasure it would have given me to kill you. But for what, revenge? I'll take my revenge from knowing that as of tomorrow morning the whole world will know what you are and what you did. You see my story is already in the hands of the press. Sue me if you want, I'd quite like my day in court.'

Vicenta turned on her heels and left the house

elevated by a curious sense of serenity.

Two days later Juan-Martin Garcia was found dead in the bedroom of his house, shot through the side of the head. The gun, ironically the same one that had been used to murder Eduardo Ripoll, rested in his own hand.

Two weeks later the last remains of Eduardo Ripoll were interred in the municipal cemetery at Benimarta. The Mayor, who at first denied the family's request, backed down when confronted by a baying pack of reporters.

In the days that followed, Vicenta reflected on her life's journey and the jeopardy she had faced and overcome. She pondered also on the path her life might have taken were it not for Garcia's evil acts. She could have felt a sense of revenge at Garcia's final demise and the manner in which it had been brought about, but she realised that her real redress came from having survived against the odds to see Reny reach maturity and raise a family of his own. Through everything she had faced her purpose had been to remain true to the pact she had made with Eduardo. Now free of that obligation, Vicenta began to write a letter to Ramón in which she would, at last, disclose the sentiments she had felt for a long time, but had never allowed herself to express.

AUTHOR'S NOTE

The historical episodes which form a backcloth to Vicenta's story are based on actual events and recorded incidents, though the precise timing may have been altered to fit the storyline.

The arrest and subsequent death of political detainees during and after the Spanish Civil War in the early years of Franco's rule are well documented in books such as Paul Preston's *Spanish Holocaust*. Estimates of the number of victims of Franco's *White Terror* vary from 200,000 to 400,000. There are those who would balance this with the executions perpetrated by the Republicans immediately before and during the war, though most put the estimated number of deaths from the *Red Terror* at between 40,000 and 75,000. Others distinguish the Republican executions as being perpetrated by anarchists motivated by revenge and precipitated by the breakdown of the state, as opposed to Franco's organised policy of *limpieza* – the systematic cleansing of opposition sanctioned and implemented by the State. Wherever the truth lies it is clear that neither side emerged from this epoch without justified criticism and condemnation. At the time of Franco's death in 1975 some 400 political prisoners were still held in Spanish jails.

The *Pacto de Olvido* was given legal force in the 1977 Spanish Amnesty Law. It meant that responsibility for the Civil War and the repression and extra-judicial murders that followed was never placed on any individual member of the government or any political party. The Amnesty Law remains in place to this day. In 2007 Spain's Socialist government passed the Law of Historical Memory which, amongst other things, condemned the Francoist regime and authorised the removal of Francoist symbols from public buildings and spaces. The Law also prohibited political events at the Valley of the Fallen and gave state help in the tracing, identification and exhumation of victims of Franco's repression. The Law of Historical Memory remains in force though the Partido Popular government elected in 2011 closed the government office dedicated to the exhumation of victims and announced the withdrawal of funding from the historical memory project.

In 2008 Judge Baltazar Garzón opened a national investigation into Franco and his allies and declared their acts of repression as crimes against humanity under international law. He ordered the exhumation of nineteen unmarked mass graves, one of them said to contain the remains of the poet Federico Garcia Lorca. A month later Garzón was forced to drop his investigation after state prosecutors questioned his jurisdiction and the courts subsequently declared that the judge's actions were contrary to the Amnesty Law of

1977. Garzón himself was subsequently charged with abuse of power and suspended. Though he was acquitted of this charge in 2012, the Supreme Court upheld the ruling that the initial investigation was contrary to Spain's Amnesty Laws.

To this day, Spain has resisted calls from the United Nations and Amnesty International to repeal the Amnesty Laws and conduct a full investigation into the atrocities of the Franco years.

In June 2011, Spain's judiciary was forced to act after ANADIR (National Association of Irregular Adoptions) an association formed to represent people searching for missing children or parents, filed its first official complaints. Attorney General Cándido Conde-Pumpido announced that 849 cases were being examined, adding that 162 already could be classified as criminal proceedings because of evidence pointing to abductions. Lawyers believe that up to 300,000 babies were taken in a scandal that continued into the 1990's.

The practice of removing children from parents deemed "undesirable" and placing them with "approved" families, began in the 1930s. At that time, the motivation may have been ideological, but years later, it seemed to change – babies began to be taken from parents considered morally or economically deficient. The scandal is closely linked to the Catholic Church which, under Franco, assumed a prominent role in Spain's social services including hospitals, schools and children's homes. Nuns and priests compiled waiting lists of would-be adoptive parents, while doctors were said to have lied to mothers about the fate of their children.

In April 2012, Sister Maria Gomez Valbuena aged 86 of the Sisters of Charity Order was accused of stealing a mother's newborn daughter at a Madrid hospital in 1982. Her signature was alleged to have appeared on hundreds of documents relating to adoptions with many parents coming forward to state they had been told their babies had died. She was the first person ever to be formally accused in connection with the scandal of Spain's missing children. When she appeared in court, Sister Maria refused to testify and never faced trial. She died in January 2013 and was buried in the grounds of her convent.

The *Sección Femenina* continued in existence throughout Franco's rule and whilst it undoubtedly made a contribution to improvements in health, education and social welfare it remained staunchly committed to Falangism and the traditional Catholic view of women's role in society. The leader of the SF for more than forty years, Pilar Primo de Rivero (sister of José Antonio, founder of the Falange whose funeral cortège is described in this book) proved herself to be a woman of significant political prowess even being appointed to Franco's pseudo-parliamentary Cortes. At the same time she moulded herself to changing times and in 1961 gave the support of the SF to new labour laws which expanded the right to work to women and prohibited discrimination in the workplace on the grounds of sex or civil status. However women still continued to need marital permission to work and Pilar herself declared, "This doesn't even resemble a feminist law, we would be unfaithful to José Antonio if we made it that way, it is only a just law for working women."

The Good Housewife guide mentioned in this book was first issued by the Sección Femenina in 1934 and continued in existence in more or less similar form until 1977. It is now much mocked and parodied, but original versions can be found on the internet by searching for "Guia de la Buena Esposa."

Universal women's suffrage, first granted in 1931 but suspended during Franco's time, was finally reintroduced in 1976. At the same time those parts of the Civil Code which gave precedence to the male head of the family were finally annulled. The SF officially ceased to exist in 1977 when the foundations of Spain's new democracy were laid. Adultery and cohabitation ceased to be a crime in 1978, and in the same year the selling of contraceptive devices became legal. Divorce was legalised in 1981 and abortion was permitted from 1983.

Spain's gradual transition to democracy was briefly interrupted by an attempted coup d'état in February 1981 when Lieutenant Colonel Antonio Tejero and two hundred officers of the Guardia Civil burst into the Spanish Congress of Deputies and held the deputies hostage. Shots were fired and Tejero barked orders before calling on the King to make a statement in the hope that military rule would be restored. Meanwhile Lieutenant General Jaime del Bosch, a supporter of Franco, declared a state of emergency and ordered tanks onto the streets of Valencia. King Juan Carlos gave a nationally televised address denouncing the coup and urging the maintenance of law and order and the continuance of the democratically elected government. The coup collapsed and the hostage takers surrendered the next day without anyone being harmed.

*****

BY THE SAME AUTHOR

MISSING IN SPAIN

The first Inspector Fernandez mystery.
A British couple disappear in Spain and as a fluent Spanish speaker, British detective Michael Fernandez seems the ideal choice to help track them down. But he finds more than he bargained for when he encounters a branch of his family he had previously tried to forget. Then a body is found and the hunt for the killer is on.

> *"An excellent read for those who like detective stories. Read from cover to cover in a couple of days, would have been less but life interfered. A complex, brisk plot with lots of side interest. I hope this will only be the first of many outings for Inspector Michael Fernandez."*

SPANISH LIES

Detective Inspector Fernandez returns to Spain to investigate a tangled web of murder, corruption and immorality on the Costa Blanca. Meanwhile, in the village where he has inherited a home, the tentacles of local life engulf him in an irresistible intrigue and a mystery that has its roots in the aftermath of the Spanish Civil War.

"This is an excellent detective novel with lots of twists and turns to keep you thinking right to the end! Just the right balance between the plot and background of the main character's private life. Really enjoyed it!"

I WANT TO LIVE IN SPAIN

In the middle of a dreary drawn out English winter, Mark Harrison and his wife Vivien suddenly took stock of their lives and decided it was time for a change.

Ten months later they had resigned from their jobs, sold their house in leafy Surrey and moved to a new home in the mountains inland from Spain's Costa Blanca.

This is the story of how they got there and how they fared in their new surroundings.

I Want to Live in Spain will make you laugh at their innocence and cry at their misfortunes. It is essential reading for anyone who has ever dreamed of moving out of the fast lane to find a new life in the sun.

"My first thought was, 'it's all been done before,' but this is different – fresh, funny and unpretentious. I just couldn't put it down."

IN PURSUIT OF THE PERFECT PAELLA
(More adventures from a new life in Spain)

Ten years on from an impetuous "lock, stock and barrel" move to the Costa Blanca, Mark Harrison recounts the events that exemplify his new Spanish lifestyle. From a serious skirmish with developers, to an encounter with wild boars and the vagaries of the weather, the story paints a humorous and yet poignant picture of life in foreign land as viewed through his own eyes and those of his stoical wife, Vivien. The story is interwoven with a series of paella experiences that epitomise Spanish culture and tradition and give a taste of everyday expat life. Forget the guides and manuals, this is real time, real life experience written with true insight and honesty. Essential reading for anyone who has ever dreamed of exchanging the rat race for a new life in the Spanish sun.

Printed in Great Britain
by Amazon